BROOMSTRAW RIDGE

A NOVEL

BETSY REEDER

BROOMSTRAW RIDGE

BETSY REEDER

Canterbury House Publishing
www.canterburyhousepublishing.com
Imprint of Dudley Court Press

Canterbury House Publishing

www.canterburyhousepublishing.com
Imprint of Dudley Court Press

Copyright © 2019 Betsy Reeder
All rights reserved under International and Pan-American
Copyright Conventions.

Book design by Tracy Arendt
Cover photo courtesy Jessie E. C. Reeder

Library of Congress Cataloging-in-Publication Data

Names: Reeder, Betsy, author.
Title: Broomstraw ridge : a novel / Betsy Reeder.
Description: First Edition. | Sonoita, Arizona : Canterbury House
  Publishing, 2019. | Summary: "In 1873, a tragic event causes Joseph Cook
  to return to his birthplace. There he finds his inheritance spent, his
  sister "imprisoned." Worse, an unexpected rejection pairs with an
  agonizing involvement with a family that could have been his. Joseph
  must overcome danger, conflict, and disappointment to approach peace in
  the Appalachian region he calls home"-- Provided by publisher.
Identifiers: LCCN 2019037034 (print) | LCCN 2019037035 (ebook) | ISBN
  9781945401442 (trade paperback) | ISBN 9781945401152 (ebook)
Classification: LCC PS3618.E43595 B76 2019 (print) | LCC PS3618.E43595
  (ebook) | DDC 813/.6--dc23
LC record available at https://lccn.loc.gov/2019037034
LC ebook record available at https://lccn.loc.gov/2019037035

First Edition: November 2019

Author's Note:
This is a work of fiction. Although an effort was made to use surnames and geographic identities of the area in the nineteenth century, names, characters, places, and incidents are either the products of the author's imagination or are used fictitiously. Exceptions are a few historic figures, namely members of the Hinton (Silas and Evan), Bennett (Jefferson and Nancy), and Waddell families, as well as Captain Thurmond and John Henry. The Ballengee family once owned the land on which Hinton was built. Otherwise, any resemblance to actual persons living or dead, business establishments, events, or locales is entirely coincidental.

Publisher's Note:
Without limiting the rights under copyright reserved above, no part of this publication may be reproduced, stored or introduced into a retrieval system or transmitted, in any form, or by any means (electronic, photocopying, recording, or otherwise), without the prior written permission of both the copyright owner and the above publisher of this book.

For information about permission to reproduce selections from this book email:
publisher@dudleycourtpress.com
Please put Permissions in the subject line.

DEDICATION

With a full heart, this book is dedicated to my enchanting grandson. As well, to the ancient New River, wondrous in every season.

INITIAL CHARACTERS, RELATIONSHIPS
(**bold** = main characters)

Lilly family:
    Suzanne and Quentin

Offspring:
    Quentin Junior ("Junior"), deceased
    Marcus, married to **Maylene Farley**
    Johnny, deceased
    Eliza, married to Mayhew Mullens
    Rachel, married to Rev. Eli Goins
    Vesta
    Louella, married to Howard Neely
    Calvin
    Lester

Children of Marcus and Maylene (Farley) Lilly:
    Jenny
    Johnny
    Sara Sue
    Quentin Marcus ("**Quencus**")

Farley family:
    Bob and Sara Mae

Offspring surviving childhood:
    Mary, married to Marcus's friend Corbin Radcliff
    Melva
    Maylene, married to Marcus Lilly
    Margaret, married

Wallace family:
   Enoch and Becky
Offspring surviving childhood:
   Amos, presumed dead
   Caroline, married
   Lura, married
   Caleb
Cook siblings:
   Will, deceased
   Joseph
   Becky, married to Enoch Wallace
Friend of Joseph Cook:
   Randall Murphy
Hinton physician:
   Dr. Mason

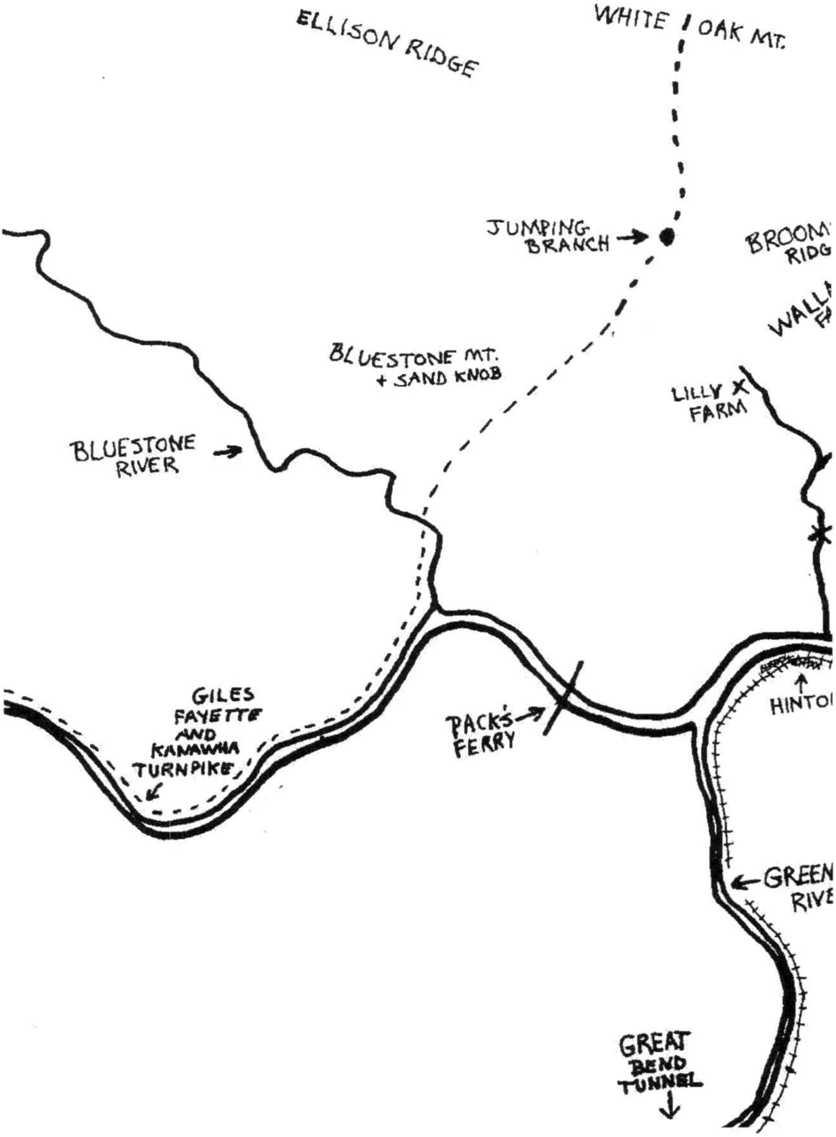
ELLISON RIDGE
WHITE OAK MT.
JUMPING BRANCH
BROOM RIDG
LILLY FARM
BLUESTONE MT. + SAND KNOB
BLUESTONE RIVER
GILES FAYETTE AND KANAWHA TURNPIKE
PACK'S FERRY
HINTO
GREEN RIVE
GREAT BEND TUNNEL

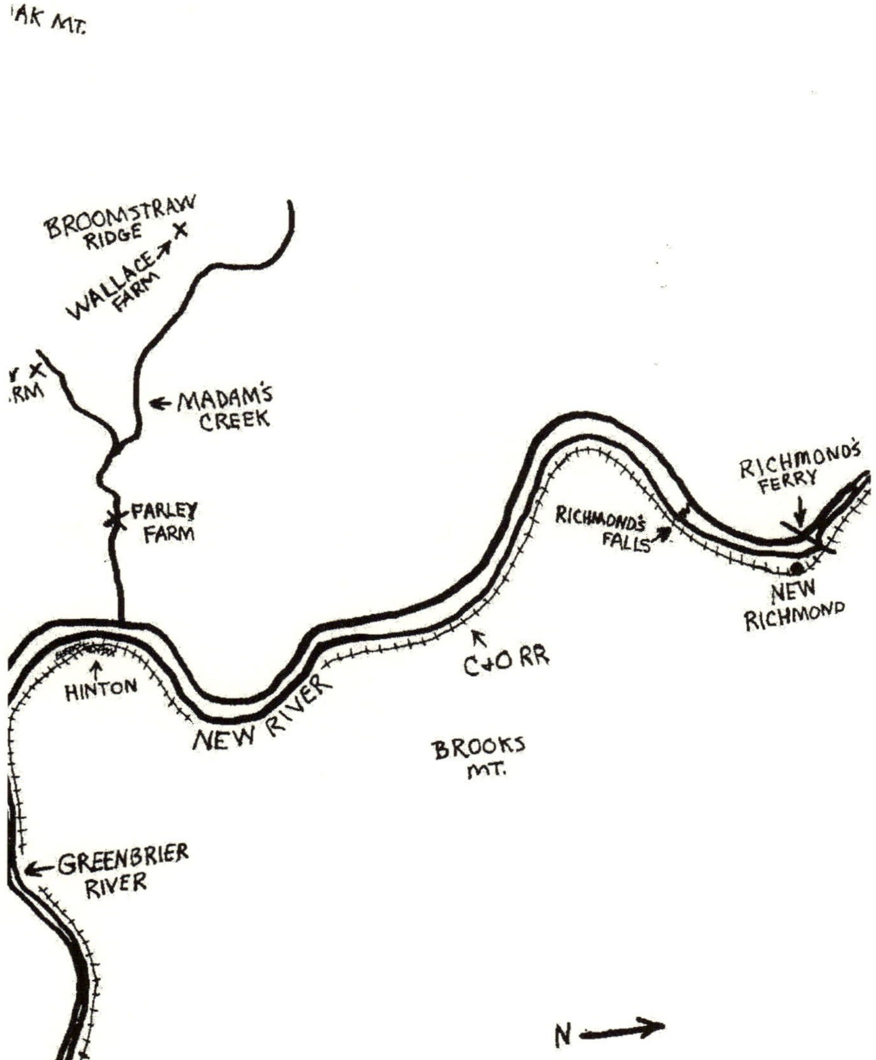
BROOMSTRAW RIDGE
WALLACE FARM
MADAM'S CREEK
FARLEY FARM
RICHMOND'S FERRY
RICHMOND'S FALLS
NEW RICHMOND
HINTON
C+O RR
NEW RIVER
BROOKS MT.
GREENBRIER RIVER
N

CHAPTER ONE

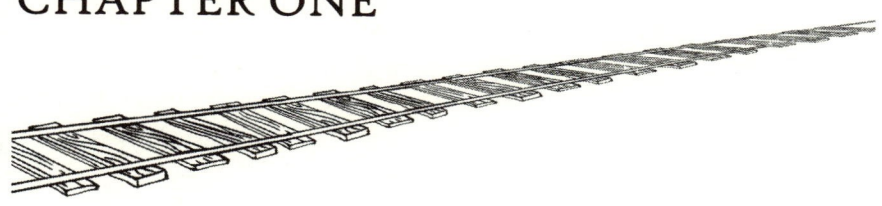

On a late-September afternoon, edging on evening, Suzanne Lilly strode onto the porch, grasped a thin leather strap above her head, and gave the dinner bell a clapper thrashing. "Where is that man?"

Rarely did she have to sound the bell a second time to get her family assembled. Was she supposed to scorch the potatoes and veal and cornbread, or let them grow cold?

Back inside, she said, "We might as well start without him. He can pick the bones if that's what's left when he gets hungry enough to show up."

Marcus, uneasy about the brief but robust storm that had come and gone an hour earlier, started to rise from his seat on the long bench. "Maybe I ought to go for him."

"Eat your supper first, son. If he's not here by then, you can see what he's up to. He's probably strayed too far up the ridge to hear. I keep telling him he's getting deaf, but he don't believe me."

Quentin had gone to cut wood above the pasture. He could still manage the smaller trees alone with an axe, and he took pride in that. He rode Reggie up the steep trail, dismounting when he spied his target. He didn't bother to tie the mule, who waited drowsily for his job of dragging the fallen tree back down to the barn.

This day, Quentin chose a chestnut little more than a foot in diameter at the base. Tall and straight, its trunk would yield fresh fence rails, its limbs firewood, its smallest branches kindling. The burly man unlatched his axe from the leather loop that held it to the saddle, hobbled to the tree, and began the wide swings, as familiar as breathing, that soon notched the tree on its downhill side.

That done, he moved to the upslope side and began chopping again as thunder rumbled beyond the slanted, canoe-shaped hollow of the Lilly farm. Chunks of bark, then wood, scattered about his feet. As an able man with a sharp blade, it wouldn't take him long to bring this one down.

Quentin paused to draw a sleeve across his sweaty brow and noticed the breeze had picked up, blowing toward him from below. He checked the sky and, sure enough, its looming darkness confirmed the approach of a storm.

Good. He'd be finished before the wind got bad, and the rain would cool him off.

He grasped the axe handle and resumed the steady whacks, allowing himself one more break before he had the trunk nearly severed. He wanted the tree felled. The wind strengthened—he knew the risks. Then, when a few more strokes would complete the job, a gust caught the tree, spinning it on its remaining sinew of intact wood. It began its earthward lean, but not downhill.

Alarmed, Quentin shifted right as the tree descended to his left. He hadn't been quick on his feet since the War, not since a horse landed on his knee and put it permanently out of commission. Fortunately, he avoided the line of fire of this wayward timber drop, an adjacent oak being the only likely casualty.

The falling chestnut clipped the oak and knocked off a dead limb, big around as a man's thigh. Quentin heard the crack and subsequent crashing but couldn't see through the leaves and didn't know which way to throw himself. He dove for the chestnut's mangled base.

The sliver of time allowed him to belly-flop and cover his head with his arms. The limb took dead aim. It broke as it struck his skull, fractured a wrist, and blackened his world. The first fat drops of rain snapped on the oak leaves, reaching Quentin's collapsed form through the canopy hole he'd made.

Marcus, the first to clean his plate, got up and headed for the door. He reached for the wide-brimmed hat he'd hung on a hook.

Maylene caught his urgency. "I'll come with you. Ma, you and Vesta don't mind watching the children, do you?"

"No, May, it's all right. I reckon Pa found a sunny spot to dry off after the rain and fell asleep. I'll find him snoring on the hillside and tell him to get his sorry arse home," Marcus said.

"You sure?"

"Yes, ma'am." Marcus gave his wife a wink with his one eye as he positioned the hat and left the house.

But he hadn't shaken his unease. Something was wrong. He felt tension like a coiled snake hidden by fallen leaves.

He debated taking his horse, Blackjack, not wanting to squander the time required to saddle him. He settled on an expedient compromise. He whistled for the black gelding, who trotted promptly to the pasture gate. Marcus slipped on a bridle, climbed up a couple of fence rails, and leapt onto the horse's bare back. Sensing adventure, Marcus's mountain cur, Chase, barked with excitement.

They were away in an instant, into the woods and up the flank of Broomstraw Ridge.

"Find Reggie," Marcus said, despite knowing Blackjack already sought him. The horse and mule disliked being separated.

Blackjack let out a whinny, and the trio heard the reply. Above them and to their left, off the trail.

Marcus saw the fallen chestnut first, immediately aware that its drop had gone awry. Quentin wouldn't have intentionally walloped another tree or taken aim cross-slope. With a dry mouth and pounding heart, he dismounted and pushed past broken branches that obscured his view of the bisected trunk.

And there he lay, face down, too still.

"Pa?"

Marcus didn't know tears already streaked his face. Or that his hand shook when he lifted Quentin's left wrist, feeling for a pulse. He rolled over the cold, heavy body and cradled the head on his lap. He sat on the wood-chip speckled ground weeping in the chill that followed sunset, smoothing the coarse wavy hair—red mingled with gray—of the man who had raised him. He tried to cover the bloody spot above Quentin's left ear, but some of the hair stuck in the dried fluid and the rest had a mind of its own, as it always had, and sprang back. He used his shirt sleeve to wipe grime off the round, large-nosed face in need of a shave, and a thumb to close the eyelids, only partially revealing a pair of hazel eyes.

Chase whined and pawed Marcus's thigh before settling next to him, using the thigh as a pillow. Reggie stepped over to the strangely quiet men and lowered his head, questioning. Trained not to wander off in the middle of a task, he'd stood his ground. Now he reminded Marcus of the lengthy wait for oats and pasture.

Marcus raised an arm to stroke the long face. "You did your job, Reg."

He resisted the urge to throw his arms around the mule's neck and sob like a child. He'd best pull himself together. As the newly anointed eldest man in the family, he must step into shoes he feared he'd never fill. There were decisions to make. For starters, he'd get his younger brothers, Calvin and Lester, to help lift their pa onto the log sled and bring him down.

With great care, Marcus eased himself out from under Quentin, and regained his feet. He had to steady himself against a sapling before whistling for Blackjack. But he found his mouth too parched for the summons, so he walked the short distance the horse had strayed in search of forage, gathered reins and mane in his left fist, and vaulted into place as if borne aloft by wings.

Riding back down the path, Marcus recalled his sole consolation, and a scant one at that. He'd kept the promise he'd made his mother years ago. Neither he nor Maylene had ever disclosed the secret that would have broken Quentin Lilly's heart.

CHAPTER TWO

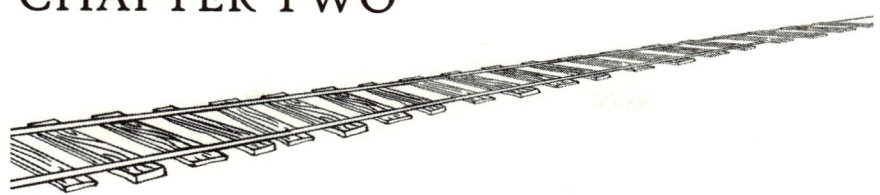

How does a man tell his mother her husband is dead? Followed by a trotting mule and led by a loping dog, Marcus agonized as he rode back down to the log house. He wanted to start with Maylene, whose comfort he craved, but predicted he'd break down and be in pieces by the time he approached his ma.

Yet there stood his wife, baby on a hip, waiting on the porch. As soon as their eyes met, she knew. "We've lost him?"

Marcus nodded.

"Dear God."

As Maylene stepped forward to hold him, he pushed forward a palm in refusal. And she understood. "Your ma's getting anxious. The boys are at the barn doing the milking and feeding, and they're getting worked up, too. I'll run get them."

Marcus found his mother in her rocker before the fire with three-year-old Sara Sue on her lap. In a willow chair next to the pair sat his daughter Jenny, now eight, reading aloud in waning light. From a third chair, five-year-old Johnny, perched on his Aunt Vesta's lap, twisted his head toward the door.

"Where were you, Papa? Where's Paw Paw?"

Marcus reflexively pulled off his hat and looked into his mother's fear-filled, blue eyes.

"Paw Paw got hurt. The boys and I will go for him."

"He can't ride Reggie back?" Johnny asked.

"No."

Suzanne set her younger granddaughter down and stood. "You can say it, Marcus. The children will have to know. He's dead."

"Yes, ma'am. A widowmaker. I'm sure he never saw it. He didn't suffer. It struck his head. We'll go for him at once."

Marcus lied. Quentin's position and raised arms had made plain his attempt to use the stump for shelter. He'd known. Marcus envisioned the entire calamity as vividly as if he'd been there watching.

Suzanne stared.

"Ma, I'm so sorry."

What seared her mind as her sons went off in the near-dark to collect her husband's corpse were thoughts like the lashes she once applied to her nine children.

Why hadn't she laid out the meal and gone herself in search of her missing spouse? Annoyed by his tardiness, she'd insisted the family eat without him, punish him by showing its indifference. And part of her annoyance, she realized now, stemmed from Quentin making her worry. She didn't like him going off by himself to cut trees. So she'd show him—she'd delay any effort to reel him in. Hell, he used his deafness at his convenience. He might have taken a jug of moonshine with him. She could picture him sitting on a fallen trunk, mocking the dinner bell as he lingered over his whiskey.

As Maylene nursed Quencus before the fire and joined Vesta's hushed conversation with the wild-eyed, older children, Suzanne scrubbed an iron skillet, unseeing.

God, here's one more thing You can add to the list. Forgive me if You can.

It was when Suzanne thought to ask Quentin for forgiveness that she began to cry.

The baby fell asleep in his mother's arms, but his siblings continued to buzz with the energy of crisis. It took extra time, care, and finally threats of spankings to settle them in an unfamiliar bed upstairs. Sara Sue cried herself to sleep, not because Paw Paw died but because Grandma scolded her the third time she crept down the steps, asking for her mama. Maylene wanted to comfort her, but one woman couldn't right all the chaos this night had spawned.

The women went to work. With Calvin's help, they placed Quentin on the dining table where they undressed him and scrubbed his gray skin with wash rags. Calvin gave his father a final shave. Suzanne then sent him for the straw tick she'd shared with her husband for thirty years, and it took the three women and one teen to get the lumpy mattress under Quentin and wrestle his stiff limbs into his seldom-worn Sunday suit. Suzanne used a fresh rag to scrub the blood out of her mate's thick hair, unable to avoid feeling the dent in his skull. It reminded her of a pipped egg on the brink of hatching. She wiped dried blood off a small cut on Quentin's chin. She had Vesta trim her father's toenails while she worked on the fingernails. Then she used the tip of a knife blade to remove every speck of dirt from under the nails.

Suzanne looked up from a thumb. "Maylene, put a cloth under his head and give his hair a little trim, will you?"

If Quentin Lilly was going to meet his Maker, he was going to look presentable.

Marcus and Lester had taken two lanterns to the barn. The sounds of saws, draw-blades, and planes came through the open door as the brothers assembled a coffin from wood awaiting other roles. The carpentry noises blended with those of crickets and katydids, offering a dirge-like nocturnal drone that scraped its way into the cabin.

The eastern sky showed first light when the family reassembled in the main house.

Suzanne said, "Marcus, you and Maylene go on home and see if you can get some sleep. The children will run up and get you when breakfast is on, not that it will be anything fit to eat. We'll make do on the porch. Then, boys, I want you to go to your sisters, and tell them to come at once. Get word to the Farleys and your Aunt Bess. I don't want no other guests. We're going to bury your pa first thing tomorrow. I can't have this house smelling like a corpse. I'm sorry for Eliza, but we can't wait on her. I want her told in person. Calvin, you'll go to White Sulphur on a Thursday train. And walk to Lewisburg if you can't find a ride. I'll have a letter for your sister. You're to give it to her after telling her the news. Stay the night and come home Friday."

Suzanne knew their pastor, Eli Goins, would drop everything to answer the call. Being his mother-in-law gave her clout.

"Ma, are you going to bed?" Vesta asked.

"No, your pa is a-laying on the tick. I'll just rest in the rocker."

"You can use mine."

"I wouldn't sleep a wink, but it's kind of you. Go on up."

Suzanne sagged when the room emptied. She wanted a quiet spell to sit with her husband. Sit and rock.

They followed Reggie up to the Lilly gravesite at the edge of the woods, not far from the log cabin Marcus had built as a teen, inspired by a competitor for Maylene's affection. It had been an uncomfortable time to begin such a task, with winter coming on, but as soon as Maylene dismissed the threat—one Amos Wallace—Marcus had chosen the site above the fields of hay, wheat, oats, and flax, with woods on one side and pasture on the other. He'd laid it flat with shovel and pick. By New Year's Day, he'd placed the first chestnut logs, squared and notched, on a stone foundation.

They climbed that mild, cloud-cloaked morning, the coffin lashed to the sled, smelling of fresh-cut wood. Reggie labored under the load and required several rest stops. Suzanne didn't mind those breaks herself.

The plot lay curiously vacant for a family in its fourth generation on the farm. Its only occupants were three stone markers, two for Quentin's parents—Jacob and Ellie Lilly—and a third that bore no name. The nameless slab stood guard over the resting place of an infant sister of Quentin's, born blue, who died within hours of entering the world. The surviving eight children, with the exception of Quentin, had dispersed. Five daughters, one now deceased, had married and moved to other farms in what was then western Virginia, prior to West Virginia's formation, and Quentin's two brothers had packed up and moved to the wilds of Ohio in search of flatter, less-stony land. And Quentin and Suzanne had been graced with the unusual fortune of not losing a single child. Their nine had grown as strong and supple as buckeye saplings. The two sons they lost in the War were buried elsewhere, Quentin Junior in a hideous mass grave at Castle Thunder in Richmond as a prisoner of war and Johnny somewhere on a farm in the shadow of Peters Mountain.

Thus Quentin D. Lilly, Sr., represented the fourth member of his family, in the year 1872, to find a resting place there above the sprawling farm on the wide hollow furrowed by a small, nameless run, a tributary of the larger Madam's Creek bound for New River several miles below.

Suzanne brushed away the thought of her missing sons, reminding herself to be grateful for the large family ringing the hole. All but a couple of the children wore hastily dyed, borrowed, or recycled black, their collective darkness matching the opening in the earth.

Next to Suzanne stood Marcus, her second child, her look-alike son. She sometimes wondered if he'd kept the beard he sprouted during the War to help conceal the likeness. She sensed his solicitousness without him uttering a word.

Chase, who had supervised the digging of the grave, remained interested. She started forward to inspect it but returned to Marcus when he snapped his fingers. Under his breath, he said *no* with a slight shake of his head. The brindle dog sat down in front of him with a sigh.

Marcus held the hand of Sara Sue, whose face reflected both father and grandmother. Her golden locks and freckles came from the Farley side, however. They were Maylene's. Marcus and Maylene had named their third child after her grandmothers, Suzanne and Sara Mae. She was Sara Suzanne. But, like so many names, the given name morphed into something shorter.

Next to Sara Sue squirmed Johnny, holding his mama's skirt. Johnny shared Marcus's brown eyes and light-brown hair but Maylene's wide face and mouth. He possessed a disarming grin that made him difficult to discipline, which his parents found problematic. Johnny stood out as the one of their four children strong-willed enough to require frequent correction.

With one hand, Maylene held the arm of Quencus, who had just begun to walk. The boy's given name was Quentin Marcus. But having another Quentin and another Marcus in the family necessitated a nickname and "Quencus" stuck. The cherubic child had his Farley grandfather's blond curls, and his eyes sparkled green with glints of gold, as if sprinkled with mica.

Looming over Quencus stood his Aunt Vesta, her red hair ablaze. Except for her bright, turbulent locks, she, like Marcus, looked strikingly like their mother. The third of four sisters born in a row, she'd always been close to her niece Jenny, whose hand she clasped.

And there was Jenny. At eight, she seemed older. Smart, responsible, tall for her age, she bore a regal look with her shiny, black hair, straight as water dropping over a ledge in Madam's Creek. Her walnut-colored eyes nearly matched the chestnut darkness of her father's one, while her skin's bronzy hue matched no one's. Maylene had named her *Jenny* soon after news arrived that Marcus had lost a second brother, Johnny, in the War. Marcus, beyond reach at the time, could not be consulted. Maylene chose the name because it sounded much like *Johnny*.

The four of them—Jenny, Johnny, Sara Sue, and Quencus—couldn't have looked less like siblings if they'd tried.

Then there were "the boys," Calvin and Lester, the youngest of Suzanne and Quentin's children. At sixteen and fifteen, respectively, they bore a resemblance. Both had round, Quentin-like faces, but Calvin carried a stouter build, mimicking his father's short-legged, bear-like shape. Calvin had blue-gray eyes, his mop of auburn hair retaining the reddish-blond highlights of his youth. Lester, with a lighter physique, shared Quentin's light-brown eyes and riotous hair, the color of which mirrored his mother's, or had until hers began turning gray. His head wore the tan of a buckskin horse.

Louella, the youngest of the daughters and the family belle, looked ravishing even in her tearful grief and late pregnancy. By now her sisters had pretty much forgiven her for the beauty she possessed by genetic accident. With coppery hair, green eyes, a heart-shaped face, a pretty mouth, and perfect skin and teeth, she turned heads anywhere she went, and she always had. Quentin said their home looked like a livery stable each Sunday during the two years every able-bodied bachelor within a ten-mile radius came a 'calling. The parade of suitors ended when Louella, defying everyone's expectations, chose one of the less handsome men with a small farm and no apparent potential for offering a life of ease. She said *yes* to the one who made her laugh.

A short, thin man and sad as a bloodhound, Howard Neely stood next to her now. It tore him apart to see Louella cry.

And daughter number two, red-headed Rachel, a dimpled and adorable female version of her father, gripped the wrists of her two sons, aged three-and-a-half and two. Suzanne called them "the ruffians" because if they weren't sleeping or eating they were engaged in a seemingly endless wrestling match. Rachel's husband, the Baptist preacher, stood inside the circle of family, at the head of the grave. Clean-shaven, dark hair slicked back, he was the Reverend Eli Goins.

Missing was Eliza, the eldest daughter, yet to learn of her father's demise. Not long after the War's close, she'd married Mayhew Mullens, nephew of the pastor who preceded Eli, and moved to Lewisburg in adjacent Greenbrier County.

Just as well, Suzanne thought, Eliza and Mayhew aren't here.

She was in no mood for their squabbling.

As if by unspoken rule, the remaining participants stood outside the circle, on the uphill side for the sake of viewing. They were Maylene's mismatched Farley parents—short and plumpish Sara Mae, tall and lanky Bob—and her older sister Melva. Also, Quentin's gray-haired sister Bess with her balding husband, Henry Bennett, who lived atop Broomstraw Ridge.

Suzanne numbly took them in, unable to elicit her usual pride in her family. More than anything, she knew a weariness that pressed upon her with the weight of the oak limb that had taken Quentin's life. She hadn't the energy to weep.

Marcus and his brothers had wrestled the coffin onto a board placed at an angle, lengthwise, from the bottom to the top of the hole. With a nod from Eli, Calvin and Lester stepped forward with shovel and sledgehammer to free the board. Calvin loosened some of the supporting soil, then stepped aside while Lester used the hammer to force the plank farther under the coffin. With a jolt, the coffin dropped about a foot before its makeshift support caught on the earthen wall. Without a moment's hesitation, Lester stepped onto the coffin, intending his weight to free the snagged board. It didn't, so he jumped into the air and came down hard on the lid. The board broke with a loud snap, and dropped the coffin with Lester aboard, to the bottom of the grave.

A collective gasp escaped the onlookers. Calvin reached for his brother's hand, but Lester hoisted himself out unaided.

The spectacle proved too much for Johnny, who squealed with laughter at the sight of his uncle riding his paw paw's coffin into the deep hole.

Aghast, Maylene leaned over and grabbed his face in one hand, tilting it toward hers. "Stop it right now, young man! This is your grandfather's funeral, and I forbid you to carry on like this."

Johnny pulled a swath of his mother's skirt over his face, bunching some of the fabric into his mouth to silence the giggles that continued to shake his frame. Marcus glanced at his mother, relieved to see no sign of anger or even attention. Although she continued to mellow with age, Suzanne Lilly had yet to outgrow her temper.

Maylene's gaze crossed the circle and took in her mother, Sara Mae, who had turned her back on the group. Bob Farley wore his poker face. This wasn't the first time Maylene had been struck by the similarity between her mother and Johnny, the only two among those gathered who were in stitches.

For a moment, she had to squelch her own urge to laugh. An odd reversal, when the sight of Quentin's box ready to descend into the earth had her teary-eyed before Lester's unscripted performance. She put an arm around Johnny's shoulders and pulled him close.

The ceremony took little time. Eli gave a short sermon and eulogy. He led the singing of "Rock of Ages." The closing prayer ended with "…ashes to ashes, dust to dust. May he rest in the peace of our Lord. Amen."

Marcus thought, we don't start out as ashes or dust. Where do we get that idea, anyhow? It don't make no sense.

Suzanne turned away and headed down the long slope when the boys began shoveling dirt into the hole. It sent a chill up her spine to think of Quentin buried in that box.

CHAPTER THREE

It was late the next year, 1873, when Jimmy Browning attacked Randall Murphy. Joseph almost saw it. In his mind he did.

In the new state of West Virginia, the rail line had made its impossible way northwest along the New River, through tortuous miles of its deep chasm, simultaneously clawing a foothold eastward from the Ohio along the Guyandotte, Mud, and Kanawha Rivers. The two lines joined in the New River Gorge at Hawk's Nest on January 29, 1873. Many of the workers subsequently migrated west to the fledgling town of Huntington, where a major terminus took form on the bank of the Ohio River.

Freed from the wilderness, Jimmy Browning and other workers seized the opportunity to get drunk, particularly on paydays. Joseph and Randall didn't normally drink. Well past the age of revelry, they preferred their own solitary company, or each other's, to the snarls of loud young *gandy dancers* who crowded into the town's lone saloon. Besides, Joseph had never befriended booze, which made him drunk and sick with humiliating speed.

But this night, this Christmas Eve, a coworker gave Joseph a bottle of bourbon, and Joseph tarried at a bonfire of defective railroad ties and wood scraps piled near the tracks, in no particular hurry to return to a cold, featureless room. Most of the men lived far from family, and the Christmas Eve bonfire had become a tradition, an excuse to drink and keep at bay the sadness that stalked a man away from home.

Besides, the saloon was closed and didn't admit Negros. Whenever possible, Joseph would have nothing of a business that shunned his friend. Tonight, he'd have one shot with Randall before retiring to the boarding house, the temporary home like so many others he and his old buddy had known during their decades of rail work. It wouldn't hurt to unwind a bit and toast the bittersweet season.

The two men sat on overturned buckets, talking little in the din of shouting and singing. Joseph reminded himself to sip from his tin cup.

What quickened his tempo was Jimmy Browning's arrival. He despised the man. Browning had been with the crew little over a year and had been nothing but trouble. A skeletal man with dark hair and acne scars, and without a trace of social grace, he enjoyed little favor with the "ladies" who found their way to camp or town. The men didn't like him either, except for a couple of tainted ones who gravitated to their own kind, violent and vulgar.

Before the War, most men fought the way they always had, with words and fists, and their disputes inflicted mendable harm. But now some of the newer hires, those of a certain breed of war veteran, carried barbed seeds of ferocity. They fought to kill. Two such men, Benton Kramer and John McMahan, accompanied Jimmy. Joseph saw the three look in his direction as they settled cross-legged on the ground a quarter of the way around the gathered circle.

He leaned toward Randall's head of close-cropped, gray hair. "Let's get out of here."

Randall glanced over his shoulder and shrugged. "They already too drunk to stand. You go on if you want. I'll be along."

Woozy, Joseph wanted to get away from the choking smoke, which kept changing direction in an erratic breeze. The smells of cigars and spat tobacco juice didn't help. But he hesitated to leave Randall alone with those venomous thugs. He downed the last of his drink, just to be done with it. He'd wait.

Randall nursed his bourbon, swirling it in the small cup, staring into it as if it were a crystal ball on the verge of revealing a portentous image. Joseph looked back at the men, who had begun a game of cards. Good, they were distracted.

Willing to tarry no longer, Joseph stood unsteadily. "I'm heading back."

"I'll be along," Randall repeated without looking up. "If I'm having only one of these, I'm taking her slow."

He gave a low chuckle. "Reminds me of the last time I lay with a woman. I weren't in no hurry then, neither."

Joseph strained to hear over the uproar. He grasped his friend's bulky shoulder and gave it a squeeze, re-positioned his wool cap on his salt-and-pepper hair, and left.

How had it gotten dark already? Joseph climbed the rough slope above the tracks, slipped between two slumbering houses, and stepped onto wooden planks that served as a sidewalk. He passed a dry-goods store and a house with porches on both floors.

As he approached another house, an elegantly dressed woman with a shawl and a hard face stepped out of the doorway. "Hey there, handsome. You feelin' a little cold and lonely tonight? If so, I have a remedy for a fair price."

"No ma'am. Not tonight."

Joseph didn't quite make it to the boarding house before he heard shouts and turned around. In the light of a gas lamp, he made out the outlines of four men, three encircling one. At once, he knew. He yelled, "No!" and started to run.

Half-drunk, he didn't sprint with the speed he willed, but he caught up with the group in time to recognize the man who held a thin-bladed knife. Joseph didn't have to see his face to know Jimmy. The features of his comrades, too, left no room for doubt. The fourth man, sprawled on the ground, clutched at his chest.

Enraged, Joseph gave chase to the cowards, who dashed around a corner and out of sight. When he got to the turn, Joseph saw nothing but an empty street bordered by houses shuttered against the cold. Where the hell did they go?

He ran a short distance before panic seized him and he spun to return the way he'd come. His best friend lay hurt, maybe dying, and needed his help.

By the time he reached Randall, the elderly Negro man lay on his back in a puddle of dark liquid. A long tear parted the front of his coat, and the heavy fabric glistened in the lamplight. Joseph came close to fainting, just as he had the first time he witnessed the butchering of the family hog, and he recalled his mother saying, "Joey, if you don't like it, you don't have to look."

He crouched, closed his eyes, and waited for the return of blood to his brain.

Randall stared at the star-spotted sky with unseeing eyes. Dead.

Hours passed before Joseph's shock gave way to grief. In the death of Randall Murphy, he'd lost his entire family. Although eleven years older, Randall had wasted no time befriending him when Joseph arrived in Cumberland, Maryland, as a twenty-year-old lost soul. For more than thirty years, Randall had been a constant ally, telling tales, prodding the recalcitrant younger man to open up, and sharing nuggets from an uncannily wise perspective on life in general. And, through all their years of toil, he offered an unquenchable sense of humor. Joseph especially needed that levity upon his arrival, having buried both parents, become estranged from his older brother, lost the woman he loved to another man, and watched his sister descend into the cavern of marriage to a man incapable of loving her but intent on keeping her locked away from her family.

Letting himself weep in the early hours of Christmas morning, he realized he hadn't cried since the day he made his way up Broomstraw Ridge, looking for his sister, Becky. That was the summer of 1843, and his tears had nothing to do with Becky.

At daylight, Joseph stopped at the brothel, a new, white-washed house already in need of multiple minor repairs. For starters, the doorknob drooped loose. He turned it, locked. Caring little if he woke the entire establishment, he knocked hard.

Nothing.

He knocked again, this time on the door's windowpane. Unable to see through the interior curtain, he heard a faint sound from within, perhaps a door creaking open. He waited.

Just as he raised an arm to rap again, the door opened a few inches and a woman's face appeared in the gap. She looked middle-aged, with puffy pouches under her eyes and graying brown hair pulled back. She wore a robe over a nightdress and a sour expression on a mouth that bore a residue of red lipstick.

"Who are you and what do you want?"

"Name's Joseph, and I need to talk to your… young ladies. There was a murder last night, and I believe one of them may have been a witness."

"I heard. It's been discussed. The sheriff was by last night. I can assure you none of my girls observed a thing. Now if you'll excuse me, I'm going back to bed."

"But, wait, there was one woman...."

The madam closed the door before Joseph finished.

He cursed himself for not remembering the prostitute's appearance. He'd scarcely glanced at her, and it had been dark. And he'd been a bit drunk.

Although Joseph didn't expect the sheriff to be in on Christmas, he found the man at his desk, writing some sort of report. Ruddy-faced and double-chinned, he offered sympathy but proved himself useless as a cow without teats.

"You didn't see what happened. Browning says Murphy pulled a knife on him, and this here knife was found on the scene. He says it was self-defense, and he's got two witnesses to back him up. There ain't a thing I can do without a witness who says different."

Joseph picked up the spotless knife lying on the sheriff's desk. It did look like Randall's.

"Well, I can swear on a Bible that man didn't wear a knife and never once drew a knife on no one. He was out-numbered three to one, and if anyone sought to save his life it was Randall. Jimmy Browning is a goddamned bully who hates Negroes. Ask anyone—all the men know it."

"They may know it, but that doesn't mean they'll say it. Do you know if Randall Murphy owned a knife?"

"He had a hunting knife, but he didn't carry it."

"And do you own such a knife?"

"I do."

"So if you produce a knife, there's no way to prove it's Randall's. And if you say the "evidence" knife doesn't match your recollection of Randall's, that's not going to stand against two eye witnesses."

Joseph instantly hated himself for his reflexive honesty. He'd already searched for Randall's knife without success. Now, as the sheriff said, he couldn't pass off his own as Randall's and claim his friend had been unarmed. But clearly that ploy wouldn't have served as proof.

"Anyway, it makes no difference," continued the sheriff. "I can't arrest a man for being a son-of-a bitch."

"But you can let a man get away with murder, by God!" Joseph stormed out of the cramped jailhouse office before he vented more of the fury churning within. He headed for the yardmaster's office, newly roofed and unpainted, down by the tracks.

The place was deserted.

Joseph groped in a vest pocket for a pencil and miniature notebook. He tore out a page, wrote a quick sentence and an address, signed his name, slid the paper under the door, and walked away.

And that marked the day Joseph Cook, after thirty years and five months, quit his railroad job.

CHAPTER FOUR

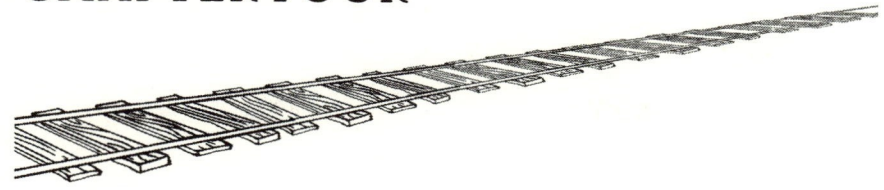

Joseph spent the rest of Christmas day in the railyard shop building a coffin. The next day, along with a dozen other friends of Randall, he got the murdered man buried at dawn in a brief ceremony with a disgruntled Baptist preacher presiding. The site, a new graveyard at the edge of town, lay stark and windswept overlooking the river. It included a "colored" section marked off in one corner, a low spot without a view, well away from the other graves. The marker, a simple wooden cross adorned with a roughly carved "Randall Murphy," looked paltry and incomplete to Joseph.

If I'd had more time, I'd have made it finer, Randall. And your middle name—why didn't I ever ask?

The time had come to go home. Joseph had always known he would someday. A man wants to be buried with his kin.

He packed his few belongings—mostly clothing and books, plus a few tools—and Randall's banjo in a trunk, bought a ticket for Hinton, and climbed aboard well before noon. Though laden with heartache and weariness, he couldn't help feeling interest in the ride through the New River Gorge. He'd seen parts of it, such as bridge locations at Falls Creek, Loop Creek, and Hawk's Nest, but this ride presented his chance, likely one and only, to see the entire route.

He and Randall had evolved into bridge specialists when they became too worn for the brutal work of slinging stone ballast and laying ties and pounding spikes. After their initial years of muscle-expanding vigor, men aged and broke doing such tasks, and rarely did any man continue in railroad labor more than a few years.

But Joseph and Randall could well have been called—and paid as—engineers many years ago, their expertise being that extensive. They cut and fit together the massive timbers of trestles and trusses with the precision of a cobbler piecing leather. They directed the exacting placement of blocks used for stone arch bridges and the oblong piers that supported longer spans. Although compensated at the lower level, they worked as middlemen between engineers and laborers, translating designs into reality. Adept with protractors, plumb lines, try squares, T-bevels, and various marking and cutting gauges, they applied keen mechanical intelligence.

Their skills were in constant demand as the B & O expanded into the Midwest. Joseph and Randall traveled south, too, onto connecting lines crossing Kentucky and Tennessee. Late in the War, they hastened back East, first recalled to Cincinnati, then used and loaned out by their employer to repair the many rail bridges burned or blown to smithereens. As soon as they erected the crucial supports, the specialists and their crew members moved on to the next project, never staying long in one place.

Exempt from the draft as rail workers, they were safe from battlefield doom, although Randall was too old anyhow.

Joseph had applied for promotions several times and been turned down. Randall never bothered. At length, Joseph gave up.

Randall said, "Joseph, it ain't no use. You may not be a Negro, but you is a shade too dark to be taken serious. Might as well accept the fact."

Hoping for better pay, they transferred from the B & O to the C & O when the push across West Virginia to the Ohio River began.

But their income remained only adequate. Joseph didn't have much to spend it on, as he avoided liquor and seldom visited a brothel. A nomadic lifestyle offered no possibility of buying a home or farm. But he did send money to his sister every few months and indulged in one habit that bordered on addiction— he bought books. Every chance he got, he'd find a book peddler or shop and snatch up whatever he could afford. Whether fiction or nonfiction, historic or contemporary, all topics satisfied. Books were his escape and his pleasure. He squandered money on them without a backward glance.

Randall had never learned to read, and resisted Joseph's efforts to teach him. "Now why on earth would I want to go to all that trouble and read at the pace of a snail when I've got you reading at me whether I like it or not?"

Randall, a captive audience in their shared rooms and tents, sometimes complained. Joseph learned early on, however, that the whining served as Randall's way of keeping them on equal terms. He wasn't going to let Joseph get a swelled head over his eighth-grade education and refusal to use the perfectly good word *ain't*.

When Joseph said, "Fine and dandy, I'll read to myself," it took no more than one evening for Randall to speak up.

"What are you readin' there to yourself?"

"It's a novel by Jane Austen, *Pride and Prejudice*."

"What's it about?"

"It's about a young woman.... Hell, Randall, it will be a lot easier for me to simply read it to you than read it and then tell you the whole thing."

"Suit yourself. Hard to imagine you bein' quiet that long anyway."

Joseph slid to the window, fixing his gaze outward. He didn't want to make small talk and hoped he made evident his disinterest in the other passengers. He did. No one joined him on his seat.

The engineer gave a whistle blast, and the wood-fired steam engine pulled its trailing cars out of Huntington, heading east, spewing a giant plume of gray smoke into the cold air. People struck up conversations, read newspapers. Children squirmed, asking questions. And Joseph stared at passing farms and low, wooded mountains. Bare, windblown branches against a gray sky. The frigid, murky swirl of the Guyandotte River.

Everywhere was Randall.

"Why the long face, Mr. Joe?" Randall asked soon after meeting the young man from southwestern Virginia. At their temporary Cumberland home, Randall worked on a track-maintenance job while Joseph received minimal training before the B & O sent them farther west.

"It's Joseph, if you don't mind, without the 'mister.'"

"Fair enough. You may call me Randall, although I outrank you in years and experience."

Randall guffawed at that, his head rocking back in merriment. As an exceptional judge of character, he knew Joseph would take no offense. "You know, most of the men call me 'Mr. Murphy,' outta respect."

Joseph smiled at that, wishing it were true. He already liked the affable man, and he knew what it was to be on the receiving end of ridicule and threats. He'd always known.

"Just been through some hard luck of late, that's all. It'll do me good to be away."

"Well, don't keep it corked forever. As an older and wiser man, I might can be of help."

They were friends from that day forward, yet it took nearly three years for Randall to tell his own tale of woe. Joseph wished he'd heard it sooner, as it would have made his own troubles pale in comparison and put his self-sorrow to shame.

The disclosure followed on the heels of Joseph's hint of loneliness. He'd always expected to have a family, and he disliked the void where wife and children should reside.

They'd gotten to the place in *Far from the Madding Crowd* where romance triumphed.

Joseph raised his head and said, "It's mighty hard to pursue matrimony when a man's got to pick up and move all the time. You ever wish you could settle down?"

"I was settled down once."

"You were? Married?"

"Yes, suh! That I was."

Randall leaned back in a wicker chair and closed his eyes. "You gonna keep readin'?"

"What happened? Do you care to say?"

Randall let out a long, tired sigh. "No, I don't much care to, but it might do you good to see how it's done."

He opened his eyes and locked them on Joseph without a trace of his usual humor.

"We had a little piece of land on the Susquehanna. That's up in Pennsylvania. I worked day labor at a big dairy farm that served

Harrisburg. Walked over three miles each way. One day, comin' home, I saw my wife, Carrie, way up on a hillside with our baby on her hip. Little Randy was three then, and he was with her. The cow'd gotten loose, and Carrie'd gone to drag her home. So there they were, the four of them, and a storm was comin' on. They didn't see me down on the road, but I could see Carrie hurryin' Randy and the cow along. They passed under one of them big spreadin' oaks, and it weren't even rainin' yet, and the sky busted open with light and split off half that tree like it was kindling. And they dropped, just like that, and didn't move no more. I run up that hill like a madman, but they was all dead when I got there. That's 'bout when I decided to try my luck with the railroad, as I'd heard they was hirin'. I got my family buried and I was gone."

Joseph looked back into the dark brown eyes, as dark as his own, and detected a blankness in them, like a cave with no exit. It took him a moment to speak.

"For the love of God, Randall, I had no idea what you been through. I'm as sorry as a soul can be."

"I thank you for that." Randall turned his attention to the window, streaked by light rain. "It was like the Good Lord reached down from heaven and took them home. I tried mighty hard to believe He done right, like he knew they was goin' to have too much hardships and sorrows, and He wanted to spare them all that. I was right sore He didn't take me, too, but I reckon I didn't pass muster."

"You are a mite ornery." Joseph's effort to trigger a smile failed. "You still got kinfolk back there?"

Randall's eyes shot back to Joseph. "Kinfolk? You think slaves get to have kinfolk? My brother and sisters and daddy got sold. That's when my mama'd had enough and took off in the middle of the night. Just me and her, and we walked near fifteen mile that night. Well, she did—she carried me some. Her feet was bleedin' by the time we holed up in a haystack. But we was lucky. We started below Frederick and got to the Mason-Dixon in two nights. The nights was clear and we could see the North Star. Mama said, 'When you feel like cryin', juss look at that big star, like the star of Bethlehem, and keep walkin' toward it. Think of Baby Jesus waitin' for us under that star and he's a'callin' to you, Randall. He's sayin', 'Come to me, and I'll give you rest.'

"Somehow my mama knew somethin' about Quakers, and we found one who carried us up near Harrisburg. He suggested we go farther, but my mama wasn't well, and we wound up stayin' with a big Negro family, the Morgans. Mama died a couple of years later, and I lived with them nine years 'til I took work at the dairy farm at fifteen. Bunked there 'til I saved enough to buy my little place on the river—weren't much more than a shack and a weed patch. But I fixed it up right smart and was mighty proud to own it and make a home there."

Joseph shook his head. "You've suffered more loss than anyone I know."

Randall nodded and formed a grimace-like smile. "Now you owe me yours. You ain't given me nothin' but dribs and drabs."

The train reached Teays Valley, an expansive, cultivated bottomland bordered by Mill Creek. Joseph, having slept only a few hours the previous night and none the night before, let his head fall back against the window frame and drifted off.

He woke well past Charleston, evident by the radically altered terrain and nature of the river, the raging New. The train had slowed to a crawl.

Aw, damn. If the train ran on the east side, as indicated by the water's northward direction and position on the opposite side of the train, he'd slept through the river crossing at Hawk's Nest. He'd liked to have seen the massive timber and stone construction, built in part by his and Randall's labor and finesse, tested by the behemoth he rode. The final-spike ceremony, almost a year earlier on that bridge, marked the culmination of a 428-mile feat from Richmond to the Ohio River. Joseph's memory heard the cheer that went up and felt Randall's huge, calloused paw as they shook hands in celebration.

He and Randall had been present at a similar event more than twenty years earlier when the B & O completed its twenty-five-year push from Baltimore to the Ohio River near Wheeling. That was a winter day, too, a Christmas Eve. The final spike preceded the arrival of two trains from Baltimore the next month, and Joseph recalled how chilled he and the other men became waiting for the delayed trains loaded with mayors, governors, and B & O officials, along with several hundred invited guests.

Now he rode a car on its hard-won track, and he must stay awake. The cinder-spewing locomotive ascended the Gorge, and the scenery grew stunning. Joseph got up and found a seat across the aisle, to stay in view of the river.

As the train wound its sluggish way and the water hurled itself downward with increasing vigor, Joseph narrated inwardly to Randall, as if continuing to read from the latest shared book.

I have to crane my neck to see the top of the slope, and in places I cannot. Higher up are gigantic chestnuts and oaks, mixed with hickories and sugar maples and others. Down along the edge of the river are the biggest hemlocks and sycamores you ever seen. And thickets of laurel you'd never get through if you was bigger than a squirrel. The river's up, but there's a cap of ice over every pool, like the water's dropped some and left a gap. There's cliffs with icicles longer than a man is tall. And the rapids are wild and loud, every one different, with great boulders crusted with ice from the spray. Makes me pity them boys who laid the line through here—I don't know how they done it. Good thing we were too old for that work. Come summer, there'll be fires from the engine sparks in the brush they left behind. You can see some burned places already from the last dry spell. Look at them blackened stumps. Must be many a thousand of trees that fell to the axe, clearing the way, cutting for ties, some for cookfires and keeping warm. We felled a few for bridges, didn't we?

Hard to believe I'm going home after all this time. Guess you already are home. Did you decide to go?

And that thought interrupted Joseph's description. Had Randall seized the opportunity to pick a fight when his friend was absent? He wouldn't have started it, but had he made the choice to provoke when he could have kept silent and kept walking. Did he say, "Someone's got to teach you manners, you brainless, worthless jackass," throw a punch, and let himself be taken out of his tired and aching body to the place he hoped his family waited? He had a tendency toward melancholy when he drank.

But no, that was madness. Randall wouldn't choose to die that way. If he wanted to go, he'd have walked into the river....

Jesus, Randall, why didn't I wait for you?

The train stopped at Quinnimont, where it swallowed one passenger, a haggard-looking man Joseph judged as slightly younger than himself. The man coughed into a stained handkerchief as he passed through the car, and Joseph exhaled relief to see the stranger continue to a car farther back. His pasty look of consumption made Joseph wonder if the man headed for a family's care somewhere.

Poor chap.

While the train rested, Joseph leaned forward to peer through the opposite window and admire a tower of stone—an iron furnace. He never failed to study the workmanship of any stone or wooden structure, and this one intrigued him more than most. With its massive and well-fitted blocks, it ought to last centuries, yet not a wisp of smoke spewed from its crown.

In contrast, the miners' homes looked like temporary shacks set in a row. They hunched along New River in its first coal mining town. It appeared deserted, almost like a ghost town, until Joseph reminded himself why the men were out of sight—they labored underground. The women and children huddled indoors, their drafty homes colder than the hellholes where their husbands and fathers worked. To Joseph, the trend away from log homes was an obvious mistake. Frame houses lacked the ability of heavy timbers to hold a fire's heat and release it for hours after flames died to embers. He felt sorrow knowing they were frigid in winter, miserable.

And coal. Joseph wondered what it could possibly do that wood couldn't. He noticed some nuggets spilled on the slope above the tracks. They shone oily-black in a weak winter sun that had squandered hours freeing itself from low clouds.

I'm showing my age, aren't I, Randall? Resisting change. You know somebody's going to get rich, and it won't be the men crawling through the earth like moles.

CHAPTER FIVE

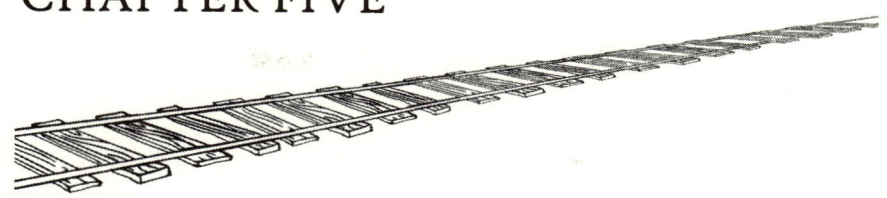

Somewhere south of Quinnimont, Joseph nodded off again. He dreamed of a tall figure with a knife, coming at him on a dark railway platform. The man's hat, its broad brim pulled low, hid his features.

"Show your face!" Joseph shouted.

Frantically, he tried to release his own blade from its sheath, but it refused to slide free.

The train's whistle blast saved him, bringing him back with a start. The brakes engaged and forced him to brace himself with an arm. He awoke thinking, Dear God, I didn't ask the sheriff if Randall wore a sheath. No one would carry an exposed blade.

He hadn't thought to look for the leather casing in his haste to leave Huntington. Was Jimmy sly enough to steal Randall's knife and leave it at the scene? Joseph didn't think so, but maybe one of the other men had the idea.

"New Richmond!" The conductor strode the length of the train, announcing the stop at a small village strung along a wide swath of the New. They'd come out of the Gorge and into a region of scattered farms. A thin crust of snow covered every north-facing slope on the surrounding mountains.

Joseph tore his mind away from the image of Randall's lifeless form. I could get off here and walk to the old farm, he thought, his restlessness urging him off the train.

But he didn't want to see the place. It had been sold nine years earlier when his brother, Will, died. Becky had gotten a letter to him by sending it to the B & O office in Baltimore, from which it had been forwarded to his worksite at Harpers Ferry, where the bridge across the Potomac was repeatedly destroyed during the War. She wrote that Will, wifeless and childless, had been drafted as a Confederate shortly before West Virginia's birth as a Union state. In his mid-forties, he missed by a few months being too old for conscription. Further bad luck followed. He died the next year from an infected hip wound received at Cedar Creek, Virginia, and left the farm to his two siblings, with instructions that they sell it and split the money. Joseph wrote back, asking his sister to keep his share in a secure place. He considered reminding her to be sure her husband didn't find a way to filch it but assumed Enoch would read the letter. Joseph didn't care if he insulted his brother-in-law, who knew full well what Joseph thought of him. The man was vermin. But why cause trouble for Becky, who surely had plenty on her hands already?

Joseph got up and stretched his long legs. His chilled feet and aching back stiff as the bench itself reminded him he'd been sitting too long. As the train lurched forward, he sat again, kept alert by familiar terrain and cascading memories it evoked.

The tracks lay between the river and the base of Brooks Mountain, which soon loomed above. There Joseph had grown to manhood on a farm up a holler created by Owens Branch tumbling down for eons toward the New. A path once meandered from the edge of a pasture into the woods, up and over a sloping rise to the next holler, that of Brooks Branch and the nearest farm. It led to the home of Suzy, his childhood playmate.

Will, nearly four years older, didn't want much to do with his kid brother. Becky, two years younger than Joseph, lacked appeal by virtue of her constant presence. But Suzy was the right age, feisty, adventuresome, and sharp. She and Joseph fed off each other's strong wills, clashing often and with the frequent outcome of Joseph storming off for home. But as soon as the boy got the go-ahead from a parent, he'd scurry right back, and the duo would resume their play.

Suzy's mother, plagued by unexplained miscarriages, had only two surviving children—Suzy and Roger—and Roger, six years older than his sister, deemed her a spoiled and bothersome pest. His avoidance of her made her especially hungry for Joseph's attention.

But he was *Joey* then.

Joseph closed his eyes, remembering. He heard Billy Scaggs at the close of a school day, "Going home to your teepee, Joey?" His laughter, joined by other boys, followed Joseph home like a rabid dog.

He arrived in tears and found Mama stirring something in a large pot on the stove. She reached down with one hand, cradling his chin, drawing his face against her hip. "What is it, Joey, my love?"

And her touch and the love in her voice eased his pain. That tender moment crystalized as his last clear memory of her.

He was seven that November, when his mother's shape foretold another baby after the loss of Joseph's infant brother. Isaac, on the brink of walking, had died the year before of an illness unknown to Joseph. Now Mama's turn came to fall ill with fever, and she took to her bed. Before long, Joseph's pa told the children to stay away and let her rest. Then Papa disappeared all day after telling Will to watch the younger ones. He rode way up on Keeney Mountain and came back late with an old, bent doctor. Papa and the doctor went to Mama's bed and stayed a long time, speaking in low voices around lengthy spells of silence. They all missed their supper that night and went to bed with noisy stomachs.

In the morning, the doctor had gone, and their pa told them their mama got the blood poisoning, and the angels had come and taken her to heaven, and the unborn baby, too. He cried telling them, which his children had never seen him do. Joseph wanted to run to Suzy that awful day, but Papa told him to stay and feed the chickens and hog and take care of Becky, and that's what he did. Will had to help dig the grave next to little Isaac's.

Joseph's father, Matthew Cook, was never the same. Something in him broke that fall night when his Cherokee wife, Faye, slipped away. Although he didn't inflict unkindness on his children, he lost interest in anything but keeping them alive. He became obsessed with the success of the farm, and agonized over every dry spell, wet stretch, late frost, wind storm, sign of insect damage. Like every farmer, he worked from dawn to dusk, but he no longer found a shred of pleasure or even satisfaction in his labors. He toiled to succeed so that his wife's children would live—he owed her that.

And he set a good example in general, holding himself to high standards of fairness and honesty. What he failed to prevent was a household devoid of joy.

Joseph, who resembled his mother in both appearance and personality, retreated into his rich fantasy life and sped through his chores to spend more time at the Harman farm, with Suzy. His pa understood and let him go.

"Bring that sassy lass over here now and again," he said. "She's a breath of fresh air."

One fall day, nearly a year after Faye Cook's death, Billy Scaggs and Homer Beckwith waited for Joseph after school, which amounted to half-day lessons in old Mrs. Gwinn's cabin up on Gwinn Ridge. After mornings with her "rowdy brood," as she called her pupils, the frail and nearly deaf widow required afternoon naps.

Homer said, "There goes the half-breed with his little darlin'. Let's scalp them both and hang their hair on a fence rail."

Joseph's mother had taught him. "Ignore them, Joey. If you fight or talk back, they'll hurt you. They are fools not worthy of your attention. You just keep walking as if they don't exist."

Suzy, beside him on the well-worn path that switch-backed down from the ridge, knew no such restraint. She turned on the boys behind them. "Shame on you, pickin' on someone younger, and there's two of you to one of him."

"What are you going to do about it, shorty?" asked Billy with a snide grin.

Suzy's brother, Roger, had finished eighth grade the year before and graduated, but Suzy flaunted him anyway. "I'll send Roger to give you the beating you deserve."

"Oooo, big, bad Roger. As if he cares," said Homer. "At least we don't have to worry about that mama-squaw coming after us with a tomahawk."

The two boys laughed and Joseph froze. He spun around and flung himself at them, fists flailing. Overshadowed in size and outnumbered, he soon found himself on the ground being kicked and punched. He scrambled to get up but fell beneath a shower of blows.

Suzy snatched two sharp-edged, potato-sized stones off the edge of the path and let one fly. It struck Homer in the forehead, dropping him with momentary shock.

Billy paused his punches to double over with glee. "Did the squirrel hit you with a nut? She beaned you!"

Homer leapt to his bare feet, wiping blood from his brow, and took off after Suzy. She sped away with a good head start. Joseph seized his chance to regain his own footing, land a punch in Billy's midriff, and run for his life. He soon passed Homer, who had enough sense to consider his pa would beat the living daylights out of him if he whupped a little girl, but took aim at the friend who ridiculed him.

"Shut up, Billy. It's not funny!"

"Look at you!" Billy laughed through his hurt. "Attacked by a chipmunk, and the chipmunk won!"

Joseph heard yells and scuffling sounds as the boys went at each other.

He wheezed for air by the time he caught up with Suzy, who stepped out from behind a wide buckeye trunk. His lower lip, cut by his teeth, bled. Though badly bruised, Joseph bore no broken bones, thanks to his friend.

"They...coulda...killed me."

"Not a chance."

Joseph saw the second rock clutched in Suzy's hand. "You takin' that home?"

"Just in case. But I reckon they got the message, don't you?"

And they did. Except for whispered insults and glares, Billy and Homer left Joseph alone after that. It helped that Joseph's pa told Will to keep his brother in view on their journeys to and from school.

Only a few meandering miles separated New Richmond from Richmond's Falls, thundering in the power and beauty Joseph knew well. There the river leapt off a sandstone ledge to crash onto massive boulders—fragments of the eroding edge—below. The water's mass and speed kept it from freezing but didn't prevent dramatic curtains of ice from forming along the falls' perimeter.

Joseph heard suckling sounds and glanced at the couple seated across from him. Their baby had been fussing since the last stop, and now fed hungrily. The mustached husband faced Joseph with a newspaper wide open. His wife, turned toward the window, concealed herself but not her infant's sounds with a cape. With a slight smile, Joseph returned his attention to the river.

Lucky baby, he thought.

And he resisted too late the stab of jealousy that followed, thinking the husband lucky, too.

Joseph studied the New, which ran quiet now, slick and dark and cold, bordered with its ice shelves. Gone were the giant hemlocks of the Gorge. Here were hardwoods—sycamores, boxelders, silver maples—as well as pastures dotted with haycocks.

The train passed a small tributary spilling through mounds of ice-capped rocks, and a memory came. It was summer, and he and Suzy played on Brooks Branch near her home. They had decided to construct a bridge but disagreed on how to go about it, so their plan turned into a contest. Two bridges, and one would be best.

They scoured the hillside for fallen branches, breaking the smaller ones into suitable sizes. Suzy laid hers from bank to bank, perpendicular to the water's flow.

Joseph said, "That's all wrong—it won't work that way."

"Why not?"

"It ain't stable, and it'll be hard to walk."

He had laid two heavy branches across, about a foot apart, and busied himself placing short cross-pieces on top, parallel to the current.

Suzy readily grasped the superiority of his design, but she wasn't about to let on.

"Your sticks is too skinny—they'll break."

"No they won't. You'll see. Just a little weight goes on each one."

"Not if I walk on tiptoe."

"Well why would you do that? No one crosses a bridge on tiptoe."

"I can if I want."

Typical Suzy, getting under his skin.

"Why do I even play with you? You're so ornery."

"You're the one who insulted my bridge. And it ain't even done yet."

"Well, let me know when your masterpiece is ready for inspection."

"So now you're the inspector? Then I get to inspect yours."

"You walk across mine and I'll walk across yours, and we'll see who gets wet."

"That's not fair! You're bigger than me. I get to walk across both."

And so it went. Suzy most often got her way, but she did have enough of an honest streak not to claim victory that day. Her pride prevented her from admitting defeat, however.

She concluded, "My bridge is best for small critters, yours for bigger ones."

Joseph said, "Maybe so. I'm due home."

She never seemed to know when he was mad.

When they turned twelve, Mrs. Harman insisted on a chaperone, which made sense to neither Joseph nor Suzy, by then *Suzanne*. Becky, their only choice, accepted her role with the enthusiasm of a long-excluded child.

One spring day, the trio traipsed down Owens Branch re-enacting the Lewis and Clark Expedition, a recent school topic. Naturally, Suzanne took the lead, declaring herself Captain Meriwether Lewis. Joseph was Second Lieutenant Clark, Becky, Sacagawea.

The forest floor, carpeted with wildflowers, cushioned their bare feet with cool, damp moss. Unopened umbrellas of mayapples, feathery leaves of Dutchman's breeches with their upside-down pairs of miniature white pants, and occasional swaths of red-blooming trilliums attracted no special attention as the children made their way downstream, the emergent display being as familiar as the mushrooms and blanket of colorful, curling leaves of fall.

Suzanne said, "When we reach the Missouri, we'll build a boat."

"We have to go upstream, remember? Toward the Rockies. That means we'll need paddles." Joseph visualized the route in his head. "Sacagawea, you can fish for our supper while we work on the boat and paddles."

"I'll catch the biggest ole catfish you ever saw," Becky said, marching more like a soldier than an Indian.

Suzanne stopped and pointed through the veil of unfurling leaves at the New. "Look! There it is! The Missouri! We're almost there."

She glanced back at her followers, and that's when Joseph caught sight of it, a copperhead sunning on a large flat rock along the stream. In another step, Suzanne's foot would be upon it.

"Watch out!" He lunged forward and grabbed Suzanne's right arm, pulling hard.

She toppled backwards and would have fallen if he hadn't caught her. His arms closed around her waist long enough to save her and prop her upright again. The disturbed snake hastened for cover under a cluster of Dutchman's breeches, continued out the other side, and found refuge in a jumble of rocks.

"Dear Holy Jesus, I woulda stepped right on that thing! It was a copperhead!"

But Suzanne shrugged off her fright and resumed command of the adventure. Joseph, however, became quiet, no longer interested in gouging out the rotted innards of a small log, the intended canoe big enough for a pair of mink. In that moment when he held Suzanne and felt her warm, firm shape in his arms, something powerful awoke in him. The sensation lingered like the taste of molasses on the tongue after swallowing, and he thought he would very much like to hold her again, although it seemed unlikely another such opportunity would present itself. And he had an inkling why Mrs. Harman wanted Becky tagging along.

By the next spring, Suzanne began to "blossom," and Joseph retreated into adolescent self-consciousness. Their years of play came to an end.

The train slowed again. It had reached Hinton, the brand-new county seat of a brand-new county, Summers, created from corners of four surrounding counties—Mercer, Monroe, Greenbrier, and Raleigh. The C & O had chosen the village as a key terminus for dispatching rail crews in both directions and sidelining cars and engines for maintenance or repair. Positioned on a broad, sloping bench above the river and tracks, Hinton bristled with the skeletons of buildings under construction. Surrounded by mountains, it reminded Joseph of a clutch of eggs hatching in a high-walled nest.

Impatient to be free of the stuffy car, Joseph sprang upright before the train shuddered to a stop. In addition, he was ravenous for the first time since Christmas Eve.

CHAPTER SIX

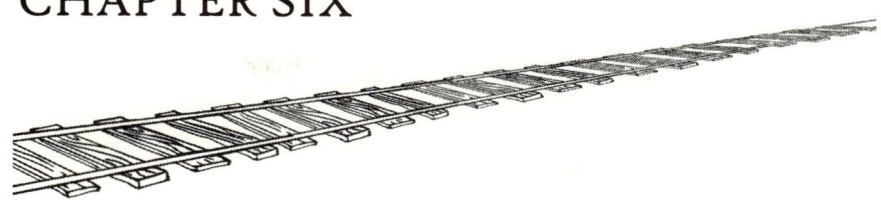

Suzanne Lilly remained mad at God. He could be mad right back if He wanted. She was plain tired of apologizing and begging for forgiveness that never came. She knew she'd done wrong, and she'd said she was sorry a hundred times, more like a thousand. She'd accepted as best she could the loss of two sons, the injury—both physical and emotional—of a third one, and the crippling of her husband. She'd tolerated Quentin's descent into the whiskey jug after the War. She hadn't complained about her own humiliating incontinence, increasingly difficult to deal with and conceal.

But, damn it, how was she to bear this hurt? God might have given some warning. Her husband could have taken sick, giving her the chance to care for him and say good-bye. She'd have held him while he took his last breath, told him of the pride and pleasure she'd gleaned in their thirty-one years of marriage.

Was God ever going to tire of punishing her?

Outwardly, however, Suzanne's habit of anger waned as she aged. How had it ever served her? She recalled with regret the welts she'd raised on her children's bared buttocks or exposed calves in fits of fury over their refusals to mind her. She'd never failed to keep a switch on hand for that purpose. But now she left discipline of her grandchildren to their parents, rarely even raising her voice in disapproval. Thankfully, her sons and daughters appeared unharmed by her temper, having grown into sound and sane folk. So she judged, with Quentin's agreement.

Now she liked to sit with a grandchild on her lap and simply talk. Relaxing into her new role, she found herself asking more than telling.

"Sara Sue, where did you get all those freckles? Let's see if I can kiss one off."

"Johnny, tell me what the shape of that biggest cloud reminds you of."

"Jenny, come sit with me and tell me what you learned at school today. Have you had another history lesson?"

And she loved to rock Quencus to sleep for his afternoon nap, the feel of his compact body going limp and heavy in her arms.

Her children marveled at her tenderness, which they recalled receiving in small, infrequent doses. Their pa, inclined to tease and give bear-hugs, had been the more demonstrative parent.

Yet they had always known they were loved by their parents, who never hesitated to stop in mid-task when a child expressed genuine need. The children were guided, protected, disciplined, and taught with an equal measure of care for each of the nine. They felt securely confident of their parents' ability and willingness to do anything required on their behalf.

Invisible to the children was their mother's exhaustion. With her petite form, she assisted in maintaining a large garden, put up countless pounds of preserved food, prepared and cleaned up after three meals each day, spun and weaved wool and flax, made clothes for the entire family, carried water from the well and milk from the springhouse, chopped wood, churned butter, and did scores of other tasks on top of caring for her multitude of children. There hadn't been time to sit and hold and talk, not until now.

Yes, Suzanne mellowed like the rounding edges of a river stone. Yet she would never forget her most shameful outburst of anger, and it had nothing to do with fatigue or a willful child.

It was the day she broke Joseph Cook's nose.

More than a year had passed since Quentin's death. Having cowed the sun, winter with its long nights drew Maylene and Marcus's family around the fireplace after supper. Maylene had conceived again, and the fatigue and queasiness of pregnancy's early weeks made her grateful for the season's quiet. Some nights Jenny, Maylene, and Marcus took turns reading from a novel, the annual gift from Maylene's widowed grandmother in Charlottesville. But many nights Marcus told stories. The older children embellished with unbounded enthusiasm these products of their father's imagination.

Maylene, only half-teasing, told Marcus she missed his tall tales of earlier years, held together by suspense and vivid imagery. They went somewhere. Now that the children were involved, however, storytelling had become a chaotic tangle of tangents and dead-ends.

Still, rocking with Quencus on her lap, Maylene appeared engrossed this night as another mangled plot unfolded.

Marcus, with Sara Sue straddling his thighs, began. "I believe we left off with Mr. Fox digging a hole to get away from Old Man McAlister. Johnny, do you remember where he surfaced?"

Johnny sat cross-legged with Jenny on a wool rug out of reach of all but the fire's farthest-shooting sparks. "In a hen house!"

"That's right," his father answered, "and he grabs himself a plump one right off her nest. Now, do you suppose the hens raise a ruckus?"

"They holler for help!" said four-year-old Sara Sue, bouncing for emphasis.

"And who wakes up?"

"The farmer!" said Johnny.

"He sure does, and his hound, too. In they come, and that hound right on Mr. Fox's tail."

"Papa, why ain't it *Mrs.* Fox? Can't it be Mrs. Fox? Her name can be *Peggy*," said Sara Sue.

"I suppose it could be Mrs. Fox, but she's mighty busy looking after all those kits of hers, who don't stay where she puts them unless she's right there to make them mind."

"*Peggy* is a dumb name for a fox," said Johnny, now six.

"It's a perfectly good name. What do you know about fox names, Mr. Smarty?" said Jenny.

"Never mind," said Maylene. "What's going on in that henhouse?"

"Well, Mr. Fox dives back down the hole with that hen in his teeth, and the hound goes right after him. Now Mr. Fox has a problem because if he goes back the way he come he'll pop up in Mr. McAlister's barnyard where he started. And he figures there's a good chance Old McAlister is still waiting around with his shotgun, just itchin' to have a shot. So what's he gonna do?"

"I'd pray!" said Sara Sue.

"He's gonna dig a new tunnel!" Johnny jumped to his feet. "He'll come up in his den with supper for his family!"

"Well, that would be a happy ending, wouldn't it?" said his pa. "But he don't want to show that mean ole dog where his den is, do you figure? We need a way to fool that hound."

The children kept quiet, thinking. Sara Sue spoke first. "Papa, is *Peggy* a dumb name for a fox?"

"No, chickadee. Your brother is a tad too full of mischief for you to believe everything he says."

Johnny beamed as if given a soaring compliment.

The word *irrepressible* arose in Marcus's mind, and he thought how well Johnny mimicked his namesake in that regard, despite looking nothing like his uncle. Marcus's brother Johnny, younger by less than fourteen months, came third in the Lilly lineup. Happy-go-lucky, wise-cracking Johnny with his wild red hair and irresistible charm. Young John Samuel possessed the same cocky confidence.

With the children momentarily distracted by discussion of the fox's name and gender, Marcus turned his attention to Quencus. His thumb-sucking, slacking off to weak, sporadic draws, signaled his descent into sleep. Maylene stroked the toddler's soft curls, nuzzled her nose in them. Marcus knew Quencus's sweetness and blond hair reminded Maylene of her brother, Robin, who died at an age not much older than Quencus. At eight, she'd been stricken with fear and grief unresolved for years. She'd told Marcus she sometimes imagined she held Robin again when she cuddled Quencus.

As the hound and fox resumed their adventure with Jenny's suggestion of a false trail of feathers, Maylene joined Quencus in departure. Her head fell back against the rocker's worn wood as the words drifted up the chimney with the smoke.

Marcus's voice had always been her compass bearing. She'd known him as long as the reach of her memory, and he'd been her closest friend from the start. As children, they'd entertained each other by the hour with their fanciful fictions, which Marcus often illustrated with a pointed stick in silt along the creek. Among others, their monsters were bears, gigantic snails, and thieves. Marcus could sketch anything his mind could invent.

The War had come close to taking them from each other. Marcus survived typhoid fever and two near-misses from snipers' bullets. He got through the three years he served, unwillingly, in a gray uniform. But he came home missing more than his right eye. The tense, short-tempered, distant Marcus wasn't the man who'd ridden away that May morning in 1862. Nearly a stranger, he inflicted more than a year of dread feasting on Maylene's innards, sickening his wife with the fear her beloved Marcus would never return.

And he might not have. He needed more than time. He needed to know a truth hidden from him his entire life, and that truth required a confession from his mother. It gave both Marcus and Maylene pause to consider that Suzanne could have remained mute, leaving them trapped in their web of unhappiness the rest of their lives.

In her prayers, Maylene thanked God for His intervention, and she thanked her father and her children. It soothed Marcus, once he got past his shock, to learn his mother's secret. It soothed him to spend hours in the woods training the puppy, Chase, his father-in-law gave him. And it soothed him to have children, whose affection, needs, and barrage of questions kept him from dwelling on the memories that stalked him like ghoulish apparitions. They were ghosts ever more distant and indistinct.

The Marcus Maylene loved might not ever get over the wariness and deep hurt he held in silence, but he had come home to her.

CHAPTER SEVEN

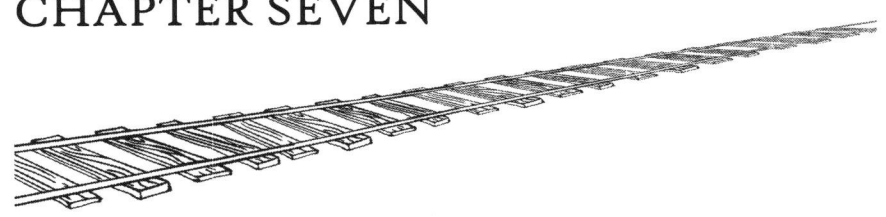

The second week of January, Johnny found his papa in the barn forking soiled straw out of the cow's milking stall. "Mama wants you," the boy said.
"Where is she?"
"In bed."
Marcus threw down the pitchfork and ran.
"Papa, why are you running?" Johnny yelled after him.
"I'm in a hurry."
He found her curled on her side, covered with a quilt. Her face lacked its usual rosiness, and Marcus saw sorrow and suffering in its blank expression.
He sat on the bed's edge and took her hand. "What is it, May?"
Tears came. "We're losing this baby. I don't want to."
"Oh, no. What can I do for you? Does it hurt awful bad?" Marcus reached out with his free hand to wipe a rivulet off Maylene's cheek.
"Not so terrible."
But he knew. With each contraction, Maylene gripped his hand hard, and her body tensed. He'd never been with her during labor, and her pain alarmed him. Was something badly wrong?
"Should I ride to town for Dr. Mason? Go get your ma? Maybe I should go."
"No, honey, I'll be alright. I just feel so awful sad. I didn't know I loved this baby already but I . . . but I do."
Another contraction. Marcus held her hand with both of his. She squeezed so hard it hurt.
As the pressure eased, Maylene said, "Will you tell me a story?"
"I'll try. Is there a sort of story you have in mind?"

"No."

Marcus's mind thrashed about, increasingly panicked to find his rich reservoir drained dry. "I'm afraid I'm at a loss. How about if I read to you?"

"All right."

Marcus turned to lift a hefty Dickens, *Bleak House*, from the bedside table and glimpsed Johnny peaking around the curtain. "Go back to the barn and finish that stall, son. You can do it. Your mama ain't feeling well and needs some quiet time."

Johnny, uncharacteristically, vanished without a word.

Marcus started where he found a bookmark, but he read without comprehension. His attention remained on Maylene's pain and sadness, and his impotence to dispel them.

After what Marcus estimated to be more than an hour, Maylene's grip began to relax, and she rolled onto her back. "I've made a mess," she said. "Will you put these to soak in a bucket?"

And she eased a wad of bloody rags out from under her. "I'll need some fresh ones."

When Marcus returned with a stack of clean diapers, he said, "We'll make another baby, I promise."

Maylene nodded without a smile, and Marcus knew he'd chosen the wrong words at the wrong time. His wife wanted *this* baby, which her heart and body had already begun preparing for. She'd made a place in August, a place in their family, for a child who would never be.

"You go on about your work, I'll be all right now. Thank you for sitting with me," she said.

"You're sure?"

"Yes, I'm just tired. I think I'll sleep a spell. Will you tell Jenny to keep the little ones at your ma's until suppertime?"

"You bet, May. Vesta will send up some food. I'll come check on you shortly." He leaned down and kissed her forehead, which felt damp and cool as a dog's nose. Then he pulled the quilt and down comforter up to Maylene's chin and paused to stoke the fire on his way out.

February came with its longer days and higher sun without bringing warmth. As always, Marcus pretended to forget Maylene's birthday, making no reference to it whatsoever. But in the darkness before dawn, when his internal alarm went off, he leaned across her and planted a kiss on her mouth.

"Good morning, birthday girl. Happy birthday."

Maylene wrapped her arms around his neck and returned the kiss. "Thank you. It's sweet of you to remember. I'd near forgotten."

Marcus knew the latter statement was untrue, but he didn't let on. "There's a little something for you under the bed."

Staying covered as best as possible against the chill, Maylene groped in the pitch dark until she located a lump wrapped in cloth.

"What is it?"

"Bring it downstairs and see. I'll light the fire."

Marcus reached for thick wool pants and sweater to pull on over his flannel underwear, doing his best to dress under the covers, the lightless room being too Arctic for any other means of donning the frigid garments. His feet already clad in heavy socks, he rose and pulled back the curtain that served as their privacy wall, and coaxed kindling and embers into a hopeful blaze in the fireplace.

Maylene, moments later, stood dressed at the table, where she set down her precious bundle. She untied twine and unwrapped the awkward shape with care. In the flickering light she made out a carved male wood-duck's head, a work of art.

"How beautiful! I love it!"

"I hoped so. Can you guess what it's for?"

"For decoration? It's too pretty to put to work."

"I'll mount it by the door. You can hang your sun bonnet and apron on it."

"How perfect! He'll be out of the children's reach, and his glorious head will show above my shabby garments."

She reached for her husband, squeezing him hard. "It's lovely and I shall cherish it."

And she gave him a lingering kiss before pulling away to light the cookstove.

One year, Marcus shaped an exquisite bowl carved from an oak burl. Another year, a fishing pole decorated with carved fish. And every year, he made the day special by finding ways to remind Maylene of what awaited her at nightfall, when the children slept.

He chose a secluded moment to kiss her throat and jaw. He massaged her thigh under the table at supper. He nibbled the nape of her neck. By the time the last child was tucked in, Maylene had reached such a state of arousal she needed no prompting to dive into the second gift, delivered with generous enthusiasm.

This year, their lovemaking complete, Marcus asked, "Did you have a happy birthday?"

"It was miserable."

"I'm a complete failure."

Maylene giggled into her husband's neck. "I love you, Marc." And she kissed him goodnight before rolling onto her side and pulling his arm across her for the delicious warmth of their fitted forms.

CHAPTER EIGHT

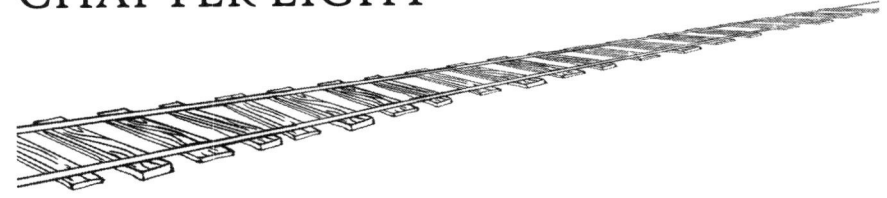

Joseph found a temporary job at Silas Hinton's general store, upriver from the railyard. The storekeeper's assistant had fallen ill, and Joseph needed a break from rail work. A closet-sized room in back would serve as his living quarters, perfectly adequate for a man whose entire possessions resided in a trunk. Offering free housing and one meal a day, Silas justified a minimal salary, but Joseph didn't object. Accustomed to making ends meet, he considered himself fortunate to find employment.

He kept the place clean, manned the cash register at dinner time, stocked the shelves, and made regular trips to the railyard for new merchandise. On one such errand to pick up a crate of iron cookware, Joseph found a young man sitting on the crate, strumming a banjo. The ruddy-haired man set down the instrument long enough to extend an arm and introduce himself as Calvin Lilly, a new freight handler. Joseph took note of the name but knew Lillys were as common as cows in these parts. He had no reason to think of Calvin as Suzanne's son. Besides, he didn't resemble her.

It was a four-mile walk from the Lilly farm to Hinton, and Calvin made that walk every day but Sunday. Inspired by a real paycheck, he answered another motive as well. At seventeen—almost eighteen—he'd grown interested in girls, and Hinton had girls. Pretty girls, smart girls, flirtatious girls, and a few musically talented girls.

Calvin, the musician of his family, had learned banjo on a homemade cigar-box version Marcus helped him craft soon after returning home from the War. Calvin picked it up with the ease of a frog jumping into the farm pond. He had a gift. By now he was an accomplished musician in search of others. Within weeks of taking the rail job, he'd found a male fiddle player and a girl, Nancy Ballengee, who played magic with spoons. Calvin soon set his cap for her.

Naturally, Nancy's parents insisted music-making be restricted to their home. Hence Calvin, Nancy, and Ben the fiddler began spending evenings in the Ballengee home, singing and playing for hours on end. What they considered "practice" drew a small audience, including those inclined to dance. Calvin thanked his lucky stars the Ballengees didn't frown on dancing.

Together, Joseph and Calvin muscled the heavy crate into the Hintons' wagon. "Thanks for your help," Joseph said as he climbed onto the wagon seat.

Damn it, just ask!

"You got a group going? Making music?"

"Sure do!" Calvin smiled. "We play every Wednesday and Saturday night. The Ballengees let me stay over. Do you play?"

"Banjo. Not as well as the man who taught me, but I reckon I can keep up."

"Do you sing?"

Joseph smiled at that. "I don't rightly know. I can't say I've tried." Randall did, but Joseph needed his full attention on his fingers.

"What kinds of songs do you play?"

Unsure if Calvin would turn up his nose at Negro gospel, Joseph said, "Gospel mostly."

"That's just what I've been wantin' to learn! We play ballads like "Omie Wise," and we've about perfected a pretty lively version of the "Virginia Reel," but we've got no gospel under our belts. Why don't you come down to the Ballengee place after work? We play at half past seven. You know the place, don't you? Big log house there, by the tracks." He pointed downriver, and there stood the two-story house.

"I'll be there if you think I can be of use."

"Sure you can. It's nothin' serious, at least not yet. We're working up to going public on the Fourth of July—that's our hope, anyway. Gives us four more months to smooth out the rough spots. We could use another picker."

With that accepted invitation, Joseph intuited he'd made his first friend on New River since losing Suzanne decades earlier.

Suzanne. When had she insisted, he stop calling her *Suzy*? They must have been about ten when she declared she would no longer go by that childish name. Not to be outdone, Joey declared himself *Joseph*. They had to correct each other for months until the new names stuck. But stick they did. Even at home, the children rejected their childhood nicknames and trained their families to call them by their given names.

Joseph's sister tried to follow suit, declaring herself *Rebecca*, not *Becky*. But she was less stubborn and forceful about the change, and it didn't take hold.

Oh, Becky. Joseph thought of her as he put the banjo back in his trunk a few nights later. He hadn't yet been to see her and collect the money she'd saved for him. Spring approached, and he wanted to buy a horse or mule and a small farm in time to plant. What was he waiting for?

It was a long-time habit to put her out of his mind. He'd been furious when she'd accepted the attention of Enoch Wallace, an eighteen-year-old encountered on his way home from a job on Virginia's newly begun Giles, Fayette, and Kanawha Turnpike. Hired to cut and split wood and assist the cook who kept the slaves fed, Enoch resented the unskilled nature of his work. When word came of his father's illness, he quit and headed north, spying Becky at Pack's Ferry when the Cook family made a rare crossing to attend a wedding. Dark-eyed and dark-haired, Becky Cook had lighter skin than Joseph's and lacked their mother's Indian facial features. Her unique blend of her parents' traits rendered her attractive in an indefinable and exotic way.

Although he despised the father he'd fled at an early age, Enoch returned home with the belief his father lay dying and the farm was his to inherit. Such was not the case. The irascible man rallied but never regained health enough to manage without Enoch's help. Enoch stayed, making Sunday trips across the river to visit Becky.

From the outset, Joseph disliked him. Too physical, too pushy, too slick. But Joseph recognized the extent of danger too late. Enoch started crossing the New on Saturday evenings, convinced Becky to sneak out at night, and applied enough charm or pressure or whatever it took to get her pregnant. As soon as he got wind of that unwelcome fact, he made himself scarce.

Becky, at fifteen, was heartbroken. She thought the son-of-a-bitch loved her—he'd said as much. Her father, livid, said he'd raise no bastard child in his home, and he'd be damned if he wasn't going to hold that good-for-nothing worm of a man accountable. He put Becky and Joseph on one horse, himself and Will on another, and off they rode for the Ferry and the Madam's Creek route up Broomstraw Ridge.

On the way, they snagged Pastor Mullens of the Madam's Creek Baptist Church. The wedding, of the shotgun variety, featured a scowling groom and a weeping bride.

Joseph had never forgiven his father for sentencing Becky to a lifetime of misery.

Joseph vowed he'd make the trip the next Sunday. He'd rent a horse at the new livery in town and gird himself with optimism. What was the worst that could happen?

He had no way of knowing Becky believed him dead. For years, Enoch had collected at the Jumping Branch Post Office and destroyed the long letters Joseph wrote twice a year—at Christmas and at Becky's July birthday. And when Becky wrote the B & O, asking about her brother, Enoch burned that letter, too.

Joseph hadn't expected responses to his messages. His erratic movements made him too hard to track down. But he wanted his sister to know he'd not forgotten her, nor had he forgotten the promise he'd made the last time he saw her.

That summer day in 1843. He'd ridden the Cook mare up Broomstraw Ridge to the site of the disastrous wedding to tell Becky good-bye and report their papa's death. Reaching the crest, he rode the meandering road along the summit to a short lane, bordered by pasture and hayfield, that ended at a modest cabin. Now-bearded Enoch, with a pistol tucked into his pants, stopped him thirty yards shy of the Wallace home.

"What are you doin' here, Joseph? I don't recall an invitation."

"I come to see my sister. I need to speak with her."

"About what?"

Joseph's blood pumped faster. Why is this man so vile?

"It's between me and her, family business."

"We don't keep no secrets in this house. If you've somethin' to tell her, I've a right to hear it."

Joseph recognized he skated on thin ice. If he was going to see Becky, he'd have to cow-tow to her husband.

"All right, then. I'll speak to you both. I don't mean no offense."

Enoch snorted with skepticism but yelled over his shoulder, "Becky, git out here. Your brother's here and has somethin' to say."

Becky materialized with such promptness Joseph surmised she'd been listening by the open door. He noticed she'd lost weight, not that she could afford to. "Good to see you, Joseph. Can you come in for a cup of coffee? Your little nephew is asleep, but I'd like you to meet Amos. I can wake him up."

"You'll do no such thing," Enoch said. "Let the boy sleep, and I don't want no stranger in my house."

"He's not...."

Enoch's scalding look silenced her.

Joseph started to dismount, but he, too, hit a wall of denial.

"Stay in that saddle. If you've got something to say, say it and be on your way." Enoch pulled the pistol out of his pants and crossed his arms.

Joseph's body churned to full boil, and he waited a moment to control his voice. He ignored his brother-in-law and looked at his sister, who stood only a foot beyond the doorway. "Becky, I come to say good-bye. I'm taking a job with the railroad—B & O—and I'm leaving in two days. And there's another thing."

He turned to Enoch, who stood like a sentry before him. "Oh, for God's sake, Enoch, let me off this horse so I can tell my sister some hard news."

Enoch answered by cocking the pistol with an audible click.

Son of a bitch, I'd kill you this instant if I had a gun in my hand.

He returned his attention to his sister to calm himself. *Ignore him—he's not here.* "Our pa died two weeks ago, Saturday. I'm sorry, Becky."

She showed no reaction. "What happened?"

"We was cutting the wheat field and he stepped on a yellowjacket nest. He got stung right bad, but not much worse than other times. Pretty soon he got all cold and shivery and went inside to lie down. Said his head hurt and he felt like he had a load of firewood piled on his chest. I wanted to keep an eye on him, but he said, 'Go on out and finish that last acre. I'll just rest a bit.' When I come back in, he was gone."

"Why didn't you come sooner, so I could be at the burial?"

Joseph gave Enoch a withering sneer. "Will come up to get you and got run off. He said Enoch took a shot at him, and he didn't feel like getting himself killed. I chose to think Enoch didn't recognize him, as no sane man would do his wife's kin that way."

Enoch said, "I don't welcome no man comes uninvited, and you wore out your welcome the minute you showed up. Now get the hell outta here."

Before Joseph composed and spat back a reply, Becky said, "Shall I ever see you again?"

"That you shall." As he turned the mare back toward the road, he said, his rigid face fixed on Enoch, "You have my word."

Was he waiting for Enoch to die? But he hadn't a clue if his brother-in-law or Becky lived. Or even resided on the same farm. All he could do was go.

He'd take his pistol this time.

CHAPTER NINE

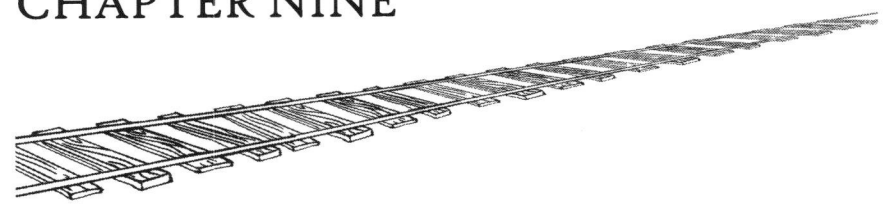

The next Saturday evening, Joseph picked up the horse—a dark-bay gelding—and tethered it in front of the store. He fired up the pot-bellied stove, brought buckets of water in from the cistern out back, half-filled a washtub, and added repeated rounds of hot water from a kettle on top of the stove. He swam in the summer to clean his skin but couldn't remember the last time he'd had a real bath.

His soaking and scrubbing completed, he dumped the water, a bucketful at a time, out the back door, its color serving as proof his winter of "birdbath" hygiene had been inadequate.

In the morning, Joseph dressed, shaved by lanternlight in front of a hoof-sized mirror hung from a nail, left money for the jerky and pickled eggs he took, re-saddled the gelding, and left before sunrise. He rode down to the ferry near the freight depot. The vessel—a long, barge-like craft—sported hinged ramps at each end. Both stood upright during the crossing, with one lowered upon landing. Secured overhead to a thick rope cable strung from bank to bank, the ferry was poled across the strong current by two muscular men. It deposited Joseph and his borrowed horse near the mouth of Madam's Creek. There Joseph remounted and started up the gentle incline of the road flanking the creek's north side.

He cursed under his breath at the horse's uncomfortable gait. He'd rented a nag, and he hoped the thousand-foot climb to the top of Broomstraw Ridge wouldn't do in the beast.

"We'll take our time, old man. I don't want you going lame."

The water, fed by snowmelt and springs, ran fast and high, alternating between small waterfalls and swirling runs. In about three miles, the road split, and Joseph took the left fork, crossing the slightly muddy water on a simple log bridge. The ascent began to steepen, and he stopped to give his mount a rest and a drink from a narrow but swollen brook racing for Madam's Creek.

Looking upward, Joseph took in the changing forest. Buckeyes, maples, and tulip poplars mixed with more oaks, ash, chestnuts, and hickories. Dark greens of white pines stood out among the hardwoods. Even without their leaves, recognizing trees by their bark, buds, and habits of growth took little effort. With wood being as essential to survival as farm crops, even children knew the trees.

Resuming the journey, Joseph allowed his mind to retrace the last time he'd followed this route, the summer day of his dispute with his brother-in-law, a day of additional drama....

It was an early morning that fateful year, 1843, when he'd passed the Lilly family heading upstream along the New, as he rode downstream from the Pack's Ferry crossing near the mouth of Bluestone River. He knew Quentin at once, having seen him on the opposite side of the same crossing almost two years earlier.

That day, Joseph, Will, and their father waited for the ferry, on their way to the baptism of a cousin. Quentin Lilly, a stocky young man with bright red hair, transported a large bouquet of wildflowers protruding from a saddlebag, and the fortyish ferryman teased him as they made landing.

"Looks like someone's getting ready to pop the question. Who's the unlucky lady?"

Quentin laughed. "She's Suzanne Harman, up on Brooks Mountain, and if these flowers are gone when I get back, she said 'yes.' I believe she shall. If she turns me down, she don't get the flowers."

"Good luck to you, young man, although I doubt you deserve it," said the ferryman.

It took no more than a second for Joseph to memorize Quentin's face.

So here was the red-haired man again, traveling somewhere with what appeared to be his parents and younger, unmarried sisters. Joseph had heard of his marriage to Suzanne, but where was she?

The Lilly quintet passed Joseph with smiles and howdies. He kept moving, to prevent their stopping and asking his name. The men walked. The older woman rode a mule, the teenaged girls a large gray workhorse. It had rained the night before, making the road muddy, and Joseph studied the boot and hoof tracks as he continued downstream.

The tracks led up Madam's Creek, the way he was headed. They went left at the fork, also in his direction. Soon thereafter, they headed up a path along a smaller creek. Joseph stopped his horse. He could keep going, on up the ridge. Or he could follow the tracks to the farm where Suzanne lived, and tell her good-bye. He could tell her he was sorry for the quarrel that left him with a broken nose and them with a fractured friendship. He hated to leave such a rift between them—it would ease his conscience to mend whatever might be mended, or at least try.

With a churning stomach and quickened pulse, he turned his mount onto the path, then into thick grass along the edge. He didn't want to leave tracks Suzanne would have to explain.

As imagined, she was alone except for her baby. Junior, teething, had spent such a fussy night that his mother was exhausted and begged off going to the Lilly funeral that would require a tiring, all-day trip. Having finally gotten Junior to sleep, Suzanne prepared for a nap when she heard the approach of a trotting horse. Going to a window, she drew in her breath. She knew the rider, well before he reached the substantial log house.

They hadn't meant to commit adultery. But there was something about the tenderness of Joseph's apology, and Suzanne's sadness in knowing she'd never see him again. Not to mention the fact that, despite their quarrels, they'd always loved each other.

Suzanne made the first move, placing a trembling finger on Joseph's healed nose. And, as was typical, she got her way. Joseph's resistance was brief. They made love in a torrent of kisses, a sizzling passion that astonished them both. Joseph's two hopes as he rode away were that Suzanne could tell neither that it was his first time, nor that he wept.

His next stop was the Wallace farm. Quite a day, all in all.

Nearly thirty-one years later, he didn't choose the Lilly-farm path, which had transformed into a wagon road. Quentin didn't deserve such disrespect, and Suzanne didn't need him blasting back into the world she'd created with a man she loved. Assuming, of course, they were both alive and living there.

The gelding labored up the steep, rutted route, requiring several more rest stops. Joseph wished he'd made a better selection. He took note of birdsong announcing the nearness of spring—cardinals, titmice, and wrens filled the still air with bright, far-reaching notes. The sun suggested warmth. Despite lacking the power to penetrate Joseph's coat, it heated the back of his neck.

At length, the plodding horse crested the ridge, and Joseph reined to the right. Less than a mile to go. How did a man ready himself for an encounter with Enoch Wallace? He checked the pistol in his right pocket. It unnerved him to carry it, was he prepared to use it?

His hands shook as he tied the gelding to a sapling near the road.

Wish me luck, Randall. I may be joining you sooner than that Charleston doctor suggested.

He walked the short lane to the cabin, which wore the defeated look of neglect. It needed cedar shingles replaced, as well as chinking. Joseph was willing to bet the roof leaked.

Joseph stepped onto the narrow porch and knocked. No response. He knocked again before deciding to check the barn.

As he reached the hard-packed clay of the yard, he heard a sound behind and turned to see a young, dark-haired man pointing a rifle at him.

Dear Jesus, he thought. This reception habit must run in the family.

"Who are you, and what's your business here?" asked the gun wielder.

"Please lower that gun. I'm looking for my sister, Becky Wallace. Does she live here?"

"Who are you?" asked the man, or boy, again. Joseph judged the lad to be in his mid-teens, more frightened than menacing.

"Joseph Cook."

"You're lying. He's dead."

"Is that a fact. Do I look like a corpse to you? Will you please set that rifle down and tell me if my sister is still alive?"

"Are you really my uncle?"

"I am if you're my nephew. What's your name?"

"Caleb."

"Well, tell you what, Caleb. If I tell you your mama's birthday, will you come here and shake my hand?"

"I guess so."

"July twenty-seven."

Caleb's tense face broke into a grin. He released the rifle stock and, holding the gun by its barrel, came down from the porch and grasped Joseph's outstretched hand.

"Now I hope you'll tell me your mama's living and well," said Joseph.

"She's alive, but she ain't real well. She's fetching eggs and feeding the hens 'round back. I'll show you."

Caleb pushed open the door of a small henhouse. Dust sifted through a beam of light that fired through the opening. Becky gave her son a quick look, then returned to her inspection of nest boxes. "Hi, son. You come to help me carry these four eggs in?"

"No, Mama. We have a guest."

Joseph stepped inside as Becky turned around, and he thought he'd have to catch her as her knees gave way. But she used an arm to steady herself against the dropping-spotted wall. Joseph hoped his expression didn't reveal his shock—he scarcely recognized his sister, owing more to how she'd aged than to the dim light.

"For the love of God. Joey."

He reached for her and she fell against him, trembling, tears streaming.

Joseph knew the money was gone. Why burden his sister by inquiring? He and Becky sat at the table by the cookstove, warm enough in the drafty cabin, while Caleb sharpened an axe and an adze on a whetstone in the barn.

"You sent letters all this time?" Becky asked in a voice rough with outrage.

"Twice a year, every year. I mailed the last one a week before Christmas, from Huntington. When did they stop?"

"Your Christmas letter after Will died. That would have been in sixty-four."

Joseph propped his forehead on a palm. "That's more than nine years ago."

"I wrote the B & O and asked about you, but I never got no answer."

"Let me guess. Enoch mailed the letter."

"I should have known he would do such a thing, but even for him it seems too low. After he convinced me you were dead, we used some of the money to buy a new mule when Paddy died. I thought the rest was safe. I kept it in a leather pouch on the mantle. But one day it went missing. I knew he'd gambled it away. He plays cards on Saturday nights, and he loses more than he wins."

"It don't matter, Becky. You did the best you could, and I'll never fault you for it. But I'd like a word with Enoch."

At that Becky shot to her feet as if confronted by a ghost. "No, you mustn't! You must leave, Joseph. I been watchin' the sun and it's getting close to time for him to be home. He's gone to the mill to see if he can trade dried apples for meal—we're running short. You mustn't be here when he gets back."

Joseph caught the fear in his sister's eyes and voice. He wondered if her missing lower tooth had fallen out or been knocked out. Her face bore deep creases from nose to mouth. Smaller ones furrowed her forehead between her eyes. Her complexion lacked color.

Joseph stood. "Becky, are you ailing?"

"I don't think so. I'm only tired."

"You don't have to stay here. There's work in town for Caleb. We can find a place for the three of us."

"You don't know how I hunger for that, but Enoch would kill you if you took me away, and Caleb won't go without me. I've tried to get him to go, but he knows we can't manage the farm without him, and he wants to look out for me. His sisters married young to get away, and their lives ain't easy, but they're better off away from here."

"Enoch can't kill me if I kill him first."

"Joseph! You ain't the killin' kind and you could get yourself hanged. Don't even consider it, I beg you. He wasn't so bad before the War. He tried not to be like his pa, he truly did. But he come home changed, and despite his suffering, I'll never forgive him about the letters. You can rest assured I learned a long time ago how to manage Enoch. I'm quicker on my feet than he is when he's drunk, and I stay between him and the door 'til he passes out. I wouldn't be here talking with you now if I hadn't learned to deal with him. Amos never did. They fought like demons until Amos enlisted. He never come back. But Caleb's not inclined to fight. He's a sweet boy, despite the impression he gave you."

A tremor shook her form, and Becky hugged herself. Joseph waited for it to pass before he came around the table to embrace her himself. She felt bony in his arms, like an orphaned child.

"Are you saying I'll make trouble for you if I stay?"

"A heap of trouble."

"Then I'll go, but I won't promise to stay away."

CHAPTER TEN

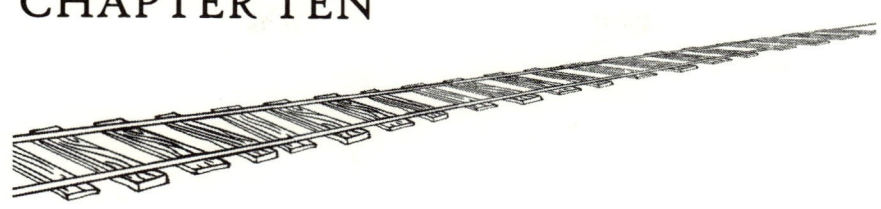

Joseph took more and more to Calvin Lilly, appreciative of the teen's good-natured gregariousness. Calvin called him *Mr. Joseph* and began to delve into topics beyond banjo tunes. They talked a little politics and explored bridge design and carpentry, horse breeding, railroad expansion, and the plans taking shape for the town of Hinton.

One night after a music-making session, Calvin followed Joseph outside. "Mr. Joseph, do you mind my asking if you've ever been married?"

"No, I don't mind you asking and, no, I haven't. I was always on the move, and I'm not much of a ladies' man."

"You think I'll be sorry if I give up my freedom?"

"That depends. Are you badly smitten?" He knew the answer.

Calvin tried unsuccessfully not to smile. "I might be."

In truth, he'd never been happier. Making music with Nancy Ballengee and staying in her home two nights a week had given him ample chance to know her, a confident, smart young woman, ever ready to tease and laugh.

He added, "She flies about inside my head like a bird in a cage—there's no releasing her."

Joseph could tell Calvin didn't care how others saw her. Nancy wasn't unattractive, but her thin, dark hair made a flimsy frame for her face, she scarcely had a bosom, and her front middle teeth overlapped. Yet the love-struck lad appeared blind to all but her charm.

Suppressing his urge to laugh, Joseph asked, "You think you could be with her day and night, and yearn for more?"

"Something like that."

"I've seen how her eyes follow you like a calf trailing a cow. She'll say 'yes.'"

Calvin's smile broadened. "You think so?"

"No, I know so. Go on and ask her, son."

Joseph tripped mentally over *son*. Why did he use that word? Calvin couldn't possibly be his son. He was much too young. And that old longing, that old what-if, loomed like a thunderhead that never shed rain. Did he have a son or daughter he'd never meet?

Calvin clasped Joseph's hand and shook it vigorously. "Yes, sir! I believe I shall."

Calvin and Nancy chose a date in May shortly after Calvin's eighteenth birthday, which allowed the groom to catch up in age with his bride. They saw no reason to waste time on the betrothal period. Ben and Joseph scrambled to prepare two instrumental versions of hymns, "Shall We Gather at the River" and "Come We That Love the Lord." The oldest and most distant of Suzanne's daughters, Eliza, took the train from White Sulphur Springs with her husband, Mayhew, and the couple stayed overnight at the Lilly farm. Maylene ensured her children's Sunday clothes were clean and pressed, and each child had a thorough washtub scrubdown. Marcus groomed his beloved cavalry mount, Blackjack, as well as Reggie. Suzanne cut Calvin's wayward hair while Vesta cut Lester's. Maylene baked two dried-apple pies, Vesta a nut cake.

The Ballengees moved furniture out of their parlor and borrowed straight-backed chairs. They shoved their dining table into a corner to make room for dancing and placed tables of various sizes and shapes on their porch. Mrs. Ballengee made bouquets of daisies and buttercups that lined the mantle, the site of a homemade altar.

A few minutes after one o'clock on that tenth of May, 1874, the Lilly contingent set out. With the aid of their wagon, the Farleys' wagon, Eli's buggy, and several loaned-out horses, everyone found a seat. Widowed Suzanne, Marcus and Maylene and their four children, Eliza and Mayhew, Rachel and Eli with their two boys and another child on the way, Vesta, Louella and Howard with their little girl, Lester the youngest, and a jittery Calvin descended the run that led to Madam's Creek. Even with the ferry crossing, they had ample time to make the four-mile trip to the four o'clock event.

Marcus drove the Lilly team, Blackjack and Reggie. Calvin sat behind him on a milking stool.

He uncrossed his legs when his ma scolded, "I told you not to do that. You'll wrinkle your pants."

"Hard to believe my baby brother's tying the knot," said Marcus. "How'd you talk that poor girl into accepting the likes of you?"

"I promised her riches," Calvin replied.

Marcus let out a hoot. "I thought you said she's a smart girl."

"Smart as a whip. She talked her folks into taking themselves and their kids to stay with friends tonight."

Marcus laughed at the sky, which threatened rain. "Oooo-eeee! I can see that would have been a right awkward request for you to make. You need any brotherly advice about your wedding night?"

Suzanne, seated next to Marcus, spoke up. "It's a little late for that, what with the children here, don't you think? Calvin, I trust you'll consummate your marriage with the gentlemanly consideration the occasion calls for."

Marcus, feigning severity, twisted his neck to eyeball his brother. "That's exactly right. Do what the occasion calls for, Cal. Listen to your ma."

Calvin smiled back with a wink. "You have my word."

"He's grinning like a mule eating briers," Marcus tattled.

Suzanne pursed her lips. "What have I loosed on the world?"

She wished to join in their merriment, but she didn't dare laugh. Every bump—and there were hundreds of them—threatened disaster. She'd had next to nothing to drink that morning and had relieved herself in the new privy just before climbing aboard, but she clenched her buttocks anyway in anticipation of what her disobedient bladder might do. She hadn't made a trip so far from home in years. She'd have to ask for at least one stop on the way to Hinton. Even with that, she worried she'd wet the two flannel diapers she'd laid between her drawers and skin. The strain showed on her face, and Marcus thought she must be missing Quentin.

Marcus savored the ride down. He seldom traveled farther than Madam's Creek Baptist Church. Now that Calvin worked in town, he brought home the salt or bootlaces or thread their ma might request from the general store. The family no longer relied on Meador's Store in Jumping Branch, though a little closer, and was too self-sufficient to require much merchandise.

So here was an opportunity to enjoy the beauty of his favorite time of year, bursting with greenery and birdsong. Marcus took in new leaves in their delicate, fresh color and extravagant white blossoms of dogwoods beneath the canopy. Every tree seemed to hold birds. Flitting, feeding, calling birds. Migration at its peak, the forest-clad mountains served as a daily feasting and resting stop for millions of songbirds, who did their traveling by night. Marcus craned his neck to scan the tops of oaks festooned with tendrils of yellow-green flowers. There warblers of more than a dozen varieties fed, but they busied themselves too high for him to discern their vivid colors.

Sara Sue climbed over the seatback and onto her papa's lap. At five, she remained his shadow. Marcus sometimes felt she'd not taken her eyes off him from the moment of her birth.

She gasped, pointing, "Papa, look!"

A male scarlet tanager had come down from the treetops for a drink. He perched above the water of Madam's Creek on a low branch, a brilliant red bird with black wings.

"Now ain't that a pretty sight! You know what that is, baby girl?"

Sara Sue shook her head.

"It's a summer redbird, and I reckon he's about the handsomest bird of all. Do you think so?"

Sara Sue wriggled around to look over Marcus's shoulder as the wagon passed. "I never seen anything so pretty. Does he sing pretty, too?"

"Not as pretty as some, but I like his song and so does his missus. She's probably nearby but hard to see. She's green."

"Why isn't she red?"

"Well, I can't say for sure, but I think it's like being a lady duck. You don't want to be all bright and flashy when you're sittin' on eggs. Think how easy it would be for Mr. Fox to see you and come gobble up a whole nest full."

"Oh." She thought for a moment. "Then why is girls prettier than boys?"

Marcus laughed. "Maybe because you girls don't sit on eggs, and us boys are too ornery to look nice."

Sara Sue giggled and put her arms around her favorite person in the world.

The Ballengee house was packed, the chairs rapidly filling. Men lined the walls, allowing women and their children to sit. Joseph, wedged into a corner with Ben, sweated more from nervousness than heat. He'd never asked Calvin about his ma's identity, and he was about to learn it. By now he had a strong suspicion, knowing Calvin walked home up Madam's Creek. And he knew Calvin's ma lived, he'd heard him mention her.

Look at me, Randall. I'm a wreck.

And there they were, Calvin leading the way. Directly behind him walked a small, buxom woman with graying hair and blazing blue eyes. Joseph could see no more than the skirt of her lavender dress until she moved out from behind her son to take a seat of honor in the front row.

Suzanne.

He looked away. Seated and stuffed into his nook of the crowded room, perhaps he'd go unnoticed. His resolve to ignore Suzanne failed almost instantly. He had to see if a son or daughter resembled him. But such a confusion of family, with hair in all colors and types. Who was a son or daughter? Who a son-in-law or daughter-in-law? And where was Quentin?

He had to stop staring.

Just as he withdrew his eyes from the Lilly procession, they snagged on a girl with black hair. Not brown but black, and thick and straight as his. Her skin a shade darker than the others'. Someone stepped in front of her. Joseph forced his gaze down to the banjo in his lap, as the instrument, the voices around him, the task at hand disintegrated into meaninglessness.

She had to be his granddaughter.

Ben stood, tucked the fiddle under his chin, and nodded to Joseph. Panicked about performing in full view of Suzanne, Joseph half-rose to relocate his chair. Perfectly natural. The duo would play better facing each other. And why shouldn't he sit if he wanted?

As he set the chair down, its back to the room, he looked up to see Suzanne, her small face with its pointed chin framed between the hats of two women, gaping at him, lips parted. There was no mistaking the shock written on her features.

Lord Jesus, Joseph thought, seating himself and picking up his banjo, how am I going to do this?

But Ben tapped his foot, rocking with the tempo—one, two, three, four—and they began "Shall We Gather at the River." Immediately, Joseph made mistakes. Ben eyed him and raised an eyebrow. The tune was simple, and they'd practiced.

Joseph sweated freshets. Focus, you damned simpleton!

But he picked and strummed so sporadically, Ben's performance became a near-solo. Fortunately, all eyes, except for Suzanne's, were soon on the bride making her way down a narrow aisle on her father's arm. The tune ended as she reached the fireplace altar.

Ben sat down and leaned his freckled face toward Joseph. "What the hell? Are you all right, Mr. Joseph?" he whispered.

"Not entirely. I'm sorry. I shouldn't have come. Can you handle the recessional by yourself?"

Ben started to respond, but the preacher in his black suit had begun with his "Dearly beloved," putting an end to all conversation.

As soon as the short ceremony concluded, the guests were ushered onto the porch for refreshments, which consisted of a mouth-watering array of desserts. The Lillys selected their sweets and found two benches long enough to hold them all, with children on laps, facing one another. Between the benches three small rectangular tables served as a dining surface crowded with heavily laden tin plates.

Suzanne had selected some sort of meringue pie—she didn't know what. Her mind swirled like a firestorm. *Joseph!* Alive! Here! She'd heard Calvin speak of "Mr. Joseph," but she'd had no reason to think he referred to her long-lost friend and one-time lover.

Good heavens, the years hadn't diminished his handsomeness. How it had angered her as a girl that he was better looking than she. With his broad face, wide mouth, and strong nose—although not too strong for her fierce fist—Joseph wore his mother's Cherokee features, and they looked even better on him than they had on her.

In comparison, Suzanne felt faded, wrinkled, spent. *How shall I speak to him? How shall I not?*

Either choice choked her with impossibility.

Her quandary was brief. Calvin approached with a quaking Joseph in tow. "Ma, I want to introduce you to Mr. Joseph. He's a good banjo player, although he won't admit it, and a better friend."

Suzanne wanted to rise but didn't trust her legs. As if reading her mind, Joseph said, "Don't get up. It's a pleasure to … meet you, Mrs. Lilly."

It didn't help Joseph's panic that he almost said, *see you, Suzanne*. He squeezed the small gloved hand.

"Calvin has spoke of you with affection." Good, her voice was under control, unlike the rest of her. "I'd like to introduce you to my family."

Calvin excused himself to join Ben and Nancy, ready to start the foot-stomping music. Food could wait.

One by one, Suzanne made her way around the loop, presenting Calvin's friend as "Mr. Joseph." Joseph willed himself to remember names, knowing he wouldn't. He took note, like all men, of Louella, who should have been banned from weddings. How any bride could feel pretty when Louella sashayed into the event was beyond imagining. She smiled demurely and took another bite of prune cake.

He avoided the girl with black hair until her turn came, but when he turned his attention to Jenny, his dry mouth went drier. He might as well have been looking into a mirror at age ten. Jenny gave a polite hello but didn't smile. She diverted her eyes after speaking.

And then, introductions nearly compete, Marcus. The man boring a one-eyed stare into Joseph from the moment he stepped onto the porch.

Maylene shot her husband a warning look.

Suzanne said, "This is my second oldest, Marcus."

Before extending his hand, Joseph, said to her, "Calvin told me he lost two brothers in the War. I'm terribly sorry."

He winced at his tactlessness. Why bring that up now? He was stalling. *Second oldest.* If one of Suzanne's was his, it would be her second, on the heels of Quentin, Junior.

"It's true. Marcus is my son who come home."

Even with the beard, Joseph discerned Marcus's resemblance, except for his dark eye color, to his mother. He took in the leather eyepatch and assumed the War had caused the loss.

As Joseph reached for a handshake, Marcus stood. "Your last name is Cook."

Taken aback, Joseph said, "That it is."

And Marcus picked up his fork and plate of apple pie and strode off the porch, into a light rain.

Suzanne barked, "Marcus, don't you dare! I raised you better!"

Heads turned and conversations stopped in mid-syllable.

And Joseph had his answer. He'd just been snubbed by his son.

CHAPTER ELEVEN

Jenny found him milking in the barn. She couldn't possibly ask her ma, but she was going to ask Papa. Even if it angered him, she had to know.

Chase clambered out of the straw and stretched before greeting her, tail wagging.

Marcus looked up from the stool. "What's up, sweets?"

Jenny patted Chase's head and took a deep breath. "That man we met today—is he my daddy?"

Marcus had to stop himself from snarling, *Oh, for God's sake, no!*

Of course, based on his behavior and Joseph's appearance, Jenny would land on such a notion. How could she not? If he hadn't been so busy fuming, he'd have seen this question written all over his daughter's pensive face at supper.

With care, he moved the pail out from under the cow and set it in a corner of the stall. He relocated the stool a few feet back, opened the stall gate, and took his daughter in his arms.

"No, baby doll. I can see from my behavior why you might think something like that. But I know for a fact who your papa is, and that man is me."

Relief ran down Jenny's cheeks as tears. She held her pa tightly.

"Laura Ann said I must be adopted."

"She did? Well, I'd like to tan her hide. When did she say that?"

"At school last year. She said I don't look like my family, so I must be adopted. Why do I look like that man we met today?"

Marcus wished he'd anticipated this question, too. "There's a family connection. On your grandma's side. It's ... complicated. It's not my place to explain it, and I have to ask you to accept that."

75

"Am I an Indian?"

"A little bit, and so am I. There's no shame in that. In fact, I'd like you to carry that bit with pride."

"So Johnny and Sara Sue and Quencus are, too?"

"Yes indeed, but this will be our little secret for now. Don't say nothing to them, or your grandma either. I'm asking you to promise. Promise?"

Jenny eyed her pa. "All right. I promise."

Marcus released her and dried her face with his thumbs.

"Why didn't you tell me before?" she asked.

"Like I said, it's complicated. Now if you ever see Mr. Cook again, I want you to treat him with respect, unlike I done today. He's a good friend of your Uncle Calvin. I ain't proud of the way I acted."

"Why don't you like him?"

"That's something I need to keep to myself. Something I need to work on. You feelin' better now, Jenny-bear?"

"Uh-huh. Thanks, Papa." She gave him another hug.

Marcus repositioned the stool and retrieved the partially filled milk pail while Jenny watched from outside the stall. His mind continued gnawing on their topic.

"Jenny? I want you to hold your head high. You pay no mind to what Laura Ann or anyone else ever says. You ain't adopted. But if you were, it'd be no cause for shame either. You'd be as much a part of this family as anyone, and your ma and I would love you the same and be just as proud of you as we are now."

"You would?"

"How could we help it, sugarplum? But the fact of the matter is your mama happened to be present at your birth and we was both present at your ... conception. There ain't no doubt where you come from."

Jenny kept quiet for a moment. Then she said, "I never did much care for Laura Ann," and left her pa to finish his task.

There lingered one question on Joseph's mind. Was Quentin absent from the wedding because of poor health or death?

The next time he saw Calvin, who strutted about like royalty after a one-night honeymoon, he asked. "Cal, it was a pleasure to meet your family. That's quite a good-looking crowd you're connected to."

"They're upstanding folks, despite having me as a representative." Calvin's smile evoked one from Joseph.

"I didn't make your pa's acquaintance. Is he living, I hope?"

Stop laughing, Randall. I'm trying to be polite.

The smile vanished. "No, he died a couple of years ago in a logging accident. A branch come down and struck his head. It felt like it struck us all—we was stunned 'bout to death."

"I can imagine. I'm sorry, Calvin. I know what it's like to lose a parent young."

"You do? What happened to yours?"

"My mama took sick and died when I was seven."

"That's a lot younger than sixteen. Did your pa re-marry?"

"No, never did. Maybe that's why I'm so useless around the ladies—I'm not real used to them."

On his way back to the store, Joseph pondered the truth of that statement. In fairness, he couldn't blame his mother for his discomfort in the presence of women. But he had felt abandoned by her. Then Suzanne, who he trusted, lied to him and blew up that awful day on Brooks Mountain. It took over two years for him to work up the gumption to court Maggie Johnson, by which time Suzanne had married Quentin. And it still pained him to think how that brief romance soured.

He'd brought Maggie home from her farm on Hix Mountain to meet his family. He was ready to propose but thought it fitting his bride-to-be assess the kin she'd be saddled with. His brother, Will, took a walk up the holler with them. Joseph got hotter and hotter as Will overtook the conversation—beyond cordial, he flirted, he sparked. By the end of the walk, Joseph's mood was so foul he decided to postpone by a week his request for matrimony. He needed time to cool off.

The next Sunday, a sky-scrubbed spring day, Joseph found the chestnut mare missing when he went to saddle her. He started to walk to the far corner of the pasture, where it dropped out of view, when he thought to check for the saddle. It was missing, too.

So he walked to Maggie's, undeterred by the heart-pounding delay, arriving forty minutes later than he'd told Maggie to expect him. And there in the yard, tied to an apple tree, slept the chestnut mare.

Joseph didn't bother to knock but opened the front door as if intent on tearing it from its hinges. A startled Mrs. Johnson looked up from her crocheting.

"Where is he!?" Joseph demanded, well aware he doubled his rudeness by omitting a salutation.

"I assume you mean your brother? He and Maggie have gone for a picnic and taken Kip along."

Joseph struggled to speak. He'd never known such rage. "I see," he squeezed past gritted teeth.

He resisted the urge to slam the door. At a breakneck, downhill gallop, he rode the mare home.

Fair, golden-haired Maggie, as it turned out, relished her power to pit the brothers against each other. The rift proved permanent, unlike her interest in Will. For Joseph, the wound was twofold. His brother had betrayed him, and the girl he loved had chosen the lighter-skinned man with brown hair. Given the choice, why wouldn't she favor the brother who could give her "normal-looking" children and freedom from the kinds of comments all too familiar to Joseph?

By the middle of summer, Joseph's father was dead from the yellow jacket stings, the farm belonged to Will, and Joseph had written for and accepted a job with the B & O.

And it wasn't like railroad work facilitated meeting promising girls. Except for a few wives who found their way to camps and towns along the way, the rest were whores.

Thus, on the surface, Joseph carried distrust of women and unease in their company. Yet deeper down lived the first seven years of his life with a devoted and affectionate mother. As well, there lived a childhood companion who stood up for him and never let him down until their final showdown at age seventeen. And there resided Becky, the younger sister he'd always loved but taken for granted until losing the opportunity to save her.

Joseph might be wary, but his caution didn't cut to the quick.

Less than two weeks after learning of Suzanne's widowhood, Joseph received an unexpected invitation. It came as a small folded note, closed with red sealing wax, offered by Calvin at the close of a rehearsal.

"Nancy and I was home for dinner last Sunday, and Mama asked me to give you this. She said she thinks you went to school together on Gwinn Ridge, and she'd like to know. If you did, she's expecting you to dinner to 'reminisce,' she said. If not, she said to just ignore it."

Joseph couldn't help but smile at Suzanne's yarn. "I did go to school on Gwinn Ridge, and I thought your mama looked familiar. That was a mighty long time ago."

Oh, what a tangled web we weave, when first we practice to deceive.

His next thought was *expecting you?* Just like Suzanne to issue an order instead of an invitation.

He didn't open the note until he got home.

> Dear Joseph. I don't know if I'll ever see you again, so there's some things I want to say. First, it has sorrowed me all these years I never apologized for lying to you that day we picked blackberries. It shames me to think of it still. The other thing is, you said you were sorry you lost your temper, but I never said I was sorry I lost mine. I never should have hit you like that and I want you to know it grieves me that I did. I was a foolish girl.
>
> If you will, come up for dinner this Sunday. I'd like to fix you a nice birthday meal. Do give me a chance to talk with you and find out where you been these 30 years. I shall send Lester down to the store this week to get your reply.
>
> Suzanne
>
> P.S. Only Marcus and his wife, Maylene, know. Their children don't. But Jenny asked and Marcus told her there is a relation. I'm afraid I must call you a cousin. I regret the lie but see no way around it.

Children? More than Jenny? How many grandchildren do I have?

With a couple of notable exceptions, the introductions at the wedding were a complete blur.

Lord, she's as direct as ever, and she remembers my birthday.

Joseph's fifty-first birthday fell on the Monday following, and its mention proved an effective bait. Despite the distasteful anticipation of another encounter with Marcus, Joseph would go.

His birthday, after his seventh, had never been celebrated. His pa remembered it some years, and would say something cheery like, "Happy birthday, and now that you're older, you'll be picking up another chore. It's time you learned to split rails." One year the promotion was "castrate the calves."

Joseph preferred the date go unnoticed.

Randall wouldn't have it, however. He insisted he and Joseph mark their birthdays—his in early September, Joseph's at the end of May—by going fishing. They'd pick the closest Sunday and find the nearest stream or river for a day of "drowning bait," as Randall called it. They normally didn't catch much but always something, and their evening meal of catfish or trout tasted better than any birthday cake.

Their hunting knives were used far more often for cleaning fish than for skinning a squirrel or rabbit. Hunting with Joseph's pistol was nearly a pointless proposition anyway, partly because of the unsuitable weapon and partly because neither man was a very good shot.

Joseph had never liked hunting. He didn't know when that strange fainting sensation would come over him, and he'd have to squat and drop his head to keep from passing out. Such incidents were excruciatingly humiliating and a source of Will's derision.

But Randall would reach for a shot rabbit, saying, "You can't skin worth a darn, Joseph. Give me that thing."

Or, "I'll clean the fish while you fix the fire. You bein' so clumsy with a knife you might take a finger off."

I'll miss fishing with you this year, Randall. Save me a seat on the bank of that creek where you're wetting a line.

I'll do just that. Sho' will, Joseph heard as he snuffed his bedside candle.

CHAPTER TWELVE

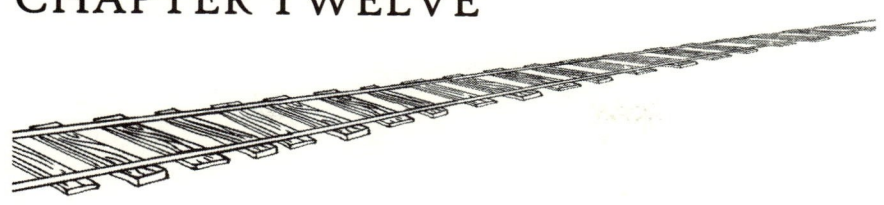

Joseph bathed again and rented a less broken-down horse. He arrived at the Lilly farm before one o'clock. Suzanne, with sweat streaking her cheeks, stirred chicken frying in a large cast-iron skillet. Vesta stepped around her to pull two steaming loaves of bread out of the oven. A crock of butter waited on the table, along with a pitcher of cold, fresh milk from the springhouse. A generous bowl of peas, dwarfing a smaller bowl of gravy, sat in the middle of the table like a centerpiece.

Maylene arrived on Joseph's heels. "Want me to ring the bell?"

"Please do," answered Suzanne. "It's time for chow!"

A stampede of footsteps came from upstairs. Others from the yard and barn. Within minutes, the children were assembled, along with Lester, Vesta, Maylene, and Suzanne. Joseph made sure not to sit at the table's head, where he assumed Quentin had presided over his family.

Suzanne chose her oldest grandchild. "Jenny, will you say grace?"

Jenny bowed her head and closed her eyes. "Thank you, Lord Jesus, for the food we are about to eat for and for bringing us a guest to eat it with. Amen."

"Thank you, honey," Suzanne said before glaring at the unoccupied place setting.

"Where's Marcus?"

Maylene felt her face flush. "He's in the barn cleaning tack."

"He don't have to do that on Sunday, and he heard the bell."

"Shall I go for him?" Maylene asked in a tone suggesting futility.

"No, don't bother. I'll have a word with him myself. For now, let's enjoy our meal."

"Amen to that," said Joseph. "It's a feast, and I thank you for including me."

Suzanne said, "We're honored to have you. Now I don't expect you to remember everyone's name, so I'll make introductions again. Lester is my youngest. You may recall Maylene is Marcus's wife and the mother of these rascally but beloved grandchildren. Jenny is the oldest, then Johnny, then Sara Sue, then Quencus. Vesta is my third daughter and a great help to me."

She swept her eyes around the table. "You all remember meeting Mr. Cook at the wedding."

She turned to Joseph. "Shall they call you 'Mr. Cook' or 'Mr. Joseph?'"

"'Mr. Joseph,' I prefer."

"Well, Mr. Joseph and I grew up on Brooks Mountain and went to school together. We are ... cousins, although I'm rather unclear on the kinship. I believe it's on my papa's side. Anyway, Mr. Joseph has been away since the forties, and I'll bet he has some stories of the world to tell."

The children fixed their attention on Joseph as if he were a magician.

"Did you go to Washington?" Johnny asked. "Did you meet President Lincoln before he got shot?"

Joseph smiled. His first question from a grandchild. He took in Johnny's deep brown eyes, light-brown hair, and broad face. Although he didn't look particularly related, it swelled Joseph's heart with pride to know he was. "No, I never met any president, or even a governor, but I did pass through Washington by train."

"Did you see any Indians?" blue-eyed Sara Sue asked, her freckled, Suzanne-like face intense with interest.

"A few. But mostly in the mirror. My mother was a Cherokee and I take after her."

"Do you talk Indian?" Johnny wanted to know.

Suzanne started to intervene, embarrassed by the children's questions, but Joseph gestured to stop her. His expectation to the contrary, she relented.

"I'm afraid not. My mama used to sing to us in Cherokee, but I've forgotten her songs." Joseph wished he remembered her Cherokee name, too. She'd pronounced it for him, but it formed a meaningless string of syllables that didn't stick in his mind. He did recall her saying her name meant *clouded moon*, and he always thought of her when he watched clouds pass before the moon's face.

As the cross-examination continued, Maylene buttered a thick slab of bread and cut it in half. When Suzanne left the table to check on baking pies, Maylene stacked the halves, buttered sides together, and slipped the bread into a dress pocket. Johnny, ever alert, burst into giggles. Maylene put a finger to her lips and shook her head. Joseph smiled at her, winking, which warmed her to the stranger.

Joseph, quick to assess a new acquaintance, didn't question his instincts regarding Maylene. She emanated an air of confidence, competence, and generosity, the kind of presence that puts others at ease. Her wide, blue-eyed face with faded freckles struck Joseph as attractive in a wholesome way, quite unlike the women he'd "known" over the years.

You chose well, my son.

Vesta helped serve dessert—juicy wild-cherry pies, offered with cream. She, Lester, and Maylene joined in the conversation while Jenny remained quiet, sneaking peeks at the face of the man who wore her features. Even his hands were larger versions of her own.

Joseph's heartbeat quickened every time he caught Jenny's eye, which caused her to examine her plate. She reminded him not only of himself but of his mother, and he couldn't deny, vanity implications aside, she struck him as beautiful.

After dispersing the children and yielding to Maylene and Vesta's insistence on washing the dishes, Suzanne and Joseph settled on the porch to talk in private. Suzanne harbored two pressing questions she wanted to address before she went after Marcus.

She tackled the first one. "What made you decide to come home?"

"I was afraid I'd kill a man if I stayed with the railroad."

"That don't sound like you, Joseph."

"He killed a friend of mine and got away with it."

"Dear Lord. Why didn't the law take care of him?"

"Partly because he had two men willing to lie for him. Partly because of the color of my friend's skin."

Suzanne nodded with understanding. "There ain't no such thing as justice for some folks."

"It's a sorry fact and one I can't tolerate."

"I regret you suffered such a sad and hateful thing. Do you want to tell me what happened?"

"No. But thank you."

"I'd like to hear more about your life on the railroad, and what's around the next bend, but first, may I ask—that day you come by, why did you? Did you come all the way up here thinking you'd get a warm welcome from Quentin?"

"Not exactly. I was on my way up Broomstraw Ridge to say good-bye to Becky."

"How did you find me?"

"I passed your family down on the river and followed their tracks. It was easy enough—the road was muddy. But I don't reckon I should have."

"I've pondered that a very long time."

"Have you found the answer?"

"No, but I've tried to make my peace with what can't be changed."

Peace, however, was not evident in Suzanne's demeanor. She sat rigidly upright on a rocker, and Joseph sensed anger brewing. "If you'll excuse me a moment, I'm going to have a word with my son," she said.

Suzanne left her guest on the porch and made haste to the log barn. There she found Marcus, seated on a bench, oiling a saddle and dismantled harness straps with a scrap of flannel.

"Young man, your behavior is inexcusable. I won't have it!"

Marcus un-straddled the bench and laid a leather girth strap across the wall of the stall behind him. "I'm sorry you feel that way, Ma, but you never asked if I want my children exposed to that man. For all I know, he's nothing but a shiftless drifter. Why don't he have a home and family of his own?"

"He's been working for the railroad thirty years—where's the shame in that? I'll not have you treating a guest so rude. You don't have to like him, but you can treat him decent."

"Decent? Like he treated Pa?"

Joseph, having "discussed" the matter with Randall, decided to try smoothing things over. Besides, what man would wait on the safety of the porch while Suzanne entered the lion's den alone?

Marcus's anger hitched up a notch when he saw him appear in the open barn doorway. It hitched up one more when a flash of shame struck him. His eye-socket crater with its ugly purple and white scar screamed in naked display—he seldom wore the eyepatch on the farm.

Joseph spoke first. "Marcus, you have every reason to dislike me, and I don't blame you. All I ask is that you put the blame on me, not your ma."

Suzanne wheeled on him as if insulted. "What are you talking about? I'm through with you taking the blame for things that ain't your fault—it ain't even honest."

Turning to Marcus, she said, "Son, maybe I should tell you what happened, how . . ."

"I know what happened! The two of you took it upon yourselves to cheat on Pa. Then I come home from the War to meet a daughter who looks so unlike any of us I thought Maylene cheated on *me*. And, Ma, you took your sweet time takin' *that* dagger outta my heart. It damn near killed me."

He shook with fury, astonished. He thought he'd set aside his anger, maybe even forgiven his mother for the fifteen agonizing months it took her to tell him the truth. Those months were pure torment for a man additionally haunted by his experience of war.

Suzanne stood as stunned as Marcus. He'd never spoken to her with such anger. Never. Tears filled her eyes, a sight unknown to Marcus. He'd been away when she grieved the loss of her sons, and she'd reserved her weeping over Quentin for times alone.

Marcus had never seen his mother cry.

His anger fizzled like a match in water. "Aw, Ma, don't cry. I'm sorry."

Joseph, unused to family drama, willed the earthen floor to open and swallow him on the spot. Like Marcus, he didn't know Suzanne was capable of tears. "I've done nothing but stir up trouble. I'll be going."

Suzanne swiped away tears with two fingertips and said, "Wait, there's things I want you both to hear." Her voice, although soft, conveyed unequivocal command. The father and son waited as she took charge of herself.

"I been on this farm over thirty years, and there was in-laws here when I moved in. There was one day—just one—in all those years I spent here alone, and it was because Junior had kept me up all night a'fussin' over a new tooth. I was supposed to go with the family to a funeral that day and I refused. I told Quentin I needed to stay home and sleep as soon as that screaming baby settled down. One day in near thirty-three years. And that happened to be the day Joseph come up Broomstraw Ridge looking for his sister to tell her good-bye, and he decided to stop and say good-bye to me as well. It's like God was testing me, and I can tell you—as if you don't know—I failed the test. It wasn't for lack of caring for your pa, Marcus. It was because Joseph and I had parted years earlier over a terrible fight. All I wanted was to put things right and let us have the chance to part as friends, not enemies. We'd been friends all our lives, just like you and Maylene. The blame is more mine than Joseph's. I can't say why or how, but I lost my senses, and I've had to live with that shame ever since. I don't believe God has ever forgiven me, and if He can't, I don't see how you can either. The most I can ask is for you not to hate me for it."

"I couldn't hate you, Ma. I just don't understand why you didn't tell me sooner."

"I was wrong not to, but I didn't see the tension building between you and Maylene. I thought the War caused all your hurt. Maybe I was blind because I wanted to be. Looking back, I can't figure how I didn't see. Despite my dislike of Mrs. Nivens, Lord knows it was a blessing she spilled the gossip about Maylene."

Marcus abhorred that Joseph Cook remained, taking in this second-most revealing of disclosures his private mother had ever allowed.

Suzanne continued. "The night you and Johnny rode away, I heard a voice, plain as day. It said, 'One of them shan't return.' I dropped to my knees by my bed and prayed and cried. I loved you both the same, but I knew in that moment if it was you didn't come home I'd never recover. Marcus, I know I sinned, and it grieves me that it caused you such pain, but I can never completely regret what

I done because if I hadn't, I wouldn't have you. I suppose there would have been some other child between Junior and Johnny, but it wouldn't have been you."

Suzanne's vision blurred with tears again.

What's wrong with me, blubbering like a baby?

Marcus caught something unfamiliar in his mother's blue eyes. Something soft and tinged with longing. He took her in his arms and kissed the top of her head—as he would one of his children—as Joseph slunk away.

He said, "I'm still missing Pa. Maybe that's the main thing wrong with me."

"Lord knows, that's the main thing wrong with all of us."

Suzanne packed a large wedge of pie and a half-loaf of bread for Joseph to take home. He hesitated to request more generosity, but he had a favor to ask.

"I have a dilemma," he said after mounting the horse.

"What's that?"

"I'd like to visit Becky again, but her husband won't allow it. I must go on a Saturday night when he plays cards, but the ferry will be closed by the time I get back. Do you think I could stay here, sleep in the barn? I'd leave before sunrise—I wouldn't have to see Marcus or the children at all."

"The barn is out of the question. Besides, Blackjack and Reggie would react to a visiting horse, and Marcus would check to see. You'll stay upstairs with Lester—it's not a scrap of trouble. Don't worry about Marcus. He'll come around."

"No, no, I distress him too much. I'll sleep down by the river and take the ferry in the morning. I'm not too old to sleep under the stars. Not yet."

"May I remind you this is *my* house, and I may decide who may or may not be my guest."

Oh, there she goes. Miss High and Mighty.

"Joseph, I insist. I don't need to know when. Come when it suits you. Lester misses Calvin—he'll be glad for your company and so will I. We do have some more catching up to do, don't you think?"

Joseph blew out a breath of air. What was the point of arguing with this woman? Had he ever won?

"Thank you—it's kind of you. I'll see you in a week or two."

Marcus didn't want to ruminate on the seduction that spawned him, but his mother's attempt to cast it in a less sordid light failed, and his imagination pounced on the topic. He'd been with enough men for three years as a cavalryman to know the type. Smooth, sweet-talking. The sort he'd first encountered in Joseph's own nephew, Amos Wallace, when he came down Madam's Creek to court Maylene.

Joseph did his best to hide his character with a polite facade, but his good looks weren't lost on Marcus. The man's face and quiet confidence were those of one accustomed to having his way with women. Marcus vividly pictured the encounter. His ma showing Joseph to the door, thanking him for coming by. Joseph saying, "Please, just one little kiss and I'll be on my way. I'm unlikely ever to see you again." And before Suzanne could protest, he had her in his arms, with the "little kiss" turning out to be a real scorcher. Suzanne, flustered, pushing him away. Joseph saying, "Oh, my darling, I'll miss you so," and pulling her in for another impassioned kiss....

At the moment Joseph lifted his ma to carry her to bed, Marcus lurched to a stop, forbidding his runaway mind to go further.

Still, an old question resurfaced. Did they have the gall to do it in the very bed his parents shared for decades? With Junior right there? Disgusting! Joseph was a soulless seducer and his mother, though not without blame, his victim. Why did she try to protect him? Marcus could only conclude she attempted to ease his pain, to cast his father in as favorable a light as possible.

Yet this was the man who'd made him feel like a bastard child in his own family. Who'd made him cringe internally when Pa called him *son*, which he frequently did. Who'd made him ashamed of his mother. Who'd made him nauseated with outrage the day Suzanne confessed. Who'd been the cause of the deepest hurt of all—his suspicion of Maylene.

I'm sorry, Ma. Don't expect me at dinner.

He told Maylene as they turned in for the night, "I don't want him around the children."

Maylene did her best. "I wish you'd been there at dinner. He's perfectly proper, but he's stiff as a plank around them. I can't begin to imagine him tossing a child in the air or giving a giddyap knee-ride like your pa would do. If he continues to visit, he'll be nothing but a dull sort of uncle to them. They know who their Paw Paw was, and nothing will change that."

"I don't want him visiting. Especially for Jenny's sake. He's made me lie to her."

"I don't like it either, but I don't know what else we can do. You couldn't pretend he's not related to her. It's obvious he is. And that would be another lie. The children are too young to know the truth, and then they'd have to keep it a secret unless your ma is ready for the whole family to know. We can't put that on them. I think you done right, but it makes us both dishonest, and I ain't easy with that either."

"He reminds me of Amos."

"Oh, Lord, Marcus, leave that be! I doubt he even knew his nephew. Don't turn him into a monster."

"I know what he done."

After a moment, Maylene sighed and said, "It's for God to judge, not us. Try to sleep."

Minutes later, however, they both lay awake. Maylene, pregnant again, stroked Marcus's cheek. "Do you need help relaxing?"

Marcus pulled her close, kissing her. "I believe I do. Do you feel up to it? You've not been feeling so well."

"Only if you promise to stop brooding."

"Brooding? Was I brooding? I've already forgotten," He slipped his hands under his wife's summer nightdress, welcoming the powerful amnesia of arousal summoned by Maylene's skin.

CHAPTER THIRTEEN

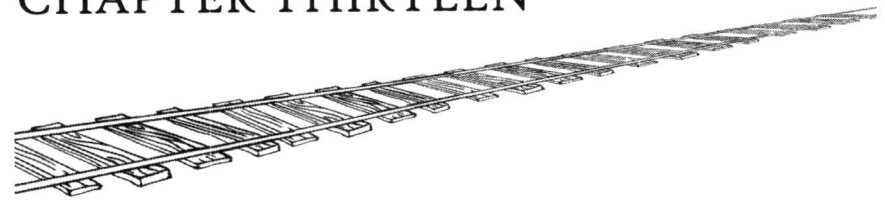

The next horse did go lame on the way up Broomstraw Ridge. Anxious about the roan mare's condition, as well as the ire of the livery owner, Joseph dismounted and walked the last quarter mile to the top. He'd taken a new route Marcus had sketched and labeled for him, a shorter, steeper way, scarcely more than a deer path, that spared him a mile of travel.

The map served as peace offering for his ma—Marcus entertained no interest in helping Joseph.

Just before the path met the road along the crest of the ridge, Joseph tied the mare and went forward to crouch behind a large, rounded boulder. From there he spied on the road above, and there he waited for Enoch to pass by on his way to his card game in Jumping Branch. He'd been foolish not to ask Becky about the appearance of Enoch and the mule. Would he recognize them?

He nearly missed Enoch. He'd been hunkered down no more than five minutes when a mule appeared, ridden by a thin man with a long gray beard. Enoch? Joseph wasn't sure. As he passed, the man coughed and reached into a vest pocket for a small flask. His profile looked familiar as he took a swig. Joseph reassured himself the man was his brother-in-law.

As before, he tied his mount near the road before approaching the shabby cabin. Again, he checked for the pistol, patting his bottom-button-only closed vest, under which the weapon nestled in a hidden holster.

Gunslinger that I am, huh, Randall? It's nice to know it's there, though.

This time Becky opened the door, greeting Joseph with an expression of joyous surprise.

"You *did* come back! Come in and have a little supper. There's some greens left, and I'll fry up a few eggs."

"Think Enoch will notice?"

"No, like I said, I can handle him. I often feed leftover greens to the chickens, and he don't know how many eggs I collected this morning. That goes for the milk, too."

Joseph smiled at his sister. "I'm glad he hasn't broke your spirit."

Settling on a chair with a missing slat, he asked, "Where's Caleb?"

"He goes fishing when his pa goes card-playing. He don't care if it's light or dark. He's got a favorite hole down on Jumping Branch, and it's his time for his self. We eat fish on Sundays if he catches any, but they ain't much longer than your thumb."

"What do you do with your Saturday nights alone?"

"Who says I'm alone? My friends Ethel Crook and Clara Bennett oftentimes come by, and we sew and spin and sing. I never had such dear friends in my life. Enoch has no idea—he don't like folks being here."

"Why does he want to keep everyone away?"

"He's ashamed of how run-down the place is, I reckon. Or maybe he don't want me talking the truth about him."

Joseph fiddled with a fork. "Becky, there's something I'd like to get off my chest."

She looked up from stirring eggs in a skillet. "What's that?"

"After you left, Will and I had a terrible falling out."

"Oh, what a shame—that had to hurt you both. What happened?"

"He stole a girl from me."

"No! Why would he do that? That don't sound like Will."

"I never asked him. She was comely—maybe he did it for sport, to see if he could. I was ready to ask for her hand, and I never forgave him."

"Did he marry her?"

"Did you never hear from him? You don't know he never married?"

"No, I only knew he was single when he died. I wondered if he'd lost a wife."

"Good God, Becky, have you not been off this farm?"

She fixed her attention on the stovetop, avoiding his eyes. Joseph took in the gray streaks in her hair and lines scrawled on her face by sun and worry. His younger sister appeared at least ten years older than he.

"I been on Ethel's and Clara's farms, and I walked the children to Jumping Branch a couple of times during the War. Tell me the rest of your story."

"All right. She dropped Will like a sour apple and moved on to someone else. By then I knew she wasn't right for me, but I was too proud and hurt and bulled up to let Will know he'd likely done me a favor by taking Maggie off my hands."

"You men! You're stiff-necked, every one of you."

"That's true enough. The point is, I left home without ever making right with Will. When I heard he died, I berated myself for holding a grudge absurdly long. And I promised myself I'd do better by you. The money wasn't enough."

"What money?"

Joseph lowered his head to the table's scarred surface and groaned. "I feared you'd say that."

"You sent money?"

"All these years. It wasn't much but I sent what I could, every few months. I stopped after seeing you in March."

Becky's mouth fell open and the unstirred eggs began to scorch. She slid the pan off the stove and banged it onto the table. "I wondered how Enoch always seemed to have enough for another card game and another jug of moonshine."

"I'm afraid I hurt more than helped by sending it."

"Oh, no, you mustn't think so. If he'd had to, Enoch would've traded food for 'shine and let the children go hungry. And I believe he put it to good use on occasion. He come home from Meador's Store with a new plowshare in the cart one day, and I thought he'd been lucky with the cards. But he gambles away every penny he makes and don't come home 'til he's broke. That must have been your money."

"I'm no good at forgiveness, Becky. I never forgave Will 'til it was too late, and I never forgave Pa for making you marry Enoch. There's little hope I'll ever pardon Enoch for how he's treated you and stolen what was yours, as well as mine. I want to get you and Caleb out of here. We'll live in town and if Enoch comes looking for trouble, he'll have it. It's the least I can do. I didn't look out for you when we were young 'cause I was too busy feeling sorry for myself and running away to Suzy's, but I can look out for you now."

Becky shook her head slowly. "I can't do it, Joseph. It's kind and brave of you, but Enoch is wicked mean when he's crossed. I'd live in terror for all of us. I can manage. I *do* manage. You know, Enoch was conscripted in sixty-two, when they raised the draft age, and gone two-and-a-half years...."

"Then you must have gotten mail from me during the War, surely after West Virginia entered the Union as a state."

"Oh, Lordy, he's a clever man. He had me sign a note before he left saying Elmer Sizemore could pick up the mail. He'd drop it off on his way back from the mill or store. Paddy was getting old, and Enoch said I mustn't use him for trips to Jumping Branch no more. That made sense to me—I couldn't run the farm without him. Elmer must have kept everything you sent."

"Son of a *bitch*," Joseph muttered under his breath. "How'd you cope, Becky? You said Amos enlisted."

"I wasn't about to let my children starve. Ethel and Clara were in the same pickle, and we worked together, plowing, planting, everything. Nancy Bennett sent her boys when she could spare them. It's the hardest I ever worked in my life, but those were happy years. I learned I could do whatever I needed to survive and keep my children safe. When Enoch come back—and God forgive me, I began praying he wouldn't—I stepped around him like he wasn't there and kept right on working. He got drunker and lazier, and that suited me fine. I intend to outlive him, and he's not well."

"What's wrong with him?"

"Some illness of the lungs. It's getting worse."

Joseph choked down the buttered greens and dry eggs. "Will you think about it anyhow, moving to town?"

"I shall, but don't expect me to change my mind."

They moved on to smoother ground, reminiscing about the old farm and sharing their scant memories of their mother until Becky became uneasy.

Clearing the table, she said, "You'd best go. Thank you for coming—it means the world to me to know you're alive and living so close."

Joseph gave her a hug. "I'll be back before the leaves fall. If you need to get word to me, see if Caleb can get to the Lilly farm above Madam's Creek. Folks will know the place if he asks, and the Lillys'll get ahold of me."

Then he remembered Marcus's map and fished it out of his vest pocket. "Wait. Here, keep this hid. It shows the way down."

Joseph, leading the lame horse, approached the Lilly farm when Chase loped up the path to greet him and escort him the remaining distance. He had to cross behind Marcus and Maylene's cabin on his way to the paddock below. Hearing voices on the porch, he paused, wishing to pass unseen. After some hesitation, he tied the mare and sat down on a stump, a residue of the cabin's creation, to wait for the family to turn in for the night. Chase reappeared to check on him and then trotted back around the log home. Fireflies crawled out of hiding, up stems and twigs, to lift into the twilight and keep Joseph company with their mesmerizing blinking.

He heard someone who sounded like Jenny. "Does the eagle carry the wildcat on its back or with its feet?"

"What do you think? Shall we put the wildcat on its back for a better ride?"

The next voice sounded like Johnny's. "It can hold on with its claws, like this."

Joseph imagined Johnny holding his hands in claw-like shapes.

Marcus laughed. "Exactly like that. Now that we've got that ole wildcat aboard, Mr. Eagle is going to take him where?"

"No, Papa. *Miss* Eagle."

"I forgot, Sara Suzy, we promised you our next adventure would feature a lady beast. Miss Eagle. Have you a name for her?"

After a moment of silence, during which Joseph picked up the squeak of a rocker on the porch planks, Sara Sue burst out with enthusiasm, "Ruthie!"

"Very well. Ruthie the Eagle. She has something up her sleeve, or wing. What if she follows the New to its end. What will she find there?"

"I know. The Kanawha. And it flows to the Ohio River." That must be Jenny again.

"And where does that river go? Jenny, let the others guess."

The story continued with the eagle and wildcat surviving several calamities, one of which involved a ruthless riverboat captain, and ultimately reaching the mouth of the Mississippi where an octopus—Johnny's invention—crawled up on the beach and grabbed hold of the wildcat, which turned out to be part of Ruthie's ill-intentioned plan all along. Joseph felt almost as disappointed as the children when Maylene announced it was time for bed. Marcus promised the story would resume the next night and reminded the children he needed their help figuring where it would go next.

"Come here, cuddlebug." The rocker stopped squeaking, and Joseph's mind saw Marcus lifting a sleepy Quencus from Maylene's lap.

As he retrieved the mare, who was restless with hunger, Joseph heard a young voice say, "I ain't going to bed!"

A child Johnny's size leapt off the side of the porch and dove underneath. Marcus materialized on the other side, jumping down and vanishing from view. Scuffling sounds followed by squeals and giggles preceded Marcus's reappearance with a child slung under one arm.

"May, looky what I found under the porch, a squirming, screaming little piglet. I reckon I'll put him to bed in the sty with the sow tonight. Don't suppose she'll mind one more piglet, even if he is a cantankerous one."

"Noooooo!" wailed Johnny, struggling to free himself, his mock terror evident to Joseph. Ah, he knows the jest of the pig-sty threat.

"Well then, you tell me, mop-top. Shall it be your bed or the sow's pen for you tonight?"

Johnny relented. "I'll take my bed, just for tonight."

"Good choice. In you go."

Easing away, Joseph fought a crushing sadness. Four grandchildren he didn't know how to embrace. And Marcus, his son. He'd not gotten his playfulness from either true parent—he must have learned it from Quentin.

Until now, Joseph hadn't been able to see himself in Marcus. This night, however, the reality of their relatedness broke upon him with the storytelling. The fanciful tale reminded him of ones he'd used as a child to distract himself from the sorrow and loneliness he suffered after his mother's death, as well as when he needed escape from stewing about classmate bullies.

Marcus was truly his very own son, a son who despised him.

Marcus heard hoofbeats and stepped back out the open door. He observed a man lead a limping horse down to the paddock, where he began taking off tack.

Ma had told him Joseph would be spending the night at the house after a trip to Broomstraw Ridge. He'd planned to ignore him, but what was wrong with the horse? Marcus knew horses, and he'd saved several injured ones from being slaughtered during his cavalry years. He often cured lameness, if it didn't go too far.

Damn it to hell.

He walked barefoot to the paddock to see about the horse before Joseph turned it out. After clearing his throat to announce his presence, he said, "She been favoring that leg all day?"

"No, not until we were close to the top of the ridge. I been walking since then."

Marcus ran both hands down the mare's far hind leg below the hock, feeling for swelling and tenderness. As he suspected, the back of the leg bulged slightly, warm to his touch.

"She's got a strain here—it's not the hoof. You'd best leave her and walk back down tomorrow. Tell the livery man she needs to rest a week or so. I'll have Lester bring her back when she's ready. Or, if you're looking to buy a horse cheap, you can see if she's got a history of lameness. You might get her for a song."

"I'd like to buy a horse, but I've no place to keep one. If I could talk my sister into moving to town, I might look for a construction job and my own place with a stable. I thank you for looking after her. She's a likeable one with some spirit."

"I'll rub some turpentine on that leg in the morning and wrap it good. I'll put her right." And he took a rope off a rail, slipped it over the mare's head, and led her toward the barn.

"If you'll be keeping her in, I'll pay for her feed."

"No need for that," Marcus said as he disappeared into the barn's blackness.

Joseph continued to Suzanne's home.

Go ahead and laugh, Randall. Here I am running to Suzy with my tail between my legs. I could use some of your jolly company about now, but she does have a habit of taking me in.

They settled on the porch rockers again. Marcus had made the second one for his pa after coming home to find him crippled. Quentin would prop his bad leg on the porch railing in the evenings, lean back in the comfortable chair, and drink whiskey until the ache subsided. Joseph assumed he rested in Quentin's seat, but he made no complaint.

Suzanne offered leftover biscuits with honey, explaining that Marcus had learned beekeeping from his father-in-law, allowing the family the luxury of producing its own honey the past few years. Joseph stuffed down three plump ones before moving past small-talk.

As they gazed out at the sparkle of stars and lightning bugs, Joseph said, "I did a little eavesdropping just now. I didn't mean to, but I heard Marcus and his family on their porch as I come down the path, and I didn't want to…. It seemed prudent to avoid him, so I waited behind the cabin. Has he always been a storyteller?"

Suzanne laughed. "Oh, Lordy, yes! That boy was forever making up tales and a'drawin' pictures with a stick or a scrap of charred wood. He'd scribble on the porch, the steps, in mud, anywhere he could find a surface. But he shared his stories with Maylene and no one else. I overheard them a few times, though, and it was a wonder. The two of them was like magic together, their minds going on and on, feeding off each other. I never saw two little souls so well matched. What makes you ask?"

"I only wondered. I used to daydream as a boy."

"You did? That's something I didn't know about you. Probably because I kept so busy telling you what to do."

"You were a bossy little thing."

"It's a good thing you resisted. It's one of the reasons I liked you so much. You gave as good as you got."

"I didn't see it that way, but I recall trying."

They smiled without letting their eyes meet.

"What I recall is your love of reading, and that was one of my strongest clues Marcus was yours," Suzanne said.

"He likes to read?"

"Like a fiend. The only book we had was our Bible, and he used to carry it all over the farm. I'm surprised it's still in one piece. What saved it was the Farleys—that's Maylene's family. They used to get books sent from Maylene's grandma in Charlottesville, and they'd pass them along to Marcus. He'd read to us before the fire at night. It was a great pleasure."

"Why did he read instead of Junior or you or Quentin?"

"Because he was better at it. If anyone else tried, a chorus of complaints went up—we all wanted Marcus to read."

"What was he like as a child? Did he stay out of trouble?"

"Pretty much. He was always different. Nothing was black or white to him. He wanted reasons for rules, and I'd get exasperated at times. But I can tell you, despite his treatment of you, which grieves and embarrasses me, he don't have a mean bone in his body."

"That's my sense of him. I saw his concern for the mare. And for you."

"He don't like suffering. It's why he became the best marksman in the family. When he shoots something, he's sure of success before he fires. He always wanted a quick kill. I knew soldiering would be hard on him, and I worried myself half-sick. He went because he had to—he would've never enlisted. Turned out I wasn't wrong. He come home a near wreck. It took a couple of years before he was his self again. Maylene and I have talked about it, and we agree there's still a part of him that ain't healed yet—and it may never be—but he's our Marcus again."

"It feels wrong to have a son and not raise him. I have to thank you and Quentin for that."

"There's nothing to thank us for. It was a pleasure raising that boy, and I thank God every day he's still here."

She looked at Joseph. "One of the pleasures was that he made you feel less far away."

CHAPTER FOURTEEN

Joseph had an early breakfast with Suzanne, Vesta, and Lester. It was a belly-puffing offering of sausage, eggs, grits, and more biscuits—this time with elderberry jam. All washed down with buttermilk and coffee. When it came to meals, Marcus and Maylene maintained their tradition of coming down to the larger home solely for supper, as well as Sunday dinner. In addition to sparing Suzanne extra work, they secured a sense of privacy and independence, rare commodities in a large family.

Joseph thanked Suzanne and headed out, pausing to say, "Tell Marcus I thank him, too, for looking after the mare."

"I'll do that," Suzanne lied. She wasn't about to bring up Joseph if she didn't have to.

Watching Joseph walk away that June morning, Suzanne pondered her own sadness. She'd always loved him, but the man she missed was her husband. No one could take his place. It occurred to her that she and Joseph were too much alike.

We take things so serious. I need my Quentin.

As she cleared the table and heated water for dishwashing, her mind turned to Quentin and his decades of teasing. She heard him, not long after Junior's birth, saying in a muffled voice, his head burrowed between her milk-engorged breasts, "Suze, you grow these any bigger and I may suffocate in here. But I'd surely die a contented man."

She saw their son Johnny toddling about in front of the house, Quentin stepping off the porch to fetch him. "Johnny, you've got such a load in that diaper you're walking bowlegged. Let's see if your mama's got a fresh one we can trade for."

And, years later, when Calvin was about eight months old and constantly carried like a baby doll by four older sisters, she recalled Quentin saying, "I don't see how that boy's ever going to learn to walk if his feet don't never touch the ground."

What she'd so often passed off as flippant comments, owing to her distraction and fatigue, had metamorphosed into endearing, inimitable words she'd bargain her soul to hear again.

"Oh, Quen," she said after Vesta left to hoe the garden, "it's you I need."

Joseph went straight to the livery stable and reported the lame mare.

The owner, a graying man with a large mustache, shook his head. "That's the third time this year that mare's gone lame. I've a mind to sell her for horse meat. I can't afford to keep a horse that ain't sound."

"What would you ask for her?"

"Hell, I don't know. You offering to buy her?"

"I might, if the price is right." Joseph's small cache awaited use.

"Make me an offer."

Joseph wished he'd asked Marcus what a "song" would be. "I'll give you thirty dollars for her."

"I won't take less than forty—I can get that for the meat."

Joseph didn't believe him. "I can't offer more than thirty-five. That's a lame horse with no guarantee of healing."

"If you return the tack, you've got yourself a deal."

The agreement came with such expedience, Joseph suspected he'd been had.

Joseph wanted to get out of town. The place was a madhouse, having grown from six families to over five hundred residents in less than three years. Its burgeoning expansion showed no signs of slowing. Sounds of saws and hammers filled the days. Loads of bricks strained teams of oxen delivering them to the site of the courthouse planned as a permanent replacement for one built of wood. Trains carrying freight and passengers screeched through with their loud whistles and black smoke several times a day. Wagons hauled goods, their horses and wheels turning the streets into quagmires after each rain. Dogs barked, teamsters yelled.

Hinton bustled with all the activity and noise Joseph disdained.

He hadn't expected to keep the shop job so long, but the worker he "temporarily" replaced had taken construction work with better pay, and Silas and Mary Jane Hinton urged Joseph to stay. Also, the lighter demands on his frame had rejuvenated him, reducing to a mild ache the back pain he'd suffered for years. Would it be a mistake at his age to pound nails and lift heavy beams?

What he coveted was the farm he'd dreamed of buying, but that dream had been spent on a mule and gambled away in poker games. Lacking a plan, he decided to stay put for the time being and focus on making music and plotting his sister's escape. He wasn't one to give up easily. He'd keep up the pressure on Becky. And he now had a schedule at the Lillys, "expected" for dinner the first Sunday of the month. With Marcus holed up, spending time on the farm relaxed Joseph.

But the mare grazed on him as if his brain wore a sheath of grass. Would she heal? And, sound or lame, what to do with her?

A week later, Calvin reported the horse responding well to Marcus's care. "Marcus will turn her out soon, and he thinks she'll be ready to ride in a couple more weeks. Ma says she can stay until fall. It don't cost them a thing to let her graze."

"I'm beholden. Do you think Lester can bring her tack the next time he comes to town?"

"Don't see why not. Or I'll do it myself. And we have a spare saddle and bridle. After Marcus come back from the War with Blackjack, we had two horses and an old mule. We replaced the mule, but not our draft horse who died a few years back, so there's extra tack you can use. Kind of beat-up, but it'll do."

"I'd like to pay for it."

"Ma won't let you, I'm sure. Oh, does the mare have a name? Marcus wants to know."

Clouded Moon rang in Joseph's head, but he said, "Her name is *Cloud*."

"Cloud?" Marcus responded. "Don't that seem more like a name for a gray horse than a red roan?"

His brother shrugged. "That's what I thought, but I figure clouds can be red at sunrise and sunset."

"True enough," said Marcus, rolling his eyes.

One evening after supper, Marcus waited with his younger children on his ma's porch for Maylene and Jenny to finish cleaning up. He noticed movement in the garden, a pair of ears.

"Johnny, go tell your sister to bring me the Enfield off the mantle while I keep an eye on that critter."

Jenny appeared with Marcus's cavalry rifle, a pouch of powder, and a small box of ammunition. Marcus loaded.

Sara Sue, who had been playing tag with Quencus, ran to the steps. "Papa, what...."

"Shhhh. There's a rabbit's got in the garden, and it needs to go."

"Where?" Sara Sue scampered up the steps for a better look. "Oh, I see it. It's so pretty. Don't shoot it, Papa!"

Marcus raised the rifle and took aim.

"Papa! No, no, no! Don't...."

The rabbit stopped chewing. Marcus fired.

Sara Sue collapsed at his feet, sobbing, "No, Papa, it's too pretty, it's too pretty! You *killed* it!"

Marcus leaned the rifle against the wall and took his child in his arms. Convulsed with grief, her entire frame shook. "Baby, I didn't kill it. I just scared it away. We don't want it eating all our hard work now, do we? Hush now, baby girl, hush. That bunny has done run home by now."

Maylene came out with a dishrag in hand.

"Sara Sue thought Papa killed a rabbit," Jenny said.

And he most certainly would have if Sara Sue hadn't been present. Maylene would've made a fine rabbit stew the next day.

The quivering child relaxed, and Maylene produced a hanky for her daughter's streaming eyes and nose. Marcus set down Sara Sue, saying, "Sugar, how am I going to keep this family fed if you won't let me kill nothing?"

"We can eat grass."

"No, we can't. But I just might eat you."

Marcus made a grab for his daughter, who charged down the steps with a scream.

Later that night, Marcus asked his wife, "What are we going to do with that child? How is she going to grow up with chickens and hogs and steers killed all around her and have a breakdown every time? We've been sheltering her too much."

"I trust she'll outgrow it. But I've never seen such a sensitive child in my life, and she worries me. Thank you for sparing that rabbit."

"I couldn't help myself."

CHAPTER FIFTEEN

Joseph, Calvin, Nancy, and Ben climbed onto the temporary stage set up in Hinton's modest wooded park for their debut performance on the evening of the Fourth of July. Nancy, weak with morning sickness, skipped supper to avoid vomiting in front of the assembled crowd of over a hundred, including Maylene, Vesta, Lester, and four mesmerized Lilly children.

Before beginning their concert of gospel and folk tunes, Ben spoke to the audience. "Thank you all for coming out. We're going to start with a song that may be unfamiliar, but the story isn't. You know about John Henry. He worked the Great Bend rail-tunnel crew on the Greenbrier and wasn't too impressed when the first steam drill was hauled in a few years ago. Seeing the threat to men's jobs, he suggested a contest between him and his shaker, and the steam drill. And who won by five feet?"

Voices shouted, "John Henry!"

"That's right. He and his shaker, Phil Henderson, beat the steam drill, which was rejected and taken apart. The workers were mighty glad to see its pieces put to other work. Mr. Henry was a well-liked man, the best driver on the crew. And they say the only one to use two hammers, one in each hand."

Joseph's nervousness made Ben's introduction too long. *Are you going to quit yapping so we can play the durn song?*

Ben relished the rapt attention of the onlookers. "Think of it! Two hammers slamming that drill on ole Phil's shoulder. Didn't give him much time to turn the shaft between blows, did it. Or to think about what would happen to his head if Mr. Henry missed his mark! But that steel driver never did, and we won't see the likes of him again working these rails."

A male voice called out, "Amen!"

"But John Henry's no longer with us. So there's folks begun singing some tunes in his honor, which is especially fitting because they say Henry was the singin'est man in the tunnel. We'd like to begin with one of those songs. Ready now?"

He turned to his fellow musicians, lifting his bow and tapping his foot, and the first ballad commemorating John Henry was performed on stage in Hinton, West Virginia.

Joseph made his July and August and September visits to the Lilly farm. He admired the growing number of grain shocks and haycocks, and his mind flashed back to the summer days he and Becky followed Will and their father, who wielded scythes for hay, grain cradles for oats and wheat. Cradles and hay rakes left neat piles that Joseph and his sister gathered into sheaves, which they tied with cut stems before helping heap them into shocks and haycocks identical to those dotting the Lillys' fields. For the grains, threshing came next, requiring seemingly endless hours with a flail to break the seed heads off their stalks. And, finally, winnowing, using wind or a specially designed basket to separate grain from chaff.

Joseph remembered his pride when he grew strong enough to master a cradle but also pitiless heat, unquenchable thirst, and muscles twitching with fatigue. Why did he long to farm again?

On those monthly occasions, the family gathered for dinner, and Suzanne no longer made any comment or excuse for the conspicuous absence. She set aside a plate of leftovers for Maylene to take up to the cabin, or wherever Marcus sulked.

Joseph sensed a change in Suzanne, a subtle distancing. We're not through grieving, neither one of us, he thought.

He hadn't forgotten his promise to visit Becky again before the leaves fell. It was time to go. The second Saturday in September, he asked off work early, walked the four miles to the farm, saddled Cloud, and headed up the ridge.

Becky blanched when she opened the door. "Oh, no, Joseph, you mustn't be here! Enoch didn't ride to Jumping Branch tonight—he's not feeling well. I sent Caleb to tell Ethel and Clara not to come. He's gone out to.... Dear God, here he comes!"

Becky grabbed Joseph's arm and yanked her brother into the cabin. "Get under the bed! There, in the corner." She pointed.

"Becky, this is absurd. Let me talk to him."

"Go, go! He's coming!"

Her fear was so palpable Joseph had to assume it was justified. He slid under the bed on his back, disappearing as the door burst open.

Why don't I shoot him and be done with this nonsense?

He heard a voice slurred by whiskey say, "The mule's in. I've got the shivers and shakes so bad I'm going to bed."

"All right. Can I fix you a bite to eat first?"

"No, I'm going straight to bed."

Oh for God's sake, this thing better be tighter than it looks.

It wasn't. The interwoven rope sagged under Enoch's weight, pressing down the straw tick on Joseph's chest.

Christ Almighty—he's heavy for a scrawny man.

Enoch felt the tick hit bottom. "Damn it, Becky, I'm all the way down to the floor. Can't you keep the rope taut?"

Becky hurried over. "Get up and I'll tighten it."

Enoch took himself off his brother-in-law and sat down at the table, coughing. He pulled a flask out of his pants pocket and took a swig, then set the flask down hard. Only the dim light and Becky's full skirt kept Joseph hidden, and a less inebriated man might have spotted him as Becky shuttled back and forth from one side to the other, using a wooden bed key to tighten the rope. Enoch knew full well the task required two people to be done effectively, with hands needed on both sides to keep the pulled rope from slipping loose again as the other side was drawn snug. But he made no move to assist. Joseph, however, motivated to get the bed firm, helped on the far side, holding the rope in place.

"There," said Becky breathlessly. "That's the best I can do. Let me make you something for that cough before you fall asleep."

Enoch landed heavily on the bed, and Joseph winced at being pinned again, although with less force.

"Jesus, Becky. It ain't much better, but I ain't gettin' up again. You and Caleb better fix it right tomorrow."

"We'll do that. I'm mixing you a tonic."

And Becky turned her back on her husband and brother stacked like a pair of plates. She added kindling to the stove's firebox and stirred water and molasses in a small iron skillet. As soon as the mixture began to steam, she took it off the stove and added Enoch's remaining whiskey. She emptied the result into a tin cup, stirred again, and brought the drink to her husband along with a prayer for quick, deep sleep.

Enoch propped himself on an elbow and drained the cup in a few gulps. "That's good stuff, Bec. You can make me that anytime."

"It should help. Rest well. You'll be better in the morning."

Joseph, worried that Enoch would feel him breathing, took shallow breaths from the top of his lungs. He waited. He heard Becky begin spinning wool by the hearth. Enoch farted.

Thanks for that. As if it's not bad enough being plastered under your ass.

Caleb came in, and Becky told him his pa wasn't well. That he must be quiet.

"What else is new?" Caleb queried in a pseudo-whisper.

Joseph couldn't make out his sister's reply but heard a stifled laugh from Caleb. Then Caleb said, "I'll do the milking before I turn in. Holler if you need me."

At last, Enoch began to snore. Joseph waited. Caleb returned from the barn and climbed a ladder to the loft. Joseph heard a bed creak as it took weight. Becky continued spinning.

Is she going to keep at it all night?

Joseph's lower back ached, as did his lower ribs. He tried moving a fraction of an inch, but he had no traction. He extended his right leg until his boot touched a chestnut beam of the wall, and pushed. There, he moved the slightest bit. He repeated the motion, but this time Enoch grunted and rolled onto his side, amplifying the pressure on Joseph's ribcage.

It wasn't that Joseph couldn't wriggle free—he didn't know how to avoid being detected. He waved to Becky with his left hand, hoping she would notice.

Nervously checking on the bed-bound duo, it took little time for Becky to leave her spinning stool and tiptoe over. Joseph pointed upward and made a flipping motion with a flat palm. She understood.

With care, Becky pushed on Enoch's shoulder, easing him onto his back. His eyes fluttered opened, startling her, but they closed again and he did not wake. Becky recommenced her spinning and Joseph waited.

Within moments, Enoch resumed his snoring, and Joseph resumed his inchworm creep across the floor. Becky got up to unlatch the door.

Just as Joseph freed himself and rolled onto his side, the pistol he'd forgotten clanked sharply through his pants pocket onto a floorboard.

Imbecile! Joseph froze but Enoch didn't move, and Becky gestured with frantic urgency toward the door.

Joseph crawled, then stood and walked, alarmed by each squeak of the floor. He didn't look back but kept his eyes on Becky, who moved toward him, studying her husband for the slightest movement, ready to descend on him with solicitude should he appear wakeful.

Joseph left without a word, closing the door without a sound.

CHAPTER SIXTEEN

On a Saturday late that month, closing in on to the two-year anniversary of Quentin's death, Marcus drove the wagon home from Charlton's Mill on Madam's Creek. The team plodded uphill with the first load of cornmeal. He stopped the horse and mule when he came to Vesta and Sara Sue collecting hazelnuts along the run.

"If you're done, I'll give you a ride."

Sara Sue sprang forward to show her papa the small nuts, wrapped in their sticky husks, overflowing her basket but stopped before reaching the wagon. Something on a yellowing milkweed distracted her.

"Look! What's that pretty, stripy worm?"

Marcus sighed as he swung down from the high seat. His distractible daughter. What gave him patience was the way she resembled him as a child, scrutinizing everything, wonder-struck. While he and Maylene complemented each other as a natural, innate pairing, Sara Sue felt more like a chip carved off his very soul. Each knew the other as self.

"It's a caterpillar, baby doll. A monarch. It'll turn into one of those orange and black butterflies we've been seeing."

Sara Sue queried her pa with wide eyes. "It do? How?"

"It makes itself a little green case and goes inside. It dreams of flying, and after a while it comes out with wings and flies away."

Sara Sue turned to Vesta. "Aunt Vesty, did you hear that? This stripy worm turns into a butterfly?"

"It's true, honey. I can't tell you how, but I can tell you it does."

Sara Sue picked the caterpillar, ringed with white and black and green stripes, off the leaf. It curled into a circle on her palm. "Can I keep it?"

Marcus gave the freckled face—molded so like his, Vesta's, and his mother's—a stern look. "Only if you're willing to risk killing it. It's running out of time and needs to do its magic soon. I don't think it will be happy in a jar."

Sara Sue raised the caterpillar to her ear.

"What did it say?" asked Vesta, retightening the ribbon that held back her maddeningly willful red hair.

"*She* say her name is Rebecca, and she'll fly back to see me when she's a butterfly."

Sara Sue placed the caterpillar back on the milkweed, where it latched on with its suction-like feet.

Her father took her hand. "Come on, sweet pea, I'll lift you up. Let's see you drive the team to Grandma's."

Back at the house, Vesta said, "Sara Sue, run to the springhouse and get two eggs while I take these nuts in. Your grandma's making a nut cake today for Lester's birthday."

"How old is Uncle Lester?"

"He's seventeen—my baby brother. But he don't like me calling him that."

Sara Sue danced away, proud to have a role in the cake-making.

Just before she reached the springhouse, a small stone structure with water running out a slot and stone-lined trough next to the door, she noticed something on the wooded hillside above the building. There, under a large oak, were round objects—brilliant white—on the ground. Sara Sue thought they might be birds' eggs fallen from a nest but reconsidered. What bird would lay eggs so late in the year? She scurried up the slope to investigate and found the loveliest mushrooms she'd ever seen. They rose on slender stalks capped with domed hoods, not yet open. In their entirety, they shone white as snow. She knelt to study them and decided to pick them as a present for her mama to cook. She knew better than to eat them, but thought it harmless to sample the smallest, pinky-sized one, which she found unappealing without the butter her mama used for frying toadstools.

After delivering the eggs, one in each fist, she ran up the hill to home. Secure in a dress pocket nestled her fungal treasures.

"Mama, I have a surprise for you. I picked you the prettiest mushrooms."

Maylene didn't answer, and Sara Sue found her mama sleeping while Quencus had his nap. She went back outside, where Chase dozed in the sun. Using the dog for a pillow, she lay down to study dark-bottomed, white clouds floating overhead. In the distance, she heard Johnny's voice as he helped unharness the team, and she soured with jealousy for his larger size and greater usefulness with the big animals.

She turned her head when something tickled her arm. There, nearby, a small anthill stood like a miniature mountain. Sara Sue flicked the small black ant away and watched, spellbound, as its colony members marched back and forth, in and out. Some toted tiny objects in their mouths.

More than half an hour passed before she lost interest in clouds and ants. Sara Sue skipped to the barn to find her Uncle Lester tending a fire just outside the doorway. Using a long-handled wooden paddle, her pa stirred the contents of a large kettle hung above it. Johnny passed him a bowlful of sliced apples, spooned from a pot by Aunt Vesta, to add to the cider brew.

"Apple butter! Can I help?"

"Not just yet, but once your mama brings them, you can add the spices. Go see if you can find your sister. I think she's down at the house with Grandma. We need her to take a turn at stirring."

Creating apple butter was an all-day task. It required ten to twelve hours to convert the juicy broth to a thick paste, and any pause in stirring resulted in scorching.

Sara Sue visited with Suzanne before heading back home. She'd not forgotten the gift she carried and ran to see if her mama was up before returning to the activity at the barn.

Maylene, having returned from taking Quencus to the privy, gathered apple-butter ingredients with one hand and rubbed the ache in her back with the other when Sara Sue dashed in.

"Mama, I picked mushrooms for you! I found them behind the springhouse." She rummaged in her pocket.

Maylene turned toward her daughter. "That's sweet of you, pumpkin. Let me see what you have."

Sara Sue produced her offering, cupped in both palms.

Maylene's legs went boneless. She dropped to a crouch, putting herself at eye-level with her five-year-old child. "Sugar, you're not in any trouble, but you have to be truthful right now and tell me if you ate any of those."

Sara Sue hung her head and studied her unshod feet. Her mother's grave tone and expression frightened her. "Only a little one. It wasn't very good."

Dear God, don't let it kill her.

Maylene tucked a stray strand of blond hair behind Sara Sue's ear. "Sweetheart, I'm going to get a bowl, and we'll see if we can get that mushroom out of your tummy. It's not good for you."

Returning, she placed the wooden bowl in her daughter's hands. "You hold this under your chin, and I'm going to put my finger down your throat a little ways. Open up, honey."

Sara Sue did as told and gagged in response to Maylene's finger, but she didn't vomit. Maylene tried again and again until Sara Sue's eyes swam with tears and she backed away.

"Stay right here and watch your brother. I'm going to get your pa," Maylene said, making a supreme effort to appear unperturbed.

Thank goodness Marcus worked nearby.

"What's wrong?" he asked, looking up from the simmering kettle. Maylene didn't normally walk with such speed late in pregnancy.

Marcus passed the paddle to Vesta as Maylene tugged him away from the group. "Sara Sue's eaten a mushroom. I'm trying to get her to vomit but she's only gagging."

"What sort of mushroom?" Marcus asked to delay having to know unequivocally. Yet Maylene had already told him all he needed to know.

Maylene reached into her apron pocket and pulled out a ghastly sample of destroying angels.

Marcus snatched them and rushed to the fire. He threw them in, where they blackened and curled and vanished.

"Papa, what...."

"Not now, Johnny."

Returning to Maylene, Marcus whispered, "Dear God—did she say how much she ate?"

"She said just a little one, but it don't take much. I thought maybe if you hold her upside down and I make her gag.... Will that work?"

They started for the house.

"I've got to help your mama a minute. Johnny, stay here and feed the fire, and don't let your uncle burn the butter." To Maylene, Marcus said, "It's worth a try. If not, we've got to get an emetic in her. How long ago did she eat it?"

"I don't know—I slept longer than I meant to. She said she found them above the springhouse."

"Then it's been a while. Vesta sent her for eggs some time ago."

"More than an hour?"

"Well more than that."

"Marc, I'm scared to death."

The experiment failed. After several attempts, the little girl sobbed and her parents gave it up.

Marcus held her, "Don't cry, pudding, we'll try something else."

"I'm sorry I ate the bad mushroom, Papa. It looked so pretty I thought it would be good to eat."

"It ain't your fault, baby. If you didn't know not to eat it, it's our fault. May, mix up some saltwater, and make it strong."

Sara Sue hated the taste of it, but she would do anything for her papa, and she drank nearly a cupful before her gag reflex stopped her. It was enough. She emptied her stomach contents into the bowl Maylene offered.

Her parents bent their heads over the bowl. There, vivid white against the dark wood, were fragments of the mushroom, but no more than adequate to reassemble into a ladybug.

"Shall we try again?" asked Maylene.

"I'm afraid so."

Sara Sue cried but she swallowed a half-cup before vomiting again. This time, saltwater alone came up, without a trace of destroying angel.

"Do you think a purgative will help?" A pale and shaky Maylene struggled to hide her panic.

Marcus knew and held their daughter, who would have felt her mother's trembling. Maylene bounced Quencus on her knee as he watched the strange proceedings.

"It's all we have left."

"Does your ma have castor oil?"

"Not since before the War."

"We don't have time to make a tincture of poke. We'll have to grind the root and mix it with something."

"With honey. I know where there's some growing near the run. I'll be right back."

Marcus found the plants, some still laden with their dark-purple berries, and shoveled several thick roots out of the ground. He cut them from the stalks, rinsed them in the run, and raced back up to the cabin, arriving out of breath.

Maylene sliced the roots thin and then ground them with a mortar and pestle. She added honey and spooned the mixture into Sara Mae, who accepted it readily after the dreadful saltwater.

"You're such a good girl, sweetie. This will have you running for the privy, but that's exactly what we want. We'll get that nasty mushroom out of you, and we'll go down to Grandma's for Uncle Lester's birthday cake."

It wasn't much of a party. By the time the family assembled, all but Johnny and Quencus knew about Sara Sue's situation, and they were frightened. Sara Sue, however, chirped about the cake and wanted to know what hid in the slender box waiting at Lester's place at the table.

"Your Uncle Calvin left it the last time he was here," her grandma said. "I haven't a clue what it is."

With the exception of Marcus's offerings to Maylene and his children, Lilly birthdays didn't normally include gifts. Instead the honoree chose his or her favorite meal—in this case, fried chicken, cornbread, and boiled potatoes—and a dessert from a limited list of options.

The only other "gift" came at bedtimes of childhoods past. Marcus retained the fond memory of staying up later than his siblings for a brief lecture from his parents on his April birthdays.

The three of them gathered at the table, and the ritual always began the same way.

"It's a sin to be prideful, son, but your father and I want you to know how blessed we feel that God saw fit to give you to us."

Then Suzanne and Quentin would take turns telling Marcus the ways he made them proud.

"You make good marks at school."

"You help your mama take care of your little sisters."

"You're getting better at minding your pa."

"You're an honest boy and set a good example for the others in that regard."

"You rarely whine or complain about your chores."

Marcus would later lie awake vacillating between feeling puffed up about his laudable traits and ashamed for his conceit. But because his parents were far more immediate and familiar than a pride-forbidding God, their words of praise held sway, and he generally fell asleep with a high opinion of himself.

Of course, Lester had outgrown such a talking-to, but he hadn't outgrown his love of cake. And he approached Calvin's gift with a look of breathless anticipation. Sara Sue made sure to find his lap before her uncle lifted the lid of the slim wooden box. There, nestled in a bed of cedar shavings, was a shiny tin whistle. As well, a note that read, *See if you can learn to play this thing Les. We need your help.*

Suzanne sighed. The brothers were the closest of her children, and they missed each other. She anticipated losing another son to the glamour of town.

Sara Sue scrambled down abruptly. "Mama, I need to go to the privy."

CHAPTER SEVENTEEN

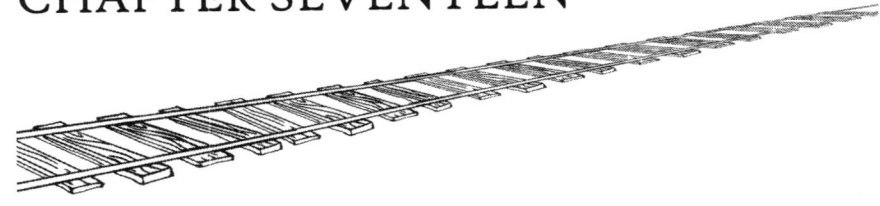

As Marcus tucked in his younger daughter that night, Maylene said to Jenny, "Wake us if you notice anything unusual. Anything at all."

"I will. She seems all right now, don't she?"

"Yes, I believe the poke root did its work and all will be well. Don't worry, honey, just keep her close."

"I will. Good-night, Mama."

Maylene kissed Jenny without rising from the rocker. Getting her oversized self in and out of the chair took effort, and she had more than two months to go.

She watched Jenny disappear up the twisting steps to the upstairs bedrooms. Only to Marcus had Maylene voiced her concern that Jenny's childhood faded with the arrival of Johnny. Instead of being envious of the attention he demanded, Jenny took him under her protective care as if he were her own child. No different with the others, she mothered her younger siblings, fretting over their every tear and mishap.

Marcus reappeared moments later. "She's already falling asleep. Maybe we're out of the woods."

"Lord, I pray so." Maylene knitted, her eyes on the fire. She regretted her long nap, which contributed to her keyed up, not-the-least-bit-sleepy state. "Why don't you turn in. I'll let the fire burn down in a while."

Maylene had just crept into bed beside her sleeping husband and started to doze off when she heard Jenny at the top of the steps.

"Mama! Sara Sue's throwing up bad. And she says her stomach hurts."

Marcus beat Maylene to the staircase and vaulted up, taking two at a time. He returned with a crying Sara Sue in his arms, her nightdress soaked with vomit.

"Oh, baby, let's get you out of that. I'll get you one of Papa's shirts," Maylene said. Needing more illumination than the dying fire provided, Marcus set his daughter down before the fireplace and used the embers to light two candles. Maylene started to lift the soiled garment over Sara Sue's head when the child heaved again, spewing more of her supper and dessert a startling distance.

"Marcus, get a bowl, will you? Jenny, see if you can sleep. We'll take care of her."

Jenny hesitated. "There's vomit all over the bed—it's wet."

"Use our bed then. We'll clean up in the morning."

Maylene hastened to re-dress her daughter before the next wave of nausea overcame her. The bowl saved the shirt. Maylene wiped Sara Sue's mouth with the sleeve of her nightdress.

"Marc, if you'll stoke the fire, I'll sit and rock with her. I don't suppose this will last long."

Marcus blindly followed instructions as his daughter cried and fear consumed him.

The poison's in her. We were too late.

"My tummy hurts. It hurts," Sara Sue wailed before throwing up again.

"I know, baby, I know. It'll be better soon," Maylene promised, praying she didn't lie.

After the vomiting turned to unproductive retching, Maylene set down the bowl and put both arms around her child. "She's shaking."

"I see that. Are you cold, sugarplum?"

Sara Sue nodded, and Marcus pushed past the curtain to retrieve a quilt from the bed, where he found Jenny weeping. He leaned down to kiss her cheek before returning to cover his wife and stricken child.

That's when they heard the dreaded sound, explosive diarrhea. The warm liquid reached Maylene's thighs before she had time to react. Sara Sue sobbed.

"It's all right, honey. It ain't your fault. Marcus, grab a couple of diapers and put them on your lap while I go change. I'll get another shirt for her. You'll have to wear undershirts tomorrow."

And so the night went. Maylene began urging her daughter to drink sips of water as the frightful diarrhea continued. It took Marcus with a story about "magic water" from a "healing spring" to get Sara Sue to swallow an appreciable amount. By then Maylene fought tears of desperation.

By first light, the fire roared and the cabin baked hot as July. Marcus held a chamber pot surrounded by two pillows under his daughter's behind and kept her wrapped as she continued to shiver. The excretions, nearly pure liquid, would not stop.

By sunrise, the little girl no longer whimpered or spoke. She drooped lethargic and confused, clearly in shock. Utterly empty at last, her beleaguered system stopped pumping out fluid, and Marcus carried her to his and Maylene's bed.

"She don't weigh no more than a newborn lamb," he said, tucking her in. "She's asleep, May. I'll tell Lester to ride to town and get Doc Mason. I know we can't pay him, but we'll find a way somehow."

"Will he come on Sunday?" Maylene asked.

"We'll find out."

"Do you think he can help?"

"Not really. But I don't feel right not trying."

"I don't either. We have to do everything we can. I'd sell my soul right now."

She couldn't speak another word, and Marcus left the house before he joined her in breaking.

Lester had the idea of selling their honey at Silas Hinton's store to pay the doctor, and Marcus agreed. They hurriedly packed the jars, wrapped in old quilts, in two large baskets secured to the saddle.

Be swift, brother, Marcus said to himself as Lester and Reggie vanished around a bend in the run.

Lester's first stop was the store, where he found Joseph, sitting on a step in the sun, engaged in his Sunday routine—playing the banjo and chatting inwardly with Randall.

"Lester Lilly, what brings you this way?"

"I've brought honey to sell. Will Mr. Hinton take it? We've got to make some money to pay the doctor, and I've got to find him quick. Sara Sue ate a bad mushroom yesterday and she's deathly ill."

"Dear Lord. Here, let's get those baskets down. I'm sure Silas'll be happy to sell the honey. He'll either buy it outright or sell it on consignment. If he don't want it all, I'll get the rest back to you. Doc Mason come by this morning. He knew we was closed, but he also knows I live here. He said he needed to buy a paper because some nervous husband was hauling him off for a delivery too soon, and he wanted something to read while he waited on the baby. Said he was heading up Possum Hollow. Come on, it's not far. I'll walk up with you."

They spied the doctor's buggy in front of a ramshackle log house. Lester, although uncomfortable intruding at such a time, knocked with force.

A bearded young man opened the door almost immediately.

"Sir, I need a word with the doctor if you can spare him for a moment," Lester said.

"Wait here. I'll see if he can step out."

The clean-shaven, middle-aged man appeared after a brief wait, his shirtsleeves rolled up to his elbows. "You fellows having some kind of trouble?"

"My niece ate a mushroom that's made her sick. She's just a little thing, five years old, and her pa never seen a child so ill. She was throwing up and had the runs all night. She's been shivering with cold and the cabin's like a forge, they've got it so hot. Her pa says she's in shock—he seen it in the War."

The men heard a moan from within the house. Joseph's stomach churned.

"I've got about another hour, I'd guess, to go here. Where do you live?"

"Up above Madam's Creek, about four miles from town. You'll do better on horseback than with a buggy," advised Lester.

"All right. Wait for me at the ferry. I'll be along as soon as I can."

"Thank you, sir."

Joseph agonized about going. Certainly, he could be of no help, and his presence would be nothing but salt in Marcus's ragged wound.

But he wanted to stand by Suzanne. He wanted to do something, anything, to help her. And, if possible, he wanted a chance to see Sara Sue.

He asked Lester, "Do you mind if I come? I'll keep away from Marcus and see if I can help your ma. If I leave now, I may arrive about the time you and the doc get there."

"It's not for me to say, Mr. Joseph. I'd wager Ma would be pleased to have your company. As for Marcus, ... why exactly is it he don't like you being around? Neither Vesta nor I can get him or Ma to talk about it."

"That's a tale for another time, I'm afraid. I'm sorry to leave you in the dark. I'm going to run back and grab a few things. Do you need fare for the ferry?"

"No, sir. Thank you."

Doctor Mason minced no words. "She's jaundiced, which means there's liver damage. How long has it been since she urinated?"

Maylene and Marcus exchanged looks.

"She hasn't all day," Maylene said. "But she's had nothing to drink since last night."

"You've got to get some fluids in her," said the doctor. "You don't want her kidneys shutting down."

Sara Sue, wrapped in a wool blanket and held on her papa's lap, stared blankly into space. Yet Marcus felt a tremor, like a leaf quaking in a mild breeze, pass through his daughter as she took in her possible doom.

"I'll make you a honey drink, baby," said Maylene. "You'll drink that, won't you?"

Sara Sue gave no indication of hearing.

"Use it sparingly, May. Lester's done sold the rest. Is there anything else we can do for her?" Marcus asked.

The doctor crossed an arm over his chest, using it as a prop to hold his chin. His thinning, sandy hair lay flat from the hat he'd removed. "I can bleed her, get some of the poison out."

Maylene took an involuntary inhale. Her eyes met her husband's one, signaling readiness to put her foot down if necessary.

Sara Sue burrowed her face into her papa's chest and spoke her first words of the day. "I want Chase."

Marcus thought, I never seen one soldier benefit from losing blood. I see no sense in it.

He shook his head. "No. We done all we could to get the poison out. I can't tolerate it."

Dr. Mason said, "As you wish. If I leave now, I can catch the last ferry. Keep her warm. Get her to drink as much as you can. Don't try to get anything down her if she's asleep or unconscious. If she gets through this, she'll have no appetite for a while, and that's to be expected. She'll let you know when she's ready to eat again."

He headed for the door, retrieving his hat on the table.

Marcus followed him onto the porch. "What would you say her chances are?"

"Not hopeless, but not good. She's going to get worse before she gets better—if she gets better. I'm sorry, son."

At Suzanne's request, Joseph stifled his desire to see Sara Sue and stayed away from Marcus. Also at her request, he picked apples with Johnny until stopped by darkness. Helpful and subdued, his seven-year-old grandson reflected the family crisis.

Joseph then sent Johnny home and shared a somber meal with Suzanne, Lester, and Vesta before Suzanne sent Vesta up the hill with leftovers. Vesta returned with news that Sara Sue lay in a deep, death-like sleep. Her frantic parents paced the floor. Jenny cried and prayed as she rocked Quencus to sleep, and Quencus, on the brink of his third birthday, had resumed his thumb-sucking habit. Johnny curled up next to Sara Sue and Chase, patting them both, telling them stories. Chase, never having been allowed in the house, recognized her role at once and refused to leave Sara Sue's side.

Suzanne teared up, and Vesta went upstairs. Lester said he had something to do in the barn. Joseph floundered. Should he hold her? Talk? Remain silent?

"Suzy, what can I do?"

She gazed up at him with her shining eyes, blue as ever they were. "Come sit with me a minute."

They brought the rockers in from the porch and set them near the heat-radiating stove.

She began. "First, before I forget, a boy come down from Broomstraw yesterday morning when Marcus was at the mill. He saw the smoke by the barn and found Vesta and Lester there. He looked about Lester's age—that's what Lester said—and said he'd been told we could get a message to you. Said he was your nephew and his ma don't want you coming up there no more. She says it's too risky and she don't want you getting hurt."

"I'm not surprised. Some other time, I'll tell you what the last visit was like."

"All right. I'd like to express sympathy for that sorry state of affairs, but for now, do you remember when I had rheumatic fever as a child?"

"I surely do. I come to play and your mama sent me away."

"But you come back with a bouquet of sarvis, and Mama said you could sit and read to me for a little while. After she went out to hang laundry, do you remember what you did?"

"I do. I sang my mother's healing song."

"You did—I've never forgotten. And I felt better by the time you left. Do you know it still?"

"I do. Because it's more of a chant than a song, the same words again and again. It's the only Cherokee I know, and I can't claim to know it because whatever it means is lost on me."

"Well, I can tell you we've been praying every last one of us for a day and a half, and that child keeps getting sicker. And the doctor was no help. Will you sing that chant for Sara Sue? It's all I can think of. I'd be beholden to you."

"Suzanne, I'd be honored to, but I can hardly imagine Marcus permitting such a thing."

"Let me handle Marcus. I'll be right back."

"He said come on up."

"Did he now!" Joseph hoped Suzanne hadn't promised more than he could deliver. He was no Medicine Man.

They entered in silence, as if approaching a shrine. Maylene rocked her daughter in the sweltering cabin. Joseph removed his vest as sweat beaded on his forehead.

Marcus, as distracted and spent as Joseph expected, said, "Good of you to come. Maylene, let Mr. Joseph hold Sara Sue there in the rocker. Do you want us to step out?"

"Please. For a few minutes."

Quencus slept upstairs. Marcus had to drag Chase by the scruff of her neck as the family retreated to the porch.

Joseph looked down at his granddaughter and wondered how a parent endured such agony. Even to him, who knew her from a distance, Sara Sue was precious, irreplaceable, this inimitable waif of a girl with her innocence and curiosity and freckles. By this stage of inner damage, her yellowish pallor and limp form rendered her horrifyingly corpse-like.

In a deep, soft voice he began the chant he'd heard his mother use whenever one of her children ailed. Old as time, the sound comforted him despite making him miss the one who taught it. He let his head fall back against the chair's frame and closed his eyes as a haunting memory came. After his mother's death, he'd wondered why his family hadn't sung for her, and held a conviction she would have lived if they had.

Joseph felt Sara Sue's breathing but detected no warmth. He willed her to live.

Marcus listened, treading the porch planks. He'd agreed only because he'd become too depleted, both physically and emotionally, for an argument. How could this nonsense help? Yet a part of him grasped at anything. He already questioned his decision not to allow the bloodletting.

No, let that be. The release of a meager amount of blood? And the procedure would have hurt and scared his daughter so. Worsened her shock.

Joseph's voice trailed off of its own accord. The chant completed, he carried Sara Sue to the doorway. "I've done what I could. God bless you all. I'll be praying for you."

"Thank you," said Maylene. She gave Marcus a pleading look as he took his child from Joseph's arms. "My husband thanks you, too."

An hour before dawn, Joseph placed a few coins on the table as he drained his cup of coffee. "This is for keeping the horse. She'll be taking hay soon, and I won't leave her here if you won't let me pay for her keep."

"I don't feel right about it, but it will help pay the doctor, so all right," said a groggy Suzanne. *Did I sleep at all? Seems like I tossed all night.*

"You'll get word to me about Sara Sue if, God forbid, there's bad news," Joseph said. He flinched to use such words without an embrace, but he hadn't touched Suzanne since clasping her hand—through a glove—at the wedding. He didn't know if she'd welcome or shun a hug.

"I'll send Lester. He didn't tell Calvin, but I see no sense anyhow, not until we know. I'd just as soon you not tell him. There's not a thing he can do but worry himself sick."

Joseph thanked Suzanne for food and lodging, and headed out.

Lot of good that damn horse does me, he thought, his leather boots immediately saturated with dew.

About the time he reached Madam's Creek, the waxing moon set behind the lofty crown of Broomstraw Ridge, depriving the woods of its soft light and cast shadows. The sky above, however, ignited with stars masked by the moon's glow. Joseph slowed his pace as his eyes adjusted to the deeper dark, and he took in the dazzling display.

Another memory bubbled up from the depths of his brain. He was a young boy, maybe four or five, waking on a spring morning. At that time of year, the sun shone straight through a small window at the end of the loft he occupied with Will and Becky. He had, as was his habit, his head burrowed under a blanket, a moth-eaten one of wool that allowed brilliant splashes of light through.

At some later time, he surveyed the night sky with his mother and viewed it transformed from a black sky decorated with lights to a dark blanket masking a blazing sky beyond.

"Look, Mama!" he said. "The whole sky is lit up, but we see only the bits that come through."

He saw the bright swath of the Milky Way as a thin place in the cloth, so worn it was close to tearing, unveiling the splendor it incompletely hid.

His mother placed a hand on his head and said, "Joey, there's magic in the way you see. Strong magic."

The pride in her voice made him remember what she said.

The quivering call of a screech owl interrupted Joseph's musings, and he quickened his steps. He wanted to catch the first ferry and make it to work on time, even if his thoughts would be with his granddaughter and her terrified family all day.

CHAPTER EIGHTEEN

That night, after Joseph left the cabin and the children were put to bed, Maylene said, "If she's going to leave us, she's going to be in someone's arms. We'll take turns holding her until she wakes up or . . . God takes her home."

The statement dropped her to a chair.

Vesta, newly arrived to check on her niece, said, "I'll sit with her a few hours. You and Marcus see if you can sleep awhile."

Maylene, nauseated with stress and fatigue, accepted the offer. Marcus fed the fire and followed her to bed.

They lay side by side on their backs, holding hands.

"Did we never teach her not to eat mushrooms without having us check them?" Maylene asked.

"I don't know. Seems like we would have, but I don't recall telling her."

"I told her about copperheads and poison ivy and black-widow spiders. Maybe I forgot about mushrooms."

"There's no point in blaming ourselves, May. We might have told her and she forgot. I don't think she would have eaten that thing if she remembered us saying 'don't.'"

"This fear is eating me alive."

Marcus stared at the ceiling and Maylene's pulse quickened.

"No, don't! *Don't!*" she whispered.

She'd prayed to never again feel him withdraw from her, retreat to that shuttered place he lived when he arrived home a man so different from the one she married halfway through the War.

"Marc, don't leave us. Not now. I can't bear it a second time."

With effort, he turned his head to fix his eye upon her. "I don't mean to. If I do, I'll be back. I promise."

He thought of his mother's words, how she'd said she wouldn't survive his death. How could he survive the loss of his inquisitive, cheerful, chatterbox of a shadow? The child who adored him, mirrored him, and, more than any of the others, healed his heart.

Maylene nestled close to her husband and shoved her sadness and apprehension into a corner of her consciousness long enough to fall asleep. Marcus returned his attention to the oak boards above them, which flickered dimly in the firelight. He'd left spaces between them on purpose, to allow the fire's heat to rise into the loft and keep his future children warm. He'd just proposed to Maylene when he placed those boards, and he burned with the wildest anticipation and desire. Their dreams—interrupted by several brutal years—had come to fruition. And now a peanut-sized, white mushroom threatened to bring the timbers crashing down, as if the house were made of twigs.

Maylene awoke close to midnight and sent Vesta home. She noticed a plate covered with a checkered cloth on the table. Ma must have brought up some food.

"Bless her heart, she can't sleep either," she said to Chase, who thumped her tail against the floor.

Rocking, holding her unconscious child, Maylene tried to sing a lullaby, but the attempt made her cry and she gave it up. She kissed her daughter's cheek and hair. She said, "Don't leave us, baby girl. Our hearts will break into pieces."

Then she closed her eyes and prayed, "God, in your mercy, spare our daughter and keep Marcus from drifting away like a duck feather floating down the river."

At her feet, Chase sighed and went back to sleep.

A few hours later, Maylene heard Marcus approach from behind.

"How is she? Any change?" he asked.

Maylene shook her head.

"I'll take her now. See if you can sleep a little more."

Maylene relinquished Sara Sue and peeked at her mother-in-law's offering. "Looks like your ma brought the rest of Lester's cake. Can I bring you a slice?"

"No, maybe for breakfast."

"I don't feel sleepy, but I'll lie down. My back's giving me fits."

"I should have brought you a pillow."

"That's sweet of you, but I can do such things. It don't hurt enough to mention."

"Then why did you?"

Maylene sighed. "I don't know. I'm too tired and anxious to know anything. See you in a little while."

She kissed him after erasing her expression that screamed she wanted to bite his head off. She walked away unsteadily, as if she'd sat long enough to forget the mechanics.

Marcus reached for the plate and slid it toward him. He flipped off the cover and tore loose a large chunk of cake. "Chase-pup, have you been fed at all the last two days?"

And he tossed the delicacy onto the floor for the hungry dog, who devoured it without chewing.

Marcus got up, cradling Sara Sue with one arm, and added wood to the fire. As the blaze brightened, it revealed the contrast of his daughter's freckles with her bleached face, as if the once-charming dots had become a ruinous rash.

Why didn't I do this before I sat down, or ask Maylene? We're useless, both of us.

Two hours crept by. Just as the moon set and Marcus noticed its rectangle of light disappear from the floor, Sara Sue stirred.

He sat bolt upright.

Without opening her eyes, she said in a hoarse voice almost too soft to hear, "Papa, I'm thirsty."

Marcus carried her to the table and sat down on the bench, reaching for a pitcher of water as tears wet both cheeks. He filled the cup Maylene had left and held it while Sara Sue drank and drank.

"Do you want more?"

She nodded and he filled the cup again. She drank half before refusing it.

Maylene heard Marcus's voice and got up. "Oh, baby. My baby girl. Thank God in heaven. How much did she drink?"

"A cupful and another half."

"Praise God. Let's get her to bed." Maylene's tears flowed as freely as her husband's.

Sara Sue slept by the time they tucked her in, but she no longer exhibited the flaccidity of the past twelve hours. Chase settled next to her patient, leaving the foot of the bed empty. There Maylene and Marcus collapsed, sideways, to hold each other and weep.

They knew their daughter remained severely ill, but they also knew she had turned her back on death.

Eight days after Sara Sue ate the destroying angel, she rode her pa piggyback to Sunday dinner at her grandma's. Having forgotten the first-Sunday-of-the-month routine, Marcus swore under his breath when he saw Joseph slicing a ham hock.

Never mind. It was good of the man to make the long walk last Sunday. What felt like an intrusion might have been a key to Sara Sue's survival. Unlikely, but possible.

Marcus stayed for the meal.

With coaxing from her grandma and both parents, the child—skeletally thin but now only faintly yellow—ate a few mouthfuls of bread and boiled cabbage and potatoes, and a small slice of ham. She yawned at the apple cobbler, shaking her head.

Seated next to her, Marcus asked, "Ready for a nap, blinky?"

She answered by reaching for his neck and climbing onto his back. Marcus piggy-backed her home, pleased to have an excuse to leave, and even more pleased to see his daughter eat the first nourishment resembling a meal in over a week. Maylene would save him a helping of cobbler.

As he pulled a pile of blankets over her, Sara Sue said, "I know a secret."

"What's that?"

"Paw Paw ain't in that box no more."

"No, he's gone to heaven."

"No, Papa. He was here. That night you gave cake to Chase. Didn't you see him? We was floating by the chimney, and we laughed at Chase eating Uncle Lester's cake. He said I should go back and have some, too, before the durn dog ate it all."

Marcus grew goosebumps over his entire body. He hadn't told anyone about feeding cake to the dog, and Sara Sue had been in a death-like state at the time, somewhere far beyond looking and seeing. How did she know?

He kissed his daughter's cheek. "Your Paw Paw was right, and I'm mighty glad you took his advice. That cake's gone, but your mama will make another one when you feel like eating it. It sounds like your mama and I ain't alone looking after you, baby. I think the good Lord sent your Paw Paw, and I'll bet he was mighty glad to get the job. Go to sleep now. When you wake up, Jenny's going to read to us."

"Read what?"

"It's a surprise. Uncle Calvin brought it, just for you."

Homing pigeon that she was, Sara Sue made her wobbly way to the barn and found her papa grooming Blackjack, who had rolled in mud. "I want to hear the book."

The family remained gathered at the main house. There Calvin explained he had borrowed the book from his in-laws, who had borrowed it from the judge, but the Lillys must keep the treasure until completed, cover to cover—*Twenty Thousand Leagues Under the Sea*.

Marcus sat down to a large square of cobbler, sharing with Sara Sue, as Joseph prepared to leave.

"Read to us before you go, will you?" Suzanne asked. "Get us started. Jenny will take over after that."

Joseph balked. "I should be getting back...."

"To what? It's Sunday. The ferry will run until seven." She thrust the thick novel at him.

The children's expectant faces fixed on him, and he sat back down. Their eagerness mirrored his own. He regretted he didn't have a copy to take home. Damn, it was irksome for him to start a book and not finish it.

So he began.

Marcus took note of the ease and expression with which Joseph read. Not like the typical man with an eighth-grade education, tripping over unfamiliar words and convoluted sentences. He read like a man who had devoured many a book. He read as Marcus read.

Marcus didn't like the rapt attention of his children.

Don't start acting like a grandpa.

After thirty minutes, Marcus interrupted. "I believe it's Jenny's turn now."

He hadn't meant to wait so long, nor had Joseph intended to read so long. Both got caught up in the tale.

"Indeed it is." And Joseph relinquished the book, thanked Suzanne for dinner, and began his walk back to the New as October's long shadows stretched beneath a cloudless sky, the air's bite promising the season's first frost.

CHAPTER NINETEEN

Suzanne loved Thanksgiving, and, after two subdued ones following Quentin's death and in celebration of Sara Sue's recovery, she was ready to pull out the stops. She wrote Eliza, her distant daughter, asking her and her husband to take the train from White Sulphur Springs on Wednesday. She instructed Maylene to invite her parents and her sister Melva, whose farm straddled Madam's Creek nearly three miles below the Lillys'. She insisted that Calvin come and bring his pregnant bride, promising she wouldn't expect them for Christmas. And she advised Joseph a place would be set for him, that she wouldn't take no for an answer.

A frenzy of preparations began well in advance of the date. Marcus and Lester made two temporary tables from sawhorses and boards. They stacked maple-trunk sections in corners of the house to serve as chairs. Then they and Chase scoured the woods for a turkey. Failing to find one, they obeyed Suzanne's command to ride to the New for a fishing expedition.

Maylene's mother, Sara Mae, sent word she would bring fresh loaves of bread. Eli stopped by to say Rachel had corn pudding in mind. Suzanne knew Eliza and Louella would bring offerings as well. She would prepare ham and fish. Maylene and Vesta would make apple and pumpkin pies. She envisioned the sagging table in her mind's eye and heard the voices of her loved ones. She'd be too busy to miss Quentin saying grace—that would be Eli's job—and adding after his *Amen*, "Suze, I ain't going to get through this meal unless you relocate the buttons on these britches. I may fire one off and hurt one of the youngsters."

Maylene had a particular task in mind, and she saved it for the pitch-black of night.

"Marc?"

"Uh-huh."

"There's something I need to tell you."

Marcus rolled in her direction. "This don't sound good."

"I done something you may not like—I broke the promise I made your ma."

"What promise? About her and Mr. Joseph?"

"I told my parents."

Marcus used an elbow to prop his head. "You swore on the Bible."

"I know, and that's why it's taken me this long to tell you."

"I didn't think we had no secrets between us."

"Now we don't. It was only that one. I must have started to tell you scores of times, but I couldn't make myself do it, thinking you'd be so disappointed in me."

"I'm disappointed you didn't tell me."

"I know I should have. I'm sorry, honey."

"Why did you tell them?"

Maylene found her husband's face and caressed a cheek. "I didn't think it was fair for them to have to carry the pain of the rumors about me. Not when I could take that hurt away. They didn't say a word, but they must have known. And I trusted them. I'm sure they've never told a soul."

Marcus reflected for a moment. "Did you think they might believe what folks said about you?"

"No. But maybe I carried a little fear. That they could have a seed of doubt planted. I decided I didn't care what anyone else said or thought, but I couldn't bear for them to have even the tiniest shred of suspicion."

She waited, her face pressed against Marcus's neck.

"Marc?"

He pulled her close. "I should've told you to tell them, May. You done the right thing. But you could've told me. Like you did just now—I would've understood. Did you truly think I'd be angry?"

"Not so much angry, but ashamed of me for breaking my promise to your ma."

"Silly girl. You think I never broke a promise to Ma?"

He kissed her smile, and Maylene let out a deep sigh, rolling over in search of a position in which her back wouldn't ache.

Maylene had yet to tell her parents about Joseph's reappearance. She planned to confide in them after church that last Sunday before Thanksgiving, but the day dawned with wind-driven sleet, and none of the Farleys or Lillys attended the modest, white-washed house of Baptist worship that morning.

As the holiday approached, Maylene grew increasing apprehensive about her mother's reaction to the unexpected guest.

The Lilly home had never contained such a crowd. Suzanne, bustling about, made the necessary introductions of her "cousin" before directing everyone to their seats. The children clustered around the makeshift tables, with Jenny in charge. Sara Sue proudly took command of her Aunt Louella's little girl, shy Annie, nearly two. One grandchild—Rachel's new baby, her third ruffian boy—joined the adults. He sat babbling in a highchair wedged in next to his mother.

Rachel's husband, Eli, cognizant of two dozen growling stomachs, sprinted from "Our Heavenly Father" to "Amen," and the feast began.

Sara Mae waited, sliding furtive looks at Joseph. As soon as Suzanne got up to check the first pies, she zeroed in on him. "I've not heard Suzanne speak of you, Mr. Cook. You grew up on Brooks Mountain?"

"Yes, ma'am. We were playmates and classmates as children."

"And you're cousins."

Maylene gave her mother a look. It had no effect.

"Are you kin on your mother's or your father's side?" Sara Mae continued.

Marcus turned his eye on his mother-in-law. *Enjoying yourself?*

A sheen of sweat appeared on Maylene's throat and brow.

Joseph shifted on his seat, avoiding Sara Mae's blue eyes. *What had Suzanne said?* He didn't remember. His pause grew awkward.

"My mother's side," he said, realizing too late it mattered not which side of his family he claimed relation. It was Suzanne's side he could not recall, and that was not the question.

Lester chased a pair of green beans with his fork. His head jerked up. He stared at Joseph, then his ma. His eyes shot back to Joseph before giving Marcus, seated across from him, a questioning look.

He knows! Marcus's stomach clenched with alarm, but he ignored his brother and asked his father-in-law to pass the butter.

Maylene's hand dropped to her belly as if she were having a birthing pain.

Sara Mae, momentarily delayed by a fishbone in her mouth, continued. "Well, it's wonderful you come home to New River. Do you have family here?"

"Only my sister's family," Joseph lied. "I've met my nephew, but not my two married nieces. My sister's up on Broomstraw, but her husband hasn't been real cordial."

"Never mind. You've got all the kin a soul could need right here."

Too late, Maylene leaned forward past Melva to give her pa an imploring *do-something!* look.

Sara Mae's face flushed the way it did when she tried to contain laughter. Her entire torso shook.

Bob hitched a knee over the bench and clambered to his feet. "Lordy, she's got food down the wrong pipe."

He helped his wife up and led her onto the porch. There, hands on her knees, Sara Mae gasped and coughed as tears streaked her flaming cheeks. Bob whacked her on the back with little hope of dislodging her mischief.

"Good heavens! Is she alright?" Suzanne asked.

"She's fine," said Maylene. "Probably just another little fishbone."

Thank goodness Jenny, preoccupied by the children's chatter, appeared to have missed the absurd exchange, if not her grandmother's abrupt exit. Marcus made another quick scrutiny of Lester. He rested an elbow on the table, his fingertips on his brow as he surveyed his plate. Without success, he attempted to tame a smile pulling at the corners of his mouth.

A belch escaping her uncomfortably full and uneasy stomach, Maylene set down her fork. This baby crowded her like none other.

She couldn't finish her meal. As conversation hummed around her, she studied her husband's face, a mask, its gaze undirected.

Sara Mae returned, drying her eyes with a napkin, hiccupped one last giggle, and re-seated herself as though nothing had happened.

Bob resumed his meal and one of his favorite topics. "Marcus, how was your honey harvest this year?"

After eating, the children tumbled outside for games of tag and crack the whip. The afternoon, fading to dusk as the sun slipped behind the southwest wall of the hollow, became winter-like in its chill. Yet the lure of squeals and laughter coaxed Marcus, Vesta, and their brothers into the melee. Eli pulled his coat from the back of a chair and called, "Come on!" to Louella's husband, Howard. The two men plunged in as well.

Joseph stood watching from the porch. A keen despair came over him as the mountainside snuffed the last of the sun's light illuminating the hollow's opposite slope.

Why am I here? This isn't my family, only a shadow one I lie about. Ain't it, damn, *isn't* it true, Randall? I can no sooner play with the children than fly to the moon. I need my own land, my own home. And a woman who don't feel like someone else's wishing I was him.

He retreated to the barn and began splitting wood. Maylene's father soon joined him. The men worked without conversation, which Joseph found soothing. He sensed the good in Bob Farley, the decency of a man whose kindness expressed itself more in deeds than words.

Meanwhile, Suzanne pulled the last two pies from the oven. She and Sara Mae cleared and stacked dishes, refusing help from Maylene, while Louella set a kettle of water to boil for dishwashing and Rachel changed a diaper. Maylene eased into a rocker, positioning a pillow behind her lower back.

"You feeling poorly?" Louella asked.

"My back's pitching a fit, but I've only a couple of weeks to go."

She rocked drowsily, half-listening as Louella and Calvin's wife, Nancy, sat at the table trading complaints about pregnancy. Both anticipated babies in late winter. The topic held no appeal for Maylene, however, and she held her tongue.

Melva Farley and Eliza set the table for dessert. Muscular and large-nosed like her father, Eliza filled space with her buxom form as well as her personality. Her blacksmith and farmer husband, Mayhew, who more than matched her bulk, fished a cigar out of a vest pocket and took a seat next to Maylene. Neither he nor Eliza found proximity to maternity talk or children comfortable. Married more than seven years, they'd resigned themselves to infertility but not without an aching envy.

"Mama," Eliza said, "there's a little orphan baby we might adopt. He's got a club foot, and Mayhew says he don't want a crippled child. We've had words."

What else is new? thought Suzanne. She'd never seen such a pair of strong-willed, quarrelsome spouses. Quentin said he'd wager they disagreed about the sun rising in the east and setting in the west.

"Mayhew," she asked, "did you respect my husband?"

"Mr. Lilly? Of course. Whatever makes you ask?" Mayhew puffed a plume of smoke.

"He was crippled from the day you met him, but wouldn't you agree there was far more right than wrong with him?"

Mayhew recognized the trap too late. "Certainly. But he was injured as a grown man, and honorably. A child would be ridiculed."

"No doubt. And that little boy needs parents and grandparents and aunts and uncles and cousins to teach him to hold his head high. Do you know the family that can do that?"

"Yes, ma'am."

"And do you believe God has a purpose for that child?"

"Yes, ma'am, I suppose He does."

"Mayhew, it'll make me right proud to see you and Eliza answer God's call."

"We'll give it serious consideration." Mayhew released another burst of smoke and cleared his throat.

"I'm sure you shall."

Eliza beamed at her mother and Maylene smiled at the fire. Mayhew never had a chance.

When the dishes were washed and dried, Rachel called the family back inside. Her one-word shout of "Pie!" started a stampede.

As Maylene lumbered to her feet, she felt the flow of warm liquid running down the inside of her leggings. "Oh! Mama?"

"What is it, dear?" Sara Mae asked, setting a steaming apple pie on the table.

"My water's broke."

Their eyes met and locked. They both knew. The baby hadn't yet dropped into birthing position.

CHAPTER TWENTY

Sara Mae's immediate priority was to get rid of her husband. Having been widowed when his first wife died in childbirth, he lost all composure when one of his four daughters endured her hours of labor. He gained a reprieve when Mary, the eldest, and Margaret, the youngest, stopped coming home to give birth. The sisters now stayed at their homes near New Richmond, ten miles down New River, with Mary serving as Margaret's midwife. Mary, mother of six, hired a local midwife, who did little more than catch and clean the latest baby. Mary and her husband, Corbin, would be the parents of seven if they hadn't lost Sallie Mae to scarlet fever soon after the War. Margaret and Harris had three of their own.

Yet Bob Farley's anxiety knew no end. It would have been far easier for him to have sons.

"Go on home, honey. You can come back Sunday after church and bring me fresh clothes and meet your new grandchild. I'll likely stay a few days longer. Why don't you invite Mr. Cook to attend church with you? Introduce him to our neighbors." Sara Mae gushed words, with tangents, when nervous.

"What's wrong?"

"Not a thing. I'm in a hurry to attend to Maylene. Sometimes babies come quickly after you've had a few."

"All right then. Give her a kiss for me."

"Oh, wait. There'll be little room for Eliza and Mayhew here tonight, what with the children staying over. Tell Suzanne they can stay with you and Melva. Melva will take care of everything. They'll be closer to the ferry in the morning."

"Good idea. I'll speak with Suzanne."

He gave his wife a peck on the cheek, and Sara Mae exhaled audibly as soon as she left the house for the uphill walk to the smaller cabin where her daughter waited. Thank goodness neither Bob nor Marcus knew she'd instructed Lester to accompany Rachel and Eli home in their buggy. He'd then borrow the buggy to fetch his Aunt Bess, an expert midwife.

Marcus would know soon enough, and his hours of torment would find no answer.

Sara Mae found Maylene alone but detected signs of Marcus's handiwork. The bed had been dragged in front of the fireplace where a hardy blaze crackled. A stack of firewood waited by the door. The stove had been lit, a bucket of wood and another of water set beside it.

Maylene, leaning on a pile of pillows, wore a flannel nightdress and a grave expression.

"Have you got your padding in place?" Her mother asked.

"Of course." Maylene flipped back her blankets to reveal three layers of felt protecting the feather tick.

"Does Marcus know the baby's breach?"

"No. Does Pa?"

"No."

"Good."

"Lester's gone for Aunt Bess."

"Can she turn the baby?"

"God willing. She's done it before. How are you feeling?"

"All right. The pains are pretty far apart yet."

"Marcus will keep away, I trust."

"Yes, he's gone to do the milking and feeding. He'll put the children to bed at their grandma's and stay with them. He knows not to show his face until you send word."

"His first night with his father." Sara Mae shook her head.

"He'll survive.... Is our baby going to?"

Sara Mae set her ample bottom on the edge of the bed and squeezed her daughter's hand. "I believe so. Let me fix you a tonic to help you relax."

"Fix one for yourself, too, Mama. Maybe you can catch a nap before Aunt Bess gets here."

Maylene shut her eyes against a contraction. It's going to be a long night.

As the vice-like pain subsided, a shiver of fear followed.

Marcus returned to the larger house to put the children to bed upstairs—Jenny and Sara Sue in one narrow bed, Johnny and Quencus in another. They chattered about the baby but soon succumbed to fatigue and their father's firm, "Not another peep, now. Your grandma's tired and heading for bed."

Descending the stairs, he asked, "Where are Lester and Mr. Joseph?"

Suzanne, hanging her apron on a hook, avoided eye contact. "Joseph rode down with Eliza and Mayhew, so he can bring Reggie and the horses back tonight. Your brother went home with Rachel and Eli."

"What'd he do that for? He's used to bunking with Mr. Joseph." Marcus cringed inwardly. Surely his ma didn't expect him to bed down with Joseph Cook.

Suzanne seated herself at the table. "Sit down, Marcus."

Marcus, continuing to stand, placed his palms on the scarred wood. He leaned toward his mother. "What?"

"Lester is borrowing Eli's buggy to go for Aunt Bess."

Marcus leaned harder as blood drained from his head. "Why?"

"The baby hasn't dropped yet—and it's breach. Sara Mae is going to need help. Your aunt will know what to do."

"What will she do?"

"Try to get the baby turned, head down."

"How the hell…. I'm sorry, Ma. What if she can't?"

"Then the baby has to come out backwards. It ain't easy, but it can be done. I'm sorry to have to give this news, son."

Marcus ran fingers through his hair. "Blessed Jesus. Does Maylene know?"

"I don't know," Suzanne lied.

Marcus yanked his coat from the back of the chair. "I'll be in the barn if you need to find me."

He turned out the cow and mucked her stall. He climbed the ladder to the loft and forked hay into three racks below. Just as he completed that task, he heard hoofbeats. Joseph led Cloud and Blackjack, followed by Reggie, into the barn lit faintly by a single lantern hung from a support post.

"I'll take care of them," said Marcus. "Thank you for your help."

"It's my pleasure," said Joseph, trying to keep his teeth from chattering. He'd dressed more for Thanksgiving dinner than a long night ride.

He hastened to the house, leaving Marcus to remove tack and feed the mule and horses. Marcus moved mechanically, his thoughts a jumble of panicky what-ifs. Must he be banished from Maylene's side? Didn't she need him most? How could she need him least?

Maylene!

He repeated her name like a drum beating a prayer.

Lester returned with a well-bundled Aunt Bess—heavyset, in her early sixties—before midnight and escorted her to the cabin overlooking the grain fields. There Sara Mae greeted her with a firm embrace.

"I hate to call you out on such a cold night, especially knowing how tired you must be after the big meal."

"Nonsense. We ate early, and I had a nice nap. I'm fresh as a daisy. Maylene, how close are your pains?"

"Getting closer. Maybe every five or ten minutes?"

Bess took off two cloaks, a scarf, and a pair of mittens, tossing them onto the table next to a basket of Thanksgiving leftovers. Unwrapped, she revealed her broad-shouldered, short-legged shape, the build of her brother Quentin. Her gray hair matched her complexion, and her sagging jowls gave her a tired, morose look. Sara Mae's face, in contrast, glowed with color. Her plump cheeks never lost their ruddy hue, her lips remained deep pink, and her blue eyes gave off a light all their own.

"Let me feel your belly," Bess said, leaning over Maylene.

With firm pressure and experienced fingertips, she traced the baby's form. "You been feeling kicks down low?"

"Yes, and a cannonball up here." Maylene put a hand between her lower ribs.

"We may be able to turn that rascal if your water ain't broke."

Maylene's face fell. "It did—hours ago."

"Never mind," Bess said, unruffled. "I want you to sit up and put your feet on the floor after your next pain. It's still worth a try."

Maylene panted through the next contraction, then swung her legs over the edge of the bed. Bess pressed on Maylene's lower abdomen with the heels of her hands, feeling for any rotation.

Nothing.

She tried again. "I don't want to be too forceful, as there's little fluid left. This one feels quite committed to its position. I wish I'd been here sooner."

"What can we do?" A slight tremor in Sara Mae's voice betrayed her alarm.

"Walk. Maylene, I want you to get up and walk between each pain. When a spasm comes, you can sit on the bed, but don't lie down. Put your knees up. We'll help you."

Marcus couldn't hold still, let alone sleep. He lit a second lantern in the barn where he used a short-handled sledgehammer and a long-handled chisel to pound boards off a chestnut bolt. When he had an adequate supply, he took a bucksaw off the wall and angled the ends of some of the slabs. He used the thicker, narrower ones to create two rectangular frames. Next, he planed and sanded the wider boards until satisfied, then selected hand-hewn nails from a tin cup, and nailed the boards onto the frames.

The work kept him warm but didn't keep his mind off Maylene. Again and again, he looked up, thinking he heard a sound and willing Sara Mae to appear with the news he ached to hear.

Marcus's constructions, two sleds, occupied most of the night. Their completion awaited iron straps Bob had promised to forge. Marcus would steam and bend oak runners to fit their protective metal coverings. For now, he stashed the sleds out of sight in the loft.

As he walked back to his mama's house, he noticed clouds had snuffed the stars. The air smelled like snow. No matter—he would send Jenny and Johnny to school in a few hours, despite their lack of shoes. The need to pay Dr. Mason for his house call rendered that purchase impossible, but Maylene had made both children a pair of thick felt slippers, tied at the top with yarn. The clumsy footwear might last until Christmas.

Reaching the porch steps, Marcus wondered whatever became of Ma's hickory switch. He could flog himself for his inability to provide his children with shoes and help his wife in her time of crisis.

Mr. Joseph had better clear out fast this morning, he thought.

Joseph slept in a series of naps until about three in the morning. Unable to return to sleep, he slid out of bed, careful not to disturb Lester, softly snoring on his back. Already dressed in half his clothes, Joseph groped in the dark for his vest and heavy wool pants. He pulled his leather satchel out from under the bed and crept catlike downstairs, where he stoked the fire back to life.

Then he turned a rocker just so, with his back to the flames, allowing the light to strike the pages of a book he pulled from the satchel. It was one of his favorites, *Moby Dick*. He knew he'd finished it the last time he read it—why had he left a bookmark in place?

Not a bookmark but an envelope. Joseph turned it over to find his name on the back as well as the return address of a law firm, Blake and Milford, in Charleston.

What the hell?

Joseph tore around the wax seal to find a single page within. Incredulous, he read the "Last Will and Testament of Randall Jacob Murphy," dated a mere four months before the man's death. Randall had left his cabin and seventeen acres in Dauphin County, Pennsylvania, to Joseph Cook.

Randall, you son of a gun! You didn't sell the place before you left home? Did Jimmy threaten you, make you fear your time was coming? Why didn't you tell me?

Guess you didn't know my middle name either. For the record, it's Crawford.

His book forgotten, Joseph sat with a swelled heart, imagining what he would do with the gift. Surely land up North was worth more than land here. Those seventeen acres might buy him forty. He'd purchase a little farm and plow, grow his own food, be a free man on no one's clock but his own.

Randall, I'll be my own boss. If you can hear me, I thank you, old man, and it's far more than I deserve for leaving you outnumbered that night.

His thoughts were interrupted by Suzanne's appearance. "I heard the fire," she said.

"I'm sorry I woke you," said Joseph, folding the will and tucking it and the envelope back inside the book.

"You didn't. I been awake most of the night, worried sick. I've known Maylene since she was a baby—she's like a daughter to me. And if she don't make it through this birthing, Marcus will come undone. I'm going up to see if I can help. Maybe Bess or Sara Mae will sleep a spell if I'm there."

"I've been praying, Suzanne. Can I do something more?"

"No, but it's a comfort having you here. To me, anyway. You may want to avoid Marcus."

"I'll go before sunrise. I don't feel right leaving, but it's probably best that I do. Shall I take care of the milking first?"

"Oh, no. Marcus needs to keep busy. God knows what he's been doing in the barn all night."

Joseph's head lifted from the novel when the door swung open. Marcus's greeting was a scowl.

The son lit a fire in the cookstove and put a kettle on for coffee. "Want some?"

"Yes, thank you. This isn't a night for sleeping."

Marcus rubbed his chilled hands together in front of the fire, impatient for the water to heat. "What're you reading?"

"*Moby Dick*. Ever read it?"

"No."

"I'll leave it here, then. I've read it three times."

"Much obliged."

The men fell silent, one staring into the flames, the other pretending to read.

Well before dawn, Marcus left the house to milk the cow. A windless snow fell, silently brightening the dark world.

On his way back to the house with a brimming jug, having left the larger milk can at the springhouse, he encountered his mother. "How's it going?" he asked, swallowing the nervousness from his voice.

"Slowly. Maylene is tired, but Sara Mae and your Aunt Bess are inexhaustible. I couldn't get either one to even lie down. I know you're worried, son, but Maylene is in good hands—the best."

Marcus smelled bacon as he pushed open the door. Vesta was up, cooking bacon and grits to serve with slabs of leftover Thanksgiving bread.

Joseph sprang from the rocker, slapping shut his book. "I said I'd go, but I can't do it. I left not knowing if Sara Sue would pull through. I don't feel right running off in the middle of a ..."—he stopped himself from saying *difficult*—"birthing. I'm expected at work, but Silas will understand."

He wanted to add that he'd ride down for Dr. Mason, if needed, but Marcus didn't need to hear that either.

As if Joseph hadn't spoken, Marcus said, "I'm getting Jenny and Johnny up. I want them to go to school."

As soon as Marcus disappeared up the steps, Joseph turned to Suzanne. "Tell me what I can do. There must be something."

"All right. Vesta and I are doing the wash today, and Lester has a paying job in Jumping Branch, rebuilding the Meadows' house that burned down last week. I'm putting you in charge of Sara Sue and Quencus. See if you can entertain them with that whale book of yours, and if the snow gets deep enough, you can take them sledding."

"Consider it done." Joseph sat back down and began thumbing through *Moby Dick*, seeking an action-packed chapter.

"Thank you." Suzanne suppressed the impulse to squeeze his hand with gratitude. The children needed distraction, and she was in no shape for Sara Sue's endless questions.

Later in the morning, with directions from Suzanne, Joseph bundled the children in wool socks, wool caps, wool mittens, wool sweaters, and wool leggings or pants to sled in the season's first snow. Sara Sue and Quencus raced to the barn for the old sled, cloaked in dust and cobwebs, leaning against the back wall.

Joseph pulled the sled up the fenced corridor leading to the pastures—one shared by horses, mule, bull, and cow, while the other held sheep. Flanking the narrow passageway lay sloping fields shorn of their hay, wheat, corn, oats, flax, and buckwheat. The steeper terrain beyond belonged to the livestock, except for the hogs penned in their sty near the barn, and offered ideal sledding hills.

Sara Sue led the way to the children's favorite spot. Although she remained reed-thin, she exuded energy. "Come on, Mr. Joseph! This is where we start."

Joseph plopped Sara Sue on his lap, Quencus climbed aboard his sister, and they were off, Chase leading the way with gleeful bounds. The sled, having endured the abuse of nine previous children, bore scarred and cracked runners more inclined to stick than slide. Its dilapidation, along with a lack of packed snow, made for a leisurely descent. In addition, the vessel stalled every time it crossed one of the many zigzagging paths made by cows over the decades. Joseph thought the children would be disappointed, yet they squealed with delight. He tried to remember the last time he'd been sledding, which must have been at Suzy's. His mind dredged up an argument about who sat in front.

On the fourth trudge back up the long hill, Sara Sue asked, "Did your wife die, like my Paw Paw?"

"No, I've never had a wife."

Sara Sue gaped up at Joseph as if he'd uttered an absurdity. "Why not?"

"I was always on the move—women don't like that sort of life. Besides, I never met one who wanted me around all the time."

"Are you going to marry Grandma?"

Joseph smiled at his granddaughter's directness. "What makes you think she wants me around all the time?"

"I don't know—I'll ask her."

"Huh! You'll do no such thing, young lady."

"Why not?" Sara Sue blinked snow out of her blue eyes.

"What if she says no and hurts my feelings?"

"Oh."

Sara Sue pointed. "Quencus, look! There's a redbird!"

"Where?" Three-year-old Quencus rode the sled, slowing their progress.

"In the cedar yonder. See? Up on top. He so pretty! I love redbirds."

"There's an Indian belief that a pair of cardinals is two birds with one spirit," Joseph said. "If one dies, so does the other. It's rare to see a cardinal without its mate nearby."

"Is it true?" Sara Sue asked. "I don't see the lady bird."

"I see it!" Quencus yelled, having spotted the brilliant male. It flew, followed by a less-colorful female.

Quencus's shout caught the attention of his father as he emptied a wheelbarrow of soiled straw. Marcus paused to take in the scene above, fuming. *For the love of God, that bastard has seized himself an opportunity for a romp in the snow, cozying up to my children while the rest of us are going through hell.*

By early afternoon, Maylene could no longer stand. Her legs had turned to mush. Her body trapped on the bed, her mind became restless, working its way into dark corners.

"Why can't I birth this baby? I'm going to die . . . without seeing Marcus again."

Sara Mae squeezed her daughter's hand. "No, you're making progress, honey. We're almost to the pushing part."

Maylene yelled with the next contraction. When it eased, she gasped, "I need Marcus!"

Sara Mae and Bess exchanged looks. The last thing they needed was an anxious husband. But her daughter's desperation urged Sara Mae to relent.

"I know it's unseemly, but she may gain strength from seeing Marcus," she said to Bess.

Bess's face puckered with disapproval as she said, "It's up to you."

"I'll see if I can find him." Sara Mae reached for her cloak and scarf.

She found him sweeping wayward stems of straw and hay out of the barn's central aisle. He started when he saw her. Did she bring good news or bad?

"Maylene wants to see you. Just for a minute."

He threw down the broom and left Sara Mae trailing him uphill through the snow.

Maylene, covered with a quilt, tried to smile when her husband approached the bed, but her face crumpled. Marcus took her hand and bent to stroke a cheek.

Confusion overcame her—what had she wanted to tell him? Oh, the mushrooms!

"The children aren't safe! Marcus, get the mushrooms out of my apron pocket and bury them."

"I threw them in the fire. They're gone, May."

Another contraction seized her, and she squeezed Marcus's hand so tightly he thought his fingers would snap. Her entire body went taut, and her grimace struck Marcus like the stone fragment that took his eye.

How could I not know?

Someone touched his shoulder. "You'd best go," said Bess. "There's some hard work coming. We're going to get this baby born."

Marcus kissed Maylene's cheek, unable to force words past his blocked throat. He bolted back outside, stumbled down the steps, dropped to all fours—his unprotected hands splayed in the soft powder—and retched. If he'd eaten any breakfast, he'd have lost it.

The snowfall tapered off as Jenny and Johnny ran home from their one-room school, nearly a mile away, on Madam's Creek. Jenny beat Johnny to the door.

"Is it a boy or a girl?"

"We're still waiting," said Suzanne, hanging the last of the laundry on indoor lines.

"Still? What's wrong?" Jenny's radiance transformed into an expression of horror.

"The baby's just slow, honey. Sometimes they take extra work to get into the world."

Jenny caught the tension in her grandmother's voice, which intensified her distress. Tears brimming, she turned to Vesta. "Will Mama be all right?"

Vesta looked to her mother for help, but Suzanne's back was turned. "Your mama's very strong, and she has her mama and your Aunt Bess at her side. She'll get through this, but it's hard as the Devil waiting."

"Aunt Bess?" Jenny hugged herself as she began to cry.

Vesta led her to the rocker, where she cuddled her niece on her lap and stroked her silky, black hair, saying, "Hush now, my darling girl. Everything is in God's loving hands."

Johnny walked backwards to the door. He needed his pa.

As Jenny cried, Maylene fought for her life and the life of her baby. She'd been pushing for hours, becoming too exhausted to be effective. Sara Mae teetered on the brink of collapse herself.

Bess said to her, "Fix yourself another tonic and sit a while. Without the head pressing down, it's taken forever to open the womb. A little rump is emerging now. We've gotta be patient and wait and pray. As soon as there's anything to grab hold of, I'll be able to help."

Maylene no longer said anything intelligible when words escaped her. Her weakness alarmed her attendants, yet her uterus continued its powerful expulsive spasms. In excruciating slow-motion, the baby moved into the birth canal.

The next time Bess made an internal check, she encountered a hard lump and said, "Glory be! There's a heel! I'll have myself a handle soon."

"Thank God!" said Sara Mae, her eyes alight with tears.

Twenty minutes later, Bess exclaimed, "Maylene! Push, push, *push!* The cord's being compressed—we've got to move fast."

And Maylene roused herself and bore down with a sequestered vestige of strength, while Bess grabbed a tiny foot and pulled. A baby boy unfolded into the midwife's hands.

But instead of pink, his skin was blue. Without waiting for the afterbirth, Bess dropped with a thump onto the edge of the bed, placed the baby face-down across a sloping thigh, and gave him a bounce and a fanny-swat. The response was immediate—a sputtering cough, then a wail.

Aunt Bess watched with weary satisfaction as the baby took on the color of life.

After an early supper of Thanksgiving leftovers, kept fresh in a basket hung from the porch ceiling to keep the varmints out, Marcus and Lester did the evening milking and feeding. The nerve-wracked family then gathered around the fire in twos—Sara Sue on her papa's lap, Quencus on his grandma's, Jenny on Vesta's, and Johnny on Lester's. Joseph opened the only possible means of escape, the book on his knees. Even Marcus, unable to follow the words, appreciated Joseph's outward calm. Ready to go mad with anxiety, he closed his eyes and took in the intonation of a steady voice.

Joseph had read no more than a few pages when a sound coming from the hillside stopped him.

The cowbell! It was rung to call the children home but sent forth a different message this night.

Marcus lifted Sara Sue down and flew to his feet like a flushed quail. "Come on, Lester! I'll send you back with news."

Neither man paused for a coat but headed uphill at a dead run, with Chase leading the charge.

"Wait . . . here," panted Marcus, too winded and frightened to say more when the brothers reached the upper house.

Please, God. He jerked the door wide.

Instantaneous tears spilled at the sight of Maylene, lying ashen and shrunken in a quilt cocoon, her blue eyes fastened to his face. Sara Mae and Bess, shedding tears of their own, turned their backs on the couple, allowing them what little privacy they could.

Marcus landed hard on his knees. Reaching under the blankets, he retrieved a hand, which he kissed and pressed to his mouth. "May, I was scared stiff."

Maylene whispered in a raspy voice, "We have a son—look."

With all but his face covered, the swaddled baby lay fast asleep next to Maylene. Marcus detected inky hair, like Jenny's, peeking out at the brow.

"He's perfect, our George Melvin."

"I'm falling asleep. Tell Mama, will you?"

Maylene closed her eyes, and Marcus tucked her arm back under the covers.

Marcus wiped his eyes with a sleeve and collected himself with several breaths. "Mama Farley? Maylene wants you to know the baby's name. He's George Melvin, after your brothers."

New cascades of tears found their way to the corners of Sara Mae's mouth. Melvin died as a teen of appendicitis. Her daughter Melva was named for him. And George fell at Sharpsburg, leaving a wife and four young children behind.

"I'm honored, Marcus. I can't tell you how much." She wanted to rise and embrace her son-in-law but didn't trust her legs. "Now you'll want to tell the others the good news. Bess and I are too tired to get down the hill and back."

Marcus remembered Lester. "I have a courier."

He swung open the door and sent a pacing, shivering brother on his way. Chase climbed into her straw-filled, wooden box under the porch, relieved to rest after Marcus's unease had kept her on edge the past twenty-four hours.

Marcus returned to the hearth. "If you've had enough to eat, I suggest you head upstairs to bed. If I knew how to thank you . . ." He choked up.

"All the thanks we need," said Bess, "is seeing those two sleeping in peace. The Good Lord's the one needs thanking, not us."

"Amen to that," said Sara Mae, wiping her face with a dishrag.

When her grandma said they must keep the cabin warm for Maylene and the baby, Jenny volunteered to tend the fire. Within minutes of his daughter's arrival, Marcus had moved his latest son to a cradle near the fireplace and fallen asleep next to his wife. Because Suzanne had ordered everyone else to bed, Jenny clutched for herself a book about a whale hunt. She settled in the rocker, watching over a bundled oval with a puffy, pink face—her newborn baby brother.

CHAPTER TWENTY-ONE

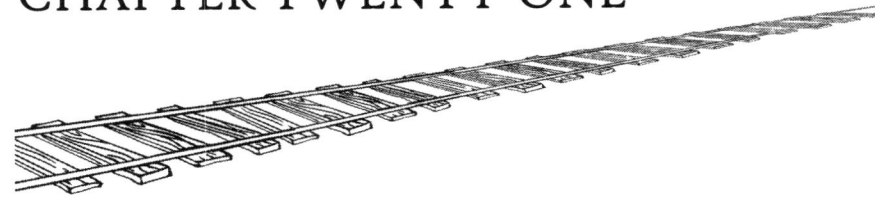

The following weekend, Joseph made the ferry crossing and long walk for his monthly Sunday at the Lillys'. He hoped Maylene could manage a brief appearance, her cordiality being a comforting offset to Marcus's silence and swift departures from the dinner table.

But when the family gathered, neither Maylene nor Marcus appeared. Joseph started to ask, "Where—"

Suzanne shook her head. Not now.

Later, while Jenny gave Sara Sue a spinning lesson, Johnny and Quencus wrestled in the hayloft, and Lester and Vesta went for a ride in the mild, snow-melting afternoon, Suzanne wiped crumbs off the table and sat down. Joseph, who had returned from grooming Cloud, straddled the bench across from her.

"Is Maylene all right?" he asked.

"Not yet. She got so swollen, she couldn't piss. Not until she was ready to burst, and then only a little. She got an infection of the bladder and was too wretched to sleep. We had to send Lester down for Doc Mason. Marcus won't leave her side, and thank God it's winter or this whole farm would be in shambles."

"Dear God. Is she on the mend?"

"Yes, finally, but it's been a week from Hell. That poor thing's been through more than enough to kill a normal girl."

"Why didn't Calvin tell me?"

"He doesn't know. I saw no point in us all going 'round the bend."

"I could've brought a remedy from the store."

"There was no need. Dr. Mason had dried bearberry and Maylene must've drunk gallons of bearberry tea by now. He told

152

her to drink water with baking soda, too, and we have that. Marcus has kept hot compresses on her belly—he's a regular nurse. But I can tell you the strain has him worn to the bone. Thank goodness Sara Mae is staying a few more days, and Georgie is an easy baby. He don't hardly fuss at all. And I'm so proud of Jenny. She's been a tremendous help, washing and changing diapers, and doing her best to comfort Sara Sue and Quencus. Those two have been the saddest little pair of orphans you ever saw, wandering about holding hands and Quencus sucking the life out of his thumb."

"Is Maylene out of danger now?"

"I believe so. But she's weaker than she's ever been—it'll be awhile before she's herself again."

"Then I shouldn't stop in."

Suzanne smiled. "No, not unless you have a new book to deliver. You can meet your grandson at Christmas. Incidentally, he has your hair, black as burnt bread."

Joseph chuckled. "Is that what I've been wearing on my head all these years? Burnt bread?"

"Well, I started to say *black silk,* but that sounded too girly."

"You do amuse me, Miss Suzanne. I'd don't believe there's anyone like you."

A change in his voice caused a thickening in Suzanne's throat.

Joseph scrutinized his worn boots. "I'll pass another book along to Calvin. Otherwise, I'm absolutely useless here. It's time I told you—"

"Told me what?" Suzanne's moment of tenderness blew away like a tufted dandelion seed.

He met Suzanne's eyes, barbed with challenge. "My friend who was killed? He left his land in Pennsylvania to me. I found his will the last time I was here. He left it in a book he knew I'd read again. I went to the courthouse and got the address of the courthouse in Dauphin County. Turns out they were sent a copy of the will. I wrote the Huntington sheriff for confirmation Randall is deceased. I'm ready to put the land on the market, and when it's sold, I'm going to buy a farm. It's time I had a plow for Cloud to pull on my own blessed soil."

"That's fortunate news for you, but it's my fault you don't find a footing here. I've treated you like a guest too long. And Marcus .

. . I thought he'd come around by now. I'm fit to be tied about that boy."

Worry lines deepened above Suzanne's nose. "Oh, Joseph, where will you go? You ain't leaving New River, are you?"

Joseph sighed. "No ma'am. Home is home."

He didn't disclose that he'd also asked the Huntington sheriff if a knife sheath had been found on Randall's body. And gotten no reply.

As the anniversary of Randall's death approached, Joseph became depressed. His mind kept turning to the previous Christmas Eve when, half drunk, he squatted at his friend's side, close to vomiting and passing out, repeating *no, no, no* to himself. He thought he'd gotten over the shock, yet reverberations emitted from within. He felt ill.

He decided to accept Bob Farley's invitation to the squat Baptist sanctuary perched above Madam's Creek. A quarter-mile from the creek's confluence with the river, little more than a ferry ride separated it from Hinton. Bob and Sara Mae greeted him warmly, inviting him to dinner after the service. Joseph rode home with them, in a wagon pulled by a team of mules, to their creek-bisected farm a mile above the church.

Sara Mae bombarded Joseph with questions about his life as a rail worker, while Bob asked about the progress of Hinton's growth. Melva, even quieter than usual, sneaked glances at the man she found uncommonly handsome.

Sara Mae's heart sank. Surely her daughter wouldn't develop a hankering for Joseph, nearly twenty years older. Melva—who mirrored Maylene's pretty mouth, petite nose, darkening blond hair, and blue eyes—wore the sharp angles of her father's face and a serious expression more often than not. She felt ungainly in her tallness, another of her father's traits. And the lisp she had borne from childhood contributed to her extreme shyness. Sara Mae despaired that she would ever have an actual conversation with a man, especially one she liked. Although Melva and Joseph enjoyed the same passion for books, Sara Mae doubted they'd share that commonality. Besides, weren't Joseph and Suzanne sparking, renewing their forbidden attraction?

The meal completed, Joseph produced two cigars. He and Bob put on their coats for a tour of the farm and beehives. Joseph marveled at the well-kept appearance of fences and outbuildings, as well as the number of sheep and dairy goats.

"Do you hire help?" he asked.

"No, sir!" said Bob, unable to cloak his pride. "I'm starting to feel my age, but Melva's about as strong as a man, and Sara Mae's handy with an axe as she is a churn. We make do."

"Well, I've been known to break the Sabbath, so let me know if I can shear sheep or guide a plow. I miss farm work."

"It gets in your blood, don't it? I appreciate the offer, and I'll let you know if we get in a bind."

Their cigars spent, Joseph said he'd be heading back. "Tell Mrs. Farley I'm much obliged for the fine dinner."

Despite his effortless rapport with Bob, Joseph's melancholy circled back, like flies waved away from honey. The solitary man lowered his head against a gathering wind and turned homeward to banjo and books. Maybe he'd have a little chat with Randall.

Marcus, in general, shunned superstition. One, however, the notion that troubles come in three, had followed him through life. A prime example was the eleven-month span when he nearly died of typhoid fever, his brother Junior perished as a Union prisoner of war, and Johnny succumbed to pneumonia during winter camp, despite Marcus's frantic efforts to save him. The next trio came in 1864, when Quentin was crippled at Cloyd's Mountain, a sniper's bullet—intended for Marcus's face—liberated a shard of limestone that claimed his right eye, and Captain Thurmond took a lethal Yankee bullet at Winfield. After the devastating frights involving Sara Sue and Maylene, Marcus wondered what the third shock would be.

He didn't have to wait long to find out. Two days before Christmas, he and Johnny chopped and grubbed locust saplings out of the sheep pasture. The annual task needed completing before the ground froze, and time ran short. Although the thorny trees made superior firewood, dense and long-burning, they were a scourge in the pastures. The inedible and prolific plants must be dug out of the ground because cutting them inspired multiple sprouts the following spring.

Marcus, in mid-swing with a mattock, heard a familiar voice scream his name. He dropped the tool and ran, with Johnny and Chase close on his heels.

"Marcus!" Maylene cried again.

"I'm coming!"

He found Maylene standing, cradling Georgie in her arms. The baby's rigid body trembled, and his eyes had gone entirely white, their pale irises seeking the top of his head. His blue-tinged lips leaked saliva down his chin.

"He's having an awful fit," said Maylene, trembling herself. "Is he going to die?"

Marcus took the baby from his wife's arms and raised him to his shoulder, rubbing the miniature back. "Easy now, easy, easy."

Georgie's stiffness relaxed into the limp inertness of a sleeping infant. His eyes closed, and his lips regained their normal color.

"There. It's over now. Does he have a fever?" Marcus asked.

"I'm sure he doesn't. He was normal as can be, nursing and content. Then his poor little body went berserk. I've never seen such a thing."

Maylene, yet to regain her strength after childbirth and illness, returned to the rocker. "I know we can't afford it, but I want Doc Mason to see him."

"I'll ride down. We can get back before dark if I leave now, assuming he's free. Don't worry too awful much, May. We've heard of babies having fits, and they're nothing, really, but a fright."

Marcus had difficulty finding Dr. Mason, who'd ridden high up Brooks Mountain to examine newborn twins and check on their invalid great-grandfather. With directions from Mrs. Mason, Marcus located the homestead an hour after arriving in Hinton and let Blackjack graze along a fence line as he waited for the doctor to appear. His hopes sank with the horizon-hugging sun. There would be no medical attention for Georgie today.

When the door opened, Marcus remounted and trotted to the cabin. "Dr. Mason," he began without introducing himself, "I've gotta baby son had an awful fit a few hours ago. My wife sent me to find you. Can you come? It's the Quentin Lilly farm again."

The unflappable man, with his ever-present, scalp-protecting hat, reached up to clasp Marcus's hand. "I know you, Mr. Lilly. I was up to see your wife a few weeks ago. How is she?"

"Much better, thank you."

"Good, good. She was quite ill. It's late for a ride that far up Broomstraw Ridge, but I'll come first thing in the morning if nothing urgent comes up. Does the baby have a fever?"

"Not that we can tell. He was fine one minute and all seized up the next."

"Your wife told me she had a long and difficult labor bringing him into the world. I'm sorry to say this may not be his last seizure, assuming he's otherwise well. I'll be along and check him over."

"Thank you, sir."

The doctor slid off a pair of spectacles and tucked them into a vest pocket before gathering the reins of his chestnut mare. By the time he took the saddle, Marcus and Blackjack had cantered out of sight. Marcus didn't like Maylene's frail and frightened look when he left.

The next day, Christmas Eve, Georgie appeared his usual self and the doctor found nothing amiss. "If he has another seizure," Dr. Mason said, "you'll have to assume there will be more. There's nothing to be done but keep him from hurting himself and let the spell pass."

Joseph made his way up Madam's Creek long after the doctor's departure. As he climbed, the terrain became dusted, then covered, with snow. By the time he arrived, well after dark, his boots slipped on a crusted, two-inch layer. He figured Suzanne didn't need to know the effort it had taken to make himself come. If not for aversion to her wrath and disappointment, he'd have spent the holiday with his latest novel, Alcott's *Little Men*.

He stomped snow off his feet before entering, relieved to find only Suzanne, Vesta, and Lester inside, along with the scent of evergreen. Fresh cuttings of pine, cedar, and hemlock, decorated with pinecones, adorned the mantle.

"I'm sorry we didn't wait on you," said Suzanne. "Maylene was so tired, we went ahead and ate. I saved supper for you. Go warm up by the fire while I lay it out. I'll have to tell you about Georgie."

The wind picked up overnight. Suzanne applauded herself for the decision to excuse her scattered children from making the journey to the farm. Marcus and Lester carried in the new sleds after completing the milking and securing all the livestock but the sheep in the barn. Marcus didn't like the animals out in a storm.

Maylene brought the children down for breakfast, after which all but Georgie lit up like meteors over the sleds. Maylene's gifts, mundane in comparison, were socks and mittens she'd knit during her convalescence. Joseph took his satchel off the back of a chair and removed three small packages wrapped in newspaper. They contained high-topped leather shoes for Jenny and Johnny—shoes that would get them to school until the barefoot days of spring— and a bag of horehound candy. Already scalded by his new debt to the doctor and his inability to provide footwear for his children, Marcus's thank-you lacked luster.

As the children eagerly opened the boxes, Marcus said, "Johnny, Jenny, aren't you forgetting something? Thank your ... Mr. Joseph for the gift."

Maylene ducked her head and grinned, reaching for a shoelace. She knew, and Marcus knew she knew, he'd almost said *your grandpa*.

Must we endure this charade forever? thought Marcus, offering Georgie a rattle made from a seed-filled gourd. Georgie managed to get the handle in his mouth and began sucking, which Johnny found hilarious.

"Look! He's just like a little calf latched onto a teat."

"And you'd have done the very same at his age," Maylene said, without deflating Johnny in the least.

Joseph stayed behind with Maylene, Suzanne, and Georgie when Marcus, Vesta, and Lester took the four older children sledding. After nursing Georgie in Suzanne's bedroom, Maylene motioned to Joseph to join her in front of the fire while Suzanne prepared gingerbread batter.

"I've been wanting to have a word with you," she began. Joseph liked the way she caught his eye.

"I'm afraid Marcus has been unkind. Please don't take it personal. He's not the same since the War. It shocked him to have you show up out of the blue, and he took it hard. He don't settle down as quickly as he used to once he gets worked up. And it bothers him greatly to lie to the children."

Joseph admired, and not for the first time, Maylene's attractive face and gracious manner. He thought his son most fortunate to have such a wife. "It don't do Marcus a scrap of good for me to be around. I'm working on getting my own farm—then I'll be here a lot less if Suzanne don't put up too big a fight."

They both smiled at the thought of Suzanne's willfulness.

"I don't mean you should make yourself scarce," said Maylene. "Just give Marcus more time, if you will. The children like you and so do I. Marcus don't get to outvote all the rest of us."

"Thank you, Miss Maylene. It helps knowing your thoughts. I admit I'm at a loss when it comes to Marcus."

"Well, Lord knows, it ain't your fault."

The pair fell silent. As Maylene rocked her baby to sleep, she studied his face. As if accepting the task of stitching together the disparate quilt squares of his siblings, Georgie exhibited aspects of each. His thick, straight hair as dark as Jenny's, his eyes almost as blue as Sara Sue's, his face and mouth shaped like his mother's and Johnny's. Even at his tender age, he exuded a quiet thoughtfulness, like that of Quencus as well as Marcus.

"Dear Georgie," she said. "He shall be our peacemaker because he carries parts of all of us."

Sleet had just begun stinging the roof and windows when Suzanne sent Joseph out to ring the bell.

Johnny, the first to push open the heavy, windowless door, blasted in, announcing that the sleds were fast as falcons. "Papa and Uncle Lester had to sit backwards and drag their feet to keep us from hitting the fence!"

At a mutton-based dinner, Suzanne revealed the news that Lester had brought a letter from Jumping Branch the day before.

It enclosed a note and gift from Eliza and Mayhew, the gift being a photograph of their adopted son, Charles Mayhew Mullens. The image passed from hand to hand, as each exclaimed over the newest family member, four months old.

After the meal, Marcus lifted the worn Bible off the mantle and read the nativity verses from the book of Luke. Eli gave a prayer of thanksgiving for the Christ child, long enough to cause Johnny to fidget and Maylene to give her son a look.

Then Lester played his tin whistle, going through his complete repertoire while the women sang and the children danced to "Barbary Allen," "Pretty Polly," and several other tunes before begging for a repeat performance. Lester complied, proud of his unexpected ability to enliven the holiday.

By the end of the second round, the children yawned.

"Quencus, if you take that thumb out of your mouth and keep it out, you can have buttermilk and gingerbread. Then it's off to bed, all of you," Suzanne said.

"But Mr. Joseph has a new book," Jenny said. "Can he read some, please?"

Joseph regretted being too slow to conceal *Little Men* when the children came in from sledding. His instincts told him Marcus wanted to take his children home, away from him.

"A few pages, but only because it's Christmas. You're all half-asleep already."

After a hurried gingerbread snack, Joseph opened the book and cleared his throat. Then he looked at Marcus. "I hear you're better at this than anyone. Why don't you read?"

"No, no—it's your book. Go ahead."

But Sara Sue, implanted on her papa's lap, squirmed around to stare Marcus in the eye. "Please, Papa. You don't read to us no more."

Marcus had to concede there'd been no books or storytelling since Maylene's labor and illness. He'd shut down as entertainer, and he'd be damned if he'd let Joseph take his place.

He studied his daughter's pleading face. Her longing for him removed all hesitation. He reached for the book.

CHAPTER TWENTY-TWO

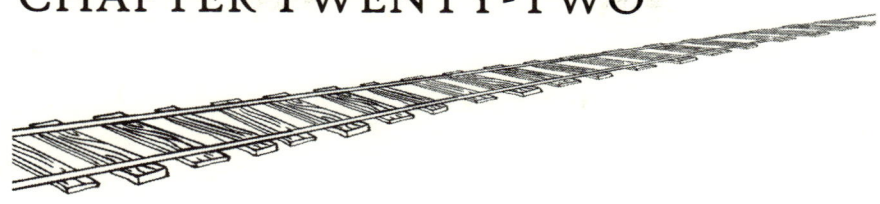

On a raw, gray February day, Joseph walked to the post office on his dinner break, impatient for word of a buyer for the Pennsylvania property. Randall's cabin had surely fallen into a state of worthless disrepair, but the acreage, which Randall had described as rich bottomland, should attract notice.

Joseph had begun checking the post office's announcement board for land listed for sale, and plotting his rescue of Becky and Caleb, assuming Enoch wouldn't do them the favor of dropping dead first. He must anticipate a showdown. Sooner or later, Enoch would find Joseph's new farm and come to reclaim, by whatever means necessary, his wife and son. The prospect unnerved Joseph. He couldn't sleep with one eye open. Maybe he'd get a dog.

Upon his return, the store's door swung open as Joseph reached for the knob. A well-dressed woman wearing a felt hat and fur stole bustled out, holding the hand of a girl about the age of Sara Sue. Her other hand clutched a bolt of fabric tied with twine. The little girl, blond and lightly freckled, hugged a doll to her chest. She gazed up at Joseph and missed the first step, stumbling. Despite her mother's quick yank, the girl fell, landing on the steps and her doll.

As she scrambled to her feet, she screamed, "Sally! Sally! Mama, she's broke!"

A large crack scrawled across the pretty porcelain face.

The woman said, "Clumsy girl! I told you to be careful with it. Now you've gone and busted your Christmas present."

The child burst into sobs. "Can't you fix her, Mama?"

"Of course not! You've ruined your doll. And all because you were gawking at a dirty Indian."

Joseph's jaw dropped. He heard his mother say, "Keep quiet, keep walking."

No, Mama, no more.

He said, "Woman, I pity your child, and her broken doll is the least of it."

"How dare you speak to me like that!" The mother's green eyes became slits.

Joseph felt them boring into his back as he entered the store and slammed the door, thinking, I let you off easy, you vile creature.

A startled Silas looked up from his newspaper spread on the counter. A dark-haired, bearded man more than twenty years Joseph's junior, he'd always treated Joseph more like an equal than an employee.

"I apologize," said Joseph without sounding the least apologetic. "I believe I just cost you a customer."

Joseph's expression gave Silas pause. He'd never seen the man enraged. The shopkeeper took a deep breath and blew it out. "Sounds to me like a patron we can do without. I heard the child pitch a fit. Care to say what the lady done?"

"No." Joseph stormed to his room and shut the door.

Silas scratched his furry chin and resumed his perusal of the paper.

Maylene chafed as her February birthday approached. Although Marcus remained solicitous, he'd made no lovemaking overture since Georgie's birth, suggesting this would be Maylene's first birthday since her husband's return from war without the treasured nocturnal gift. But Maylene didn't pressure him. Although she'd thrashed through hours of torment and exhaustion, as well as moments of despair and delirium, she'd been too busy during labor to experience the terror Marcus had endured.

As always, Marcus awoke well before dawn. He kissed Maylene before saying, "Happy birthday, honeycake. I couldn't squeeze your present under the bed this time—it's waiting downstairs. Stay here. I'll get the fire going."

Maylene shivered as soon as Marcus's warm body left her side. She pulled the down comforter over her head, listening as Marcus stirred embers and added kindling, snapping larger sticks across his knee. "You're colder than me," she whispered. "Bless your heart."

The gift was a rocking chair, shaped from black cherry. "It's about time we stopped dragging that old rocker in and out of the house," Marcus said. "I should've made this years ago."

Maylene, trying it out, said, "The wood is smooth as glass. You may never get me out of this thing." She reached for Marcus's arm and tugged him down for a kiss.

"So you like it?"

"Love it. And the man who made it."

Marcus's wide smile evoked one in return.

"If you weren't sitting on it, that fanny of yours would get a birthday swat," Marcus said as he wriggled into his coat.

As he left for the barn, Maylene got up to start breakfast. She'd treat herself to johnnycakes and sausage. She thought with a pang the honey-nut cake she'd make for Marcus's April birthday wouldn't come close to the grandeur of the chair, but it was likely all she'd find time and energy to produce.

Maylene's hope faded as the day wore on without a trace of flirtation. That night, after the children's chatter faded to sleep and the fire dimmed to silence, Marcus took his wife in his arms.

"May, we can't have no more babies. It 'bout killed you and me both getting Georgie born. If you had…. If you hadn't made it, I'd have lost all interest in living. I'd have been a worthless papa, and I'd have blamed myself. I *do* blame myself for what you suffered."

"But you mustn't! Such things happen. Like a storm or a flood. It couldn't be helped." Maylene thanked the darkness for hiding her tears. Her beloved Marcus, sometimes tender, sometimes playful, sometimes afire with passion. Excepting that searing span of time when he doubted her, he'd always made her feel cherished and done his best to give her pleasure. Did he intend to put a stop to their lovemaking?

Marcus's mouth found her lips. "I ain't saying what you think," he whispered. "I've had restraint scared into me."

He groped under a pillow and pulled out a flannel rag. "I ain't going to release inside you no more, May. No more. We've got five dear children, and that's enough. Tell me I'm right."

He kissed her again.

Maylene nodded and wept her relief. She didn't want another pregnancy, yet the prospect of a celibate marriage crippled her with desolation.

With the help of a tight embrace, she calmed herself, and Marcus delivered the second gift, keeping his promise.

Although she half-expected it, Lester's news came as a blow. Suzanne perched on a low stool at the spinning wheel, turning carded wool into yarn, when her son returned to the table after breakfast and sat down facing her.

"Ma, I know you don't want to hear this, but Calvin's friend Ben has offered me a job. He's a brick mason and they're starting the new courthouse in a few weeks. Now that we've got an extra horse, I can ride down. I want to learn a trade. The farm will go to Marcus, then Johnny. It's time I turned my hand to other work."

Suzanne's face went hard, as Lester anticipated. "How can you possibly go prancing out of here, as if it don't matter? Do you honestly think Marcus can manage without you? Have you forgotten how Vesta strained her back shearing sheep last spring and was laid up a whole week? Your brother will work his self to death. And as for that 'extra horse,' Mr. Joseph is fixing to buy a farm and take his mare. You'll be walking to town and coming home late and tired, just like Calvin used to do."

Lester's face reddened. He'd spent seventeen years avoiding confrontations with his mother, and lacked practice. "It's not as bad as you think. Calvin says I can get time off for planting—and probably at harvest time, too. And we can use the money. It's not like I'll keep it to myself."

"What we need a whole lot more than money is your help on this farm. You know that."

Lester lowered his eyes to the hands clamped onto his thighs. Suzanne sensed the way his heart raced and his desire to snap at her like an ill-tempered dog. When he looked up, he met his mother's sapphire eyes. "I'm sorry, Ma. My mind's made up. I've already told Lester to tell Ben I'll take the job. You can throw me out if you have to."

Suzanne pursed her lips and shook her head, taking in her youngest child, nearly a man, with his matching light-brown hair and eyes. His face reflected enough of Quentin's to smooth the sharpest edge of her outrage. "That's exactly what I feel like doing, son. You've got me mad as a pair of roosters. But never mind that. You're my boy, and I'd just as soon you stay here as long as you will. Maybe bricklaying won't suit you and you'll change your mind."

She turned back to her spinning, and Lester made a beeline for the door. Any delay could give his mother time to think of two additional incentives for him to go, namely making music with his brother and exploring the most alluring offering Hinton held—girls.

As he stepped across the threshold, he heard Suzanne say, "I used to have a husband and five sons."

In the golden light that followed sunrise and spilled onto the steep face of Broomstraw Ridge, Lester Lilly trod the well-worn path to the barn, his unfamiliar anger stalked and overtaken by shame.

The remaining news that February came two days apart, on the twenty-sixth and twenty-eighth. The first was the birth of a boy, Calvin and Nancy's. The next, the inexplicable stillbirth of Louella and Howard's baby, a second daughter. Louella's inconsolable grief necessitated visits from her nearest sisters—Vesta and Rachel—and her mother and Maylene, with Georgie in tow. For a week, weather allowing, the women took turns in twosomes riding to the misshapen farm scratched out of the hollow of Beech Run, a short distance upriver from Madam's Creek.

Then, just as the family relaxed into Louella's return to an approximation of life, the hounds of Hell tore free of their chains, and the real trouble began.

CHAPTER TWENTY-THREE

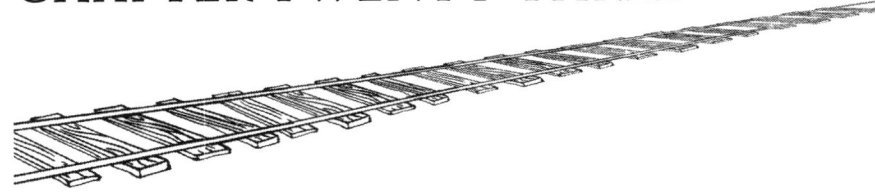

The third week of March, Maylene hung diapers on an outdoor line on a windy Sunday morning, a cold one but above freezing. The Lillys' winter recess from church would soon end when snow, ice, or mud no longer made the Madam's Creek road treacherous. Winter worship consisted of prayers, hymns, and Bible readings at the long dining table. The Sunday the family left Suzanne alone and began making its lengthy treks to church in the farm wagon marked Spring's official start.

Maylene heard Blackjack nicker and noticed his alert stance. What was he looking at? She followed his line of gaze and saw a male—a teen by the slender, unfinished look of him—climbing over the far fence. He waved, and she waved back as Chase began to bark. The lad jogged in their direction.

"Who do you think that is, girl? And why is he in such a rush?"

He opened the gate near the cabin, and there he halted, breathing hard as if the pasture crossing represented the last leg of a strenuous journey. His hatless head donned wild, dark hair. His eyes, too, were dark and shaped like Joseph's and Jenny's. Patches splotched his worn coat and a sockless big toe peeked from a shoe separating from its sole.

"Ma'am," he panted, "I'm Caleb Wallace. I been here once before to deliver a message to my uncle, Mr. Joseph Cook."

"I heard of that visit. What's wrong, Caleb?"

"I got to get word to my uncle again. Who can go for him?"

"Check with Marcus. He's in the garden despite the Sabbath, plowing for peas. He'll likely send Lester on Cloud. Does your ma need help?"

"Yes, ma'am. My pa got thrown out of his card game and come home early last night. Found her with Miss Clara and Miss Ethel and went plumb crazy. He busted her jaw and she can't eat. She's hurting bad and needs help."

"Oh, dear Lord. We'll get your uncle here on the double and fetch your poor mama. Go on down and tell Marcus. Then you can wait here and get some rest and food." Maylene wouldn't allow him to reject the offer of socks, either.

"Yes, ma'am. Thank you."

And Caleb ran.

Marcus and Caleb saddled Blackjack and Cloud, leaving the horses tied in the barn while they walked back to the cabin.

"Maylene, I'm riding down to the church. If Mr. Joseph ain't there, I'll go on to town. Tell Ma we'll explain when we get back. You may as well leave Caleb here when you go down to the house. There's no point getting Ma worked up before we must."

"Be careful, Marc. The road's bad. Take your time."

"Yes, ma'am." He started to kiss her mouth, then swerved for a cheek, wishing to spare Caleb embarrassment.

Maylene turned to the boy. "Have a seat and make yourself at home, Caleb. I'll fry up some ham and eggs. The children have gone down to the house to listen to their uncle practice hymns on his whistle. I'm guessing you didn't sleep last night."

"No, ma'am. I was a bit worked up."

"Well, you're welcome to choose a bed and have a nap after you eat. It ain't often this house is empty and quiet."

"Thank you," said Caleb, his brusque tone mismatching the words. At rest, a chill took hold, and he stood before the fading fire, arms crossed, too agitated to sit.

Marcus cursed Joseph Cook the nearly four miles to church, riding Blackjack and leading Cloud. This mild spell wouldn't last, and he wanted to get the first peas and onions in. On top of that, lambing was in full swing. With a ewe rejecting one of her twins, he'd planned to spend the afternoon on that task, either coaxing the ewe to accept the lamb or convincing another new mother to adopt the orphan before it became too weak to nurse. He had no time for this nonsense, yet how could he refuse to inform Mr. Joseph that his sister required immediate help? And what the hell kind of man would do such a thing to his wife?

Marcus shuddered to think Enoch Wallace's eldest son, Amos, had once come courting Maylene. The image of her in that godforsaken household was enough to turn his stomach.

Pushing that horror away, Marcus questioned why he hadn't sent Lester on this distasteful errand. He told himself he wished to spare his mother anxiety as long as possible, but he knew better. That was a secondary reason. Upon hearing Caleb's tale, a sense of duty he thought he'd shed re-awoke. He answered the call for a man's job.

Marcus arrived in the middle of Eli's lengthy opening prayer. Regretting that the Farleys sat near the front, he crept stealthily down the aisle, finding his way to the bench that served as a pew and settling next to Joseph as his father and the Farleys slid over to make room. He saw trepidation in Bob's and Sara Mae's eyes as they leaned forward to interrogate him with arched eyebrows. Nothing but bad news could account for his arrival, late and alone.

Melva, seated between her parents, gave Marcus a radiant smile, which he recognized at once as intended for another's benefit. He groaned inwardly but had no time to contemplate Joseph's new interest in the Farleys.

His father-in-law whispered, "Are Maylene and the children all right?"

Marcus nodded, and whispered back, "Got to speak with Mr. Joseph."

Joseph gave him a quizzical look before bowing his head again, eyes closed.

Eli droned on and on, while five of his parishioners prayed for him to stop. As soon as he announced the opening hymn, Marcus and Joseph made their escape, skewered by stares that followed them.

Untying the horses, Marcus said, "Your nephew showed up this morning. He said your sister's hurt and needs help. He'll fill you in on the details."

The blow reached Joseph's gut. "How bad is she?"

"Her jaw's broke. That's all I know."

"Damn that wretched man! And damn me, too. I should've gotten her out of there months ago."

Despite the mud, the men urged their horses into a canter, soon losing sight of the church and the sound of singing voices.

The ascent quickly tired their mounts, and the men reined them to a walk. The creek roared, muddy and high with snowmelt, and Marcus embraced the excuse to avoid conversation. The men made their way back to the farm, each lost in his brooding thoughts.

They turned the horses into adjacent stalls. Marcus went up the ladder to the loft with the speed of a squirrel scaling a trunk and forked hay into the racks below. He wasn't keen on lending Blackjack, getting on in years, to Caleb, but he would ensure the horses had food and rest before the steep climb up Broomstraw Ridge.

They found Caleb asleep on Maylene and Marcus's bed. Self-conscious about his unwashed clothing, Caleb lay atop the down comforter, unaware of the two quilts Maylene had collected upstairs to keep him warm.

Joseph took in his nephew's sunken cheeks and the dark crescents beneath his eyes. The boy looked beat. But, having no choice, Joseph shook Caleb's shoulder, and the boy reacted as if bitten by a snake. Wide-eyed, he threw off the blankets and swung his legs over the side of the bed.

"Uncle Joseph! You scared the living daylights outta me."

"I'm sorry to wake you, but I need to hear what's happened."

Caleb gulped deep breaths, like a cornered and panicked outlaw.

"Come out by the stove," said Joseph. "We'll sit and talk."

"Jenny, take the children back down to Grandma's," Maylene said. "I just now nursed Georgie. He can sleep there. You and Johnny help your grandma get dinner on. Tell her not to wait on us."

Maylene gathered hats and coats and scooted the children out the door in record time.

Caleb, unaccustomed to talking to strangers, looked about as if seeking words. "Pa's sick. He's been sick a good while. Ma couldn't hardly talk when I got home. It was my first night out fishing. Pa was passed out drunk by then. She was holding her face like this."

He cupped his lower jaw with both hands. "She said they sent him home from the poker game 'cause they're tired of lending him money he never repays, and he's got consumption and they don't want to catch it. Another man in their group already died of it. I reckon he was mad about that, then he got madder when he saw Ma had visitors. He don't allow it. So he must've run the women off, and then he done it."

Caleb's voice cracked.

Joseph placed a hand on his nephew's shoulder and said, "The goddamned simpleton busted her jaw. . . . Pardon my language, Maylene."

"I don't care," Maylene responded. "Might as well call him what he is."

She glanced at Marcus. He stood wordless, disengaged.

"Does she have other injuries?" Joseph asked.

"I don't know. Not that I could see. She told me to come here. She said, 'Get word to my brother to come tonight, meet me in the henhouse at dusk.' She said, 'If I ain't there, tell him to go and not come back.' She said, 'I'll tell your pa you run away—don't return or he'll hurt you bad.' She made me promise. She said if you don't find her tonight she's got the map, and she'll leave before sunrise tomorrow and make her way down."

Joseph paced back and forth, his hands balled in fists. "She was right to tell you to stay away, Caleb. I'll go for her this afternoon and wait for dusk. I'll not leave without your mama."

"Thank you, sir. I'm afraid for her."

"Do you believe she's caught your father's illness?"

"She may have. She been coughing."

"Damnation! Why haven't I gone sooner?"

Caleb hung his head. "I should've come sooner. It's more my fault than yours."

"Caleb, honey, you had no way of knowing this would happen," said Maylene. "None of us did. Let's go down to the house and see what Ma Lilly's got cooking. Then I'd wager Marcus could use your help with a lamb."

"Yes ma'am," said the Wallace boy without moving. Maylene hadn't seen such a lost soul since an adolescent Confederate deserter stowed away in the Farley barn more than a decade earlier. He, too, dazed by fear and fatigue, had made her heart ache.

After dinner, the children needed little encouragement to visit the newest lambs in the barn, delighting in the adoption of the rejected newborn by a benevolent ewe. The adults, along with Lester and Caleb, gathered around the table while Georgie continued his nap on an infant-sized straw tick. Uncharacteristically, Suzanne left the dirty dishes in a pile.

She was the first to speak after Joseph explained the predicament. "I don't like it, Joseph. You should wait 'til tomorrow and get the sheriff to go up with you. It ain't safe, you going alone."

Before Joseph responded, Caleb raised an arm like a schoolboy. "Ma'am, my mama said if the law showed up, Pa said he'd tell them he come home early and found her with another man. She said they won't help her none."

"For the love of mercy!" Suzanne's eyes snapped with a rage Joseph hadn't seen in decades.

"It's all right, Suzanne," Joseph said. "Enoch will twist it around, one way or another, and keep himself out of trouble. He'll likely be knocked out on moonshine by the time I show up—I don't expect any trouble from him. But I'd like to borrow a firearm, if you don't mind."

"Do you own one?" Marcus asked.

"I have a pistol."

"Then take mine," said Marcus. "We have a rifle, too, but you should take the one you're used to."

"I'm much obliged," said Joseph, tugging at an earlobe.

Suzanne flew to her feet. "This is madness! Stay here tonight. Lester will go for Sheriff Hinton first thing in the morning. We'll tell him what's happened and not to believe Enoch's lies. It don't make a lick of sense, you going up there by yourself."

Joseph rose with deliberation. Placing his palms on the table, he squared off with the small but belligerent face that challenged him from the opposite side. This time, he would not back down. "My sister is in pain and unable to eat. Every minute she stays with that monster, she's at risk of more hurt. I'll be leaving as soon as I bridle my mare and pick up the gun."

"You're making a mistake I hope you survive," Suzanne said in a tone that suggested some ambivalence about Joseph's fate.

When Marcus left his cabin with his old cavalry pistol and holster, he saw Cloud tied to the porch rail of his mother's house. He hesitated at the sight of Joseph and his ma engaged in earnest conversation at the open doorway and decided to steer clear. Setting the leather holster on the top step, he gave Joseph a nod and headed for the barn. With Lester's help, he had daylight enough to get back to his planting. He took a harness off its hook and whistled for Reggie, who never failed to respond to the bribe of a handful of oats.

Joseph set out well before dusk. As the sun sank, the wind lessened and shifted to the southwest. Cloud climbed, negotiating the muddy trail, which became splotched with patches of ice. Making it even more treacherous was a thin layer of thawed soil lying atop the frozen earth. As the slope steepened, topsoil peeled away in long, hoof-wide strips, causing the mare to slip frequently.

"Take it easy, gal," said Joseph. "This isn't a real good time for you to go lame again."

Joseph noticed the rising temperature—it must be in the forties by now. He'd lived in the mountains long enough to know what to expect. When he pulled up Cloud for rest, he scanned the woods above and spotted the snowline. Mist rose from melting snow. By nightfall, it would likely coalesce into a dense fog and blanket Broomstraw Ridge.

The mare made steady progress, her breathing labored as she made the ascent of more than a mile before taking the righthand turn onto the road along the ridgetop. After passing several farms, Joseph stopped and dismounted a quarter-mile shy of the Wallace cabin. He watched fog swallow the sun like a candle snuffed before finishing its work, then tied Cloud in a patch of woods next to the road.

Using the trees as cover, he continued a short distance past his sister's farm and sat down on an oak sampling, bowed and pinned by a hefty fallen branch, to wait. He took advantage of the chance to collect his thoughts and calm his nerves by having a talk with Randall.

Might need your help with this one, he began. *You know what a lousy shot I am and how out of practice. Might you pour some extra 'shine into that yellow-bellied fool's gullet tonight?*

Joseph heard a chuckle in his head. *Shouldn't you be askin' the Big Man, not me? You give me credit for havin' clout I ain't got.*

Well, maybe you can put in a word for me. You're closer than I am. And I'd appreciate your company tonight if that's not too much to ask.

Joseph reconsidered and said aloud, "I've got gall asking for that, don't I? I'm the one didn't stand by you."

Joseph listened for an answer but heard only the breeze stirring fog in the uppermost branches.

Suzanne needed to get out of the house. "Vesta," she said, "why don't you get the cornpone started. I'm going up the creek a ways to cut some pipestem. Miss Becky is going to need straws, bless her soul. God alone knows how long it'll be 'til she can eat."

Vesta sighed as she put down her knitting. Surely every sentence spoken to her began with *Vesta, would you,* or *Vesta, why don't you.* And ended with *watch the baby, get dinner started, help your brother, churn the butter, fetch water, feed the chickens....* Her life, though not her own, spilled its days in deep contentment by virtue of a single aspect—the farm. Like Marcus, she'd never contemplated leaving it. Although it demanded constant labor, it breathed like an animate thing with its cycle of planting, tending, harvesting, preserving, and preparing food. And every uneven square foot held memory of toil and quarrel, prank and laughter, the voices of her loved ones calling across the fields.

In addition, being an aunt graced Vesta with all the joys of motherhood without the risks. Maylene's experience served as a vivid cautionary tale, a reminder that a man might bring love, but his seed might also spell disaster.

She put on her cloak and left for milk and butter stored in the springhouse, smiling at the sight of Sara Sue following Marcus and the mule. As Lester evened the furrow's depth with a hoe, Sara Sue dropped dried peas, saved from last year's supply, into the earth, simultaneously bombarding her pa with questions.

"Papa, how do these shriveled-up old peas make plants?"

Responding to a *gee* command, Reggie turned and Marcus rocked the blade out of the soil.

Sara Sue persisted. "Papa! How do these worms know where they're going in the dark? Don't they get lost?"

"I don't know, baby. I reckon they do."

Marcus's silent distraction persisted through supper. Johnny had to ask his pa twice to pass the pitcher of milk, and Marcus seemed oblivious to the children's chatter, which normally captivated him.

When Georgie began to cry with hunger and Maylene left her place to nurse him, Marcus abandoned his unfinished meal and nodded toward the bedroom.

"You all eat up," he said. "I need to talk to your mama a minute." He pulled shut the curtain, placed two pillows for Maylene's back, and remained standing.

Maylene's mouth tightened.

Softening his voice to thwart eavesdroppers, Marcus said, "There's an hour of daylight left. I can get up to the Wallace farm before full dark if I leave now."

"Why are you even considering going? You know Mr. Wallace is a drunkard and an ill-tempered man. And it's none of your business. If Mr. Joseph wanted your help, he'd have asked for it."

"I don't feel right, him going alone. There's already bad blood between them. He needs someone watching his back."

"Marcus! May I remind you of your wife and five children counting on you to avoid foolishness and keep yourself alive. Do you owe Mr. Joseph more than us?"

"Of course not, and it has nothing to do with him being kin...." Marcus paused. How could he explain the solidarity of men who faced a common enemy? He didn't understand it himself yet wore it like his own skin.

"I can't let a man—any man—walk alone into clear danger. It's cowardly and it ain't right. Listen, May, it's not like it's the first time I've dealt with this sort of thing. I know how to protect myself. I'm providing backup, that's all."

Maylene harpooned her husband's lone brown eye. "I'm begging you, Marc, don't go. The fog up on the ridge, the way Caleb's so spooked.... I've got a bad feeling. I've never begged you for anything, but I'd be on my knees right now if I wasn't feeding Georgie. Please. Don't go."

"I can't not. I know it don't make sense to you. I'm sorry, May. I'll be back in two shakes of a lamb's tail."

"That's what you said when you rode off to war."

"This ain't nothing like that. I'll be home tonight."

Marcus stooped to kiss her, but a wave of anger jerked Maylene's face away, and his lips only grazed her jaw. Although Georgie's eyes followed Marcus, Maylene kept her gaze averted as her husband left the room.

Without a word to his sister, Marcus entered the house, strode toward the fireplace, and stopped.

Vesta straightened her back. "Who stoked a bonfire under you?"

Marcus gaped at the empty mantle above the blazing logs. "Where's the Enfield? Don't tell me Ma gave it to Mr. Joseph!"

"I didn't notice it's gone. Looks like she did."

"She's still cutting pipestem?"

"She said she figured she'd continue up the creek to visit Rachel and the boys. No doubt she accepted an invitation to stay for supper. You ain't going up to the Wallace's, are you?"

"I am. Mr. Joseph may be walking into more trouble than he can handle. But I'll be no help without the rifle."

"Then don't go."

"I'll keep my distance. I can't just sit here thinking about that man who knows nothing about fighting putting himself in harm's way. He don't have a clue what he may be getting into."

"I'll go with you," Lester offered, pushing a gravy-smeared plate away.

"Absolutely not. Ma's upset and she needs you. Caleb does, too. And I won't have you going unarmed."

"Marcus, how can you protect yourself *or* Mr. Joseph without a weapon?" Vesta asked.

"I've got my hunting knife—it'll have to do."

Chase put up her ears and tail, but she did no wagging. Something in Marcus's mood made her uneasy, and she whined, asking to come along on the grave expedition.

"No. Stay."

The dog's ears and tail drooped, and she sat on her haunches to watch Marcus swing astride Blackjack and head up the pasture at a trot. She continued watching as he dismounted, took down two rails, led his black gelding over the fence, replaced the rails, remounted, and disappeared into the woods. Only then did she return to her box under the cabin porch, where she circled and lay down. Her eyes stayed open. She would wait.

Marcus rode with growing mental torment. He seethed to think his so-called father had put him at odds with Maylene. Hadn't there been nothing but trouble since that man entered their lives, exploiting the family for free meals and feed for his horse? Under his polite exterior and occasional offer of a book lurked a self-serving man who had maneuvered his son into danger.

Why am I doing this? Armed with a knife? Marcus had set aside his memories of shooting men, most certainly killing at least one. Now his stomach clenched with a rush of emotions, the strangling tentacles of violence. Using the Enfield against Union men had eroded his sanity, but the prospect of stabbing a man, even one as deserving as Enoch Wallace, reeked of atrocity and made him feel physically ill.

No, Joseph will get his sister out. I'll help them down the ridge. It will be good to have an extra pair of hands, an extra horse. Stop inventing trouble. Enoch will be passed out drunk. Relax.

But he could not. The thickening veil of mist and Maylene's apprehension played on his nerves. A voice within said, This ain't going to go well.

Joseph waited until near-dark before edging out of the woods. He circled around the north end of the farm, approaching the henhouse from the back. Although the cabin appeared dark, the strong smell of wood smoke told him someone was up and tending the fire.

Be here, Becky.

He pushed the door with care, wishing not to disturb the hens. The sooty-black interior stank of chicken excrement.

"Becky?"

No answer.

Joseph dropped to a crouch to wait, worried he'd come too late and missed his sister. His mind digested disorganized thoughts. What was he going to do if she didn't come? He needed a solid plan.

Twenty minutes later, Joseph began to feel chilled. He considered stuffing two hens inside his coat but, despite knowing they'd quickly settle down in their darkness-imposed stupor, feared the commotion they'd make when grabbed. He smiled at the thought of approaching Enoch packing two hens, then reminded himself this was no time for jokes. He had tasked himself with a mission, a mission going poorly.

He decided he'd wait another ten or twenty minutes, then go for Becky, pistol drawn.

Becky, desperate with anxiety, exhaustion, and pain, stared at her husband's back as he lay on his side on their bed. He wasn't snoring—was he asleep? An hour earlier, when she'd headed out to feed the hens, he'd snarled, "They can wait for morning. I don't trust you not to go sneaking off to Clara's. You ain't going nowhere."

It hurt too much to talk, and what was the point? Becky wore a bandage, a strip of cloth cut off the bottom of her one other dress, intended to hold her swollen lower jaw still. It didn't work very well—thus speaking caused stabs of misery when the bone ends ground together. So she tended the fire and took sips of whiskey from a cup, waiting for Enoch to fall asleep. She prayed Joseph would return home, not come to the cabin.

Just when she thought Enoch had been still long enough that she might slip out, he rolled over, coughing, and sat up. "Gotta piss," he said.

He picked up the rifle leaning in the corner by the door.

Becky pointed. "Why?" she murmured without parting her lips.

"You said Caleb run off, said he can't live here no more? I'll be ready for him if he changes his mind, and God help him if he brings the law."

With a shaky hand, Joseph removed the pistol from the holster at his hip and left the henhouse. He could barely make out the cabin in the thick fog. Assuming the three sagging steps would creak, he took one long stride onto the porch, then inched his way to the door, wincing at each complaining squeak of a plank.

He raised his free hand and hesitated as a tremor shook his form. He mustn't let Becky down. He wouldn't. He tapped gently on the door.

A voice in his head cautioned, Beware the Ides of March.

Inside, Becky slumped with the unbroken side of her face resting on the tabletop. She'd meant to rest her eyes for a moment, not fall asleep. She dreamed Caleb rapped at the window, and she looked up to see him smiling, holding up two bottles of medicine. Wondering why he'd come to the window, she motioned for him to come around to the door. Instead, he knocked again, three times.

Becky was jolted awake, as if slapped, by her husband's voice. "Drop the pistol!"

Joseph jumped, then froze, shifting only his eyes to see the murky outline of Enoch standing to his left, off the porch. Clear enough was the rifle aimed at his torso.

"I said *drop it!*"

Joseph let the gun clatter onto the boards at his feet.

"Now kick it off the porch," Enoch commanded.

Joseph swung a boot but without much force. The pistol landed on the top step.

He had to grit his teeth to keep his voice even. "You know why I'm here. I come for my sister."

My sister! Enoch reeled with the shock of Joseph's identity. Hadn't the cessation of mailed money signaled his brother-in-law's death, turning his lie into a truth?

"Becky sent Caleb for you! They both knew you wasn't dead and where to find you."

Enoch's ire spilled over the edge of a boiling cauldron, preparing him to end the life that reduced him to a fool. He raised the cocked rifle, taking aim. "I done told you about coming uninvited—you don't get no more warnings. It's the last time!"

Joseph, aware of a strange suspension of time, inhaled what he believed to be his last breath.

Good God, he's going to kill me.

Despite the futility of escape or defense, Joseph's body responded to lethal danger involuntarily. An arm lifted to cover his head as his legs folded him into a crouch, minimizing the size of a target even a drunkard in the fog couldn't fail to strike.

At that moment, Joseph flinched as a rifle fired. The bullet struck the barrel of Enoch's rifle, just above the stock, sending the gun scuttling across the porch. Joseph started to dive for the pistol, but Enoch leapt onto the low porch, and both men lunged for the rifle. Enoch, closer to the gun, grabbed the stock as Joseph stomped a desperate foot on the barrel.

Blackjack heard Cloud's whinny and led Marcus to the mare. By this time, Marcus had concluded he pursued a fool's errand. Maylene was right. He owed her everything, Joseph nothing. He would overcome his soldier's instincts. He would wait. If he remained alone an hour after nightfall, he'd head home no matter how ashamed he felt for turning his back on Joseph's peril.

True to his plan, he placed his left boot in the stirrup to remount the gelding when he heard a rifle shot. His brain shut down but his body did not. Protecting Blackjack, he abandoned the horse and ran in the direction of the sound.

Maylene finished nursing Georgie and trailed the children upstairs to bed. She did her best to reassure the frightened four that their pa had gone to prevent Joseph from becoming lost on his way home. Frantic with worry, she hugged herself as she watched the fire's last flames subside to ruby embers. Never had she refused Marcus's kiss, not since his first shy offering that summer day in the shade of the Farley barn. Unthinkable. And suppose it was the last?

Tears welled in Maylene's eyes. Could her husband's final memory of her be that rejection, that insult of turning away?

Georgie should sleep for hours. She must go to her man. She covered the embers with ashes, checked the beeswax in the lantern, lit the wick with a candle, snuffed the candle, put on her hooded cloak, stepped soundlessly out, called softly for Chase, and was on her way. Knowing Reggie needed rest from plowing and too impatient to fetch and saddle him, she walked.

Enoch snatched the rifle stock with both hands and pulled hard. Joseph, off balance, tried to get a second foot on the barrel but failed. He felt the smooth metal sliding under his boot. From the corner of an eye, he saw the cabin door open. At the same instant, the barrel's metal loop, where its carrying strap attached, caught on the edge of his heel. Joseph bore down with all his weight as he grasped the reason not to hurl himself at Enoch.

"God dammit!" Enoch, his back to the cabin, continued his effort to yank the rifle free. He didn't see his wife raise her weapon, a heavy iron skillet, above her head and bring it down.

The sound of metal on skull rang through the night, and Enoch pitched forward in a senseless heap.

"God Almighty, Becky! Well done!" Joseph picked up the rifle. "I'm going to discharge this thing before it causes any more trouble, and permanently relieve Enoch of it."

He fired into the opaque sky.

"But…" Becky couldn't force another word past her lips, yet Joseph understood.

"That's exactly what I'd like to know. Who fired the shot that saved me? Stay here a minute. I'm going to go find out. Then we'll get going. Wait. Take the pistol just in case. But he don't look like he'll be moving for a while."

"Dead?" Becky asked.

"Good question." Joseph reached down for a wrist, then let it fall, disappointed by its vigorous pulse.

Joseph heard someone running toward him before he made out the shape of a thin man. "Who goes there?" he called out.

Relieved to recognize the voice, Marcus replied, "It's me, Marcus. You and your sister all right?"

"Thanks to you we are." Joseph wanted to embrace his son, but Marcus stopped short.

"What do you mean? I ain't done a thing. I heard the Enfield, then a loud clang and another rifle shot. Did you shoot Enoch?"

"The Enfield! All I brought was your pistol. Someone fired at Enoch—who the hell? Caleb?"

"Caleb!" Joseph shouted. "Are you here?"

From the direction of the cabin, came a weak response carried clearly, eerily on the fog's breath. "Joseph."

The men exchanged stunned looks. They knew the voice.

It was Suzanne's.

CHAPTER TWENTY-FOUR

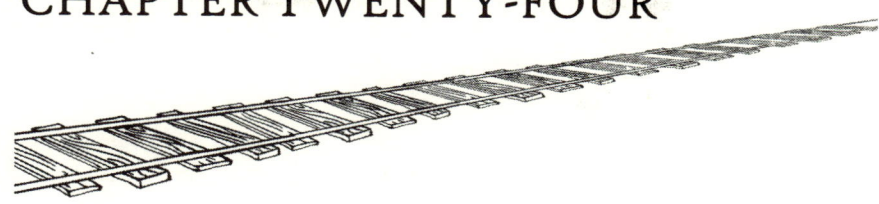

They found her sitting at the base of a walnut tree no more than twenty yards from the cabin, the Enfield across her lap.

"For the love of God, Suzanne," Joseph said, squatting before her. "You could've gotten yourself killed."

"I may have," Suzanne said in a breathless, almost-inaudible voice.

Marcus dropped to one knee, removing the rifle. "Ma, what's wrong?"

"Don't rightly know. I got so lightheaded I had to sit down before I fell down. I'm weak as a baby bird."

"I'll go back for the horses," Marcus said. "We've got to get you and Becky home."

"Come on, Suzy," Joseph said in a tone new to Marcus. "Easy now. Let's get you inside by the fire."

He gathered and carried her like a child. They both trembled. Joseph hoped Suzanne thought he was cold.

Walking away, Marcus glanced back, taking in the tender scene. Suzy? He loves her. Melva don't stand a chance.

Maylene found the climb more difficult than she remembered. It had been years, and she hadn't completely regained her strength. Every time she stopped to rest, Chase trotted ahead, then circled back to find her. The dog's ability to track Blackjack proved invaluable as Maylene could discern nothing beyond the feeble circle of lanternlight.

The slope of mud, ice, snow, and loose rocks made for terrible footing, but her lifelong experience with mountain terrain allowed

Maylene to reach the summit without falling. In less than a mile, Chase yipped joyously at Marcus's scent and headed straight for the Wallace cabin. Maylene picked up her pace.

Marcus led the horses onto the road and mounted Blackjack. The gelding took no more than a few steps before balking, however. He curled his neck to look behind, his ears forward, listening.

"What is it, Black?" Marcus asked. "Come on now, we got to get going." He nudged with his heels, but the horse didn't move.

Marcus picked up the sound, the panting of a dog. And there, emerging from the mist, tail swinging madly, loped Chase. She bounded up to Blackjack, standing on her hind legs to greet Marcus.

"Who's next?" said Marcus. "I thought I told you to stay." He gave Chase a knuckle-rub on her head.

"Marcus!"

"Maylene?" Marcus peered into the blackness.

Like an apparition, his wife took form, her swaying lantern confirming her realness as she neared.

Marcus dismounted and took her in his arms.

"Thank God! I'm sorry. I'm so sorry," Maylene said, her tears adding moisture to Marcus's weather-dampened cheek.

"What are you sorry about? You were right. All I could think about was what I was putting you through and how you didn't deserve it. And here you are making me feel ten times more a jackass for driving you mad enough to climb the ridge on such a night. You ought to horsewhip me, May. But you oughtn't have come, and I'd be right mad if it weren't my doing."

Speechless with emotion, Maylene kissed her husband before releasing him and mounting Cloud. She wiped her nose with the hem of her cape. "I prayed you'd come to your senses before it was too late. Where are we going?"

"To pick up Joseph and Becky. And you won't believe who else."

"Who?"

"My ma."

Although Joseph was tempted to leave his brother-in-law outside, he and Marcus dragged Enoch in by his feet and left him on the hearth. Then Joseph tightened his sister's bandage and helped her aboard Blackjack. Maylene straddled the gelding behind the saddle, reaching around Becky to hold the reins.

Suzanne remained so woozy and weak-kneed that Joseph carried her out to the waiting mare. She asked to be set down and told the men to turn their backs while she relieved herself, annoyed by the dampness of her flannel padding. With Marcus's help, Joseph got her into the saddle, then insisted on seating himself behind her, with one arm for reining, the other tightly wrapped around her waist.

Chase led the way. Marcus followed with the lantern, and the horses trailed him. "We'll have to stick to the road," Marcus said as they started out. "It'll add a good mile, but the trail's too slick and steep in the dark."

Suzanne hated the way her pendulous breasts rested on Joseph's forearm. If she hadn't been in such danger of toppling out of the saddle, she'd have told him to remove his arm. On the other hand, it had been a long time since she'd been pressed in a man's embrace. She relaxed her back and shoulders into Joseph's chest, grateful for the support, and tried to quiet her shaking. Her mind, like a recoiling slingshot, flung her backward in time to the other instance when Joseph had made her tremble. The day of the fight with Billy and Homer. She'd thought her best friend, her only friend, faced death, and she had shaken uncontrollably while she waited for him behind the buckeye. She'd gripped her unspent stone in one hand and shoved the other hand into her dress pocket to keep Joseph from seeing the fright her fingers would have revealed.

I'm too old for this. Quit getting yourself in trouble I've got to get you out of.

Joseph, having never known Suzanne to be at a loss for words, concluded she was gravely ill. Maylene, persisting in relief's teariness, kept her thoughts to herself. Marcus watched for ruts, icy spots, and downed limbs on the snow-covered road. And Becky's acute discomfort rendered her silent as the fog.

If not for squeaking saddle leather, Chase's breathing, Becky's sporadic coughing, and hooves striking stones, not a sound would have accompanied the mute travelers.

Close to midnight, Lester, Vesta, and Caleb heard the bray of the lonely mule. Minutes later, they picked up voices nearing the house and barreled onto the porch.

"Ma, don't tell me you walked all the way up the ridge!" said a bulled-up Vesta. "We been worried sick! We thought you fell in the creek and drowned 'til Lester found the bundle of stems you cut. Then we knew you come back. You must of sneaked off when I was helping Lester in the barn. Why on earth would you do such a thing?"

"Vesta, Ma's not well," Marcus said. "Leave her be. We've got to get her straight to bed. We'll sort out what happened tonight, but this ain't the time."

Wobbling between Marcus and Lester, who supported her by her elbows, Suzanne said, "Put Becky in my bed. I'll sleep with Vesta."

Vesta heated buttermilk, which Becky had no difficulty drinking through a pipestem straw, thanks to her missing lower tooth. But Suzanne refused to wait for the milk to warm. Joseph tucked one arm under her knees, and she folded backwards against his other arm to be carried upstairs.

Marcus, Maylene, and Lester followed. "What's wrong with her?" Lester asked as they climbed the steps.

"Hard to say," Marcus answered. "Could be she's in shock, and she'll sleep it off."

Maylene offered to help her mother-in-law into her nightclothes, but Suzanne waved her off. "I'll sleep in my dress," she said, her eyelids fluttering with the effort of keeping open.

Maylene pulled back the comforter and quilts, and untied and removed Suzanne's shoes as Joseph held her. Feeling extraneous, Marcus watched while Joseph tucked in his mother.

"I'll run downstairs for her cap," he said, returning with the knit-wool garment and securing it with ties under his mother's chin.

"Are you warm enough, Ma?"

"Snug as a bug," she said without opening her eyes.

Joseph stroked her cheek with the back of a hand.

Marcus thought, It's as if they're alone.

"Sleep now," Joseph said. "You'll be good as new in the morning."

Back downstairs, after seeing Becky settled, Joseph accepted Vesta's offering of dried-pumpkin chowder and cornbread. "I'll be on the first ferry in the morning," he said. "No one's getting to Doc Mason's door before I do."

Marcus bristled. What right had Mr. Joseph to decide who would go for the doctor? But the night had drained him beyond argument, and Maylene itched to check on the children.

She said, "I'll wake Georgie for a feeding. Then we can sleep a few hours before dawn."

Joseph stopped at the store to tell Silas about Becky's need for a doctor—he saw no reason to complicate matters with Suzanne's illness.

Silas said, "I didn't know you have a sister. By all means, do what you need to take care of her. I can manage here."

"Thank you, my good man. With any luck, I'll be back this afternoon."

Joseph rode Cloud at a canter to the stately yellow house on the floodplain's edge, a short distance below the New's great widening where the Greenbrier River entered. It struck him as precariously positioned, pinned between the water and the tracks.

His knock brought Dr. Mason—dressed in white shirt, dark pants, and suspenders—to the door. He held a steaming cup of coffee.

"Mr. Cook. Won't you come in? The missus and I are just finishing breakfast. We like to eat after the youngsters are off to school. It's quieter," he said with a smile. "Have you eaten?"

"Yes, sir," Joseph lied. "I come to see if you'll accompany me to the Lilly farm again. My sister's down from Broomstraw Ridge with her jaw broke, and Mrs. Lilly's in a bad way. I'm concerned it could be her heart."

The doctor frowned. "Did someone strike your sister?"

"Yes, sir. Her husband."

"Do you want Sheriff Hinton to ride up with us and take a statement?"

"Not 'til I've had a chance to talk to her about it. But I'd be pleased to see that man behind bars."

"Very well. Our chore boy isn't here yet. If you don't mind saddling my mare, I'll be ready in a few minutes."

With Joseph, Marcus, Vesta, and Caleb in attendance, Dr. Mason started with Becky, who rested, cocooned in a quilt, in the rocker before the fire. He felt the broken bone beneath the swollen bruise and shook his head. "It's fractured, no question."

He opened Becky's mouth to check for loose or broken teeth. Vesta held the stoic patient's hand, squeezing in sympathy with the pain.

A coughing fit ended the dental inspection. "I don't like the sound of that," said Dr. Mason. "Have you been exposed to consumption?"

Becky nodded.

"Who? Your husband?"

She nodded again.

Without comment, the doctor turned his attention to preparing a bandage. With great care, he swaddled Becky's face until she resembled a mummy. Only her eyes, nose, and lips remained exposed.

"I'm afraid it's tight enough to give you a headache, but don't loosen it. You're lucky you're missing that tooth—you'll do fine with a straw." Turning to Vesta, he said, "Give her soup broth, buttermilk, and cider. But you'll have to find another place for her. There's risk of contagion. I suggest you locate other housing by the end of the day."

Vesta and Marcus exchanged looks. Marcus thought, Another gift from Mr. Joseph, danger to my wife and children.

Leaving Caleb to assist his mother drink cider laced with whiskey, the others found Suzanne asleep upstairs. She opened her eyes when Dr. Mason nudged her shoulder. "Why are you here? Is someone ill?"

She wondered why her voice wavered.

"I'm here to examine you, Mrs. Lilly. I understand you're not well."

Suzanne tried to sit up, but the effort made her so dizzy she lay back down. "You may be right."

"Can you tell me what happened?"

"I walked up Broomstraw last night, and it was more taxing than I expected. Then there was a ... confrontation. It had to do with getting Becky—Mrs. Wallace—away from her husband. He's the one broke her jaw." She paused to rest.

The doctor took a wrist to feel her pulse. After several moments he asked, "Are you able to stand?"

With assistance from Marcus, Suzanne climbed shakily to her feet and stood while Dr. Mason continued to measure her heartrate.

"Fast as a rabbit's," he said. "Let's get you back in bed."

Suzanne surrendered to gravity without argument.

"Tell me more. Take your time." His patient held Dr. Mason's full attention.

Marcus didn't like the concern evident on the man's face.

"I went weak. I had to sit, so I sat. I had trouble catching my breath, and I felt sick to my stomach. I thought I might faint, but I didn't. That was the worst of it, but I'm still loose-kneed as a new foal. Can you make any sense of it?"

Suzanne shuddered and longed for privacy to use the chamber pot. Make it short, Doc, she thought.

"Tell me about your childhood illnesses."

"I was a healthy girl," Suzanne said. "The one serious illness I can recall was rheumatic fever, but I recovered nicely." *Off you go, now.*

Dr. Mason released Suzanne's wrist. "I'm sorry to say, Mrs. Lilly, rheumatic fever in childhood can damage the heart. I believe the combination of exertion and excitement last night caused you a heart attack. You are to have complete bed rest for a week. Then I'll be back to check on you. You'll use the chamber pot. No trips to the privy. Let your family feed you in bed. I want to be sure you understand this is serious."

"Yes, sir," said Suzanne. *A heart attack? My heart don't hurt.*

"Do you have any questions for me?"

"No, sir. Thank you for coming." *Now get out of here, so I can relieve myself.*

She said, "I need to sleep some more," to clear the room. She'd be damned if she was going to ask for help pissing in the pot.

As her family filed out, Suzanne tugged on Vesta's skirt and motioned for her to bend down close. "Take Joseph's money," she whispered, "the money he's been giving us to feed Cloud. Use it to pay Dr. Mason, and if there's enough, pay him for coming about Maylene and Georgie, too."

Back downstairs, the doctor cornered Marcus, Vesta, and Joseph. "Try to keep the bandage dry. I'll change it next week, but let me know if you see sign of infection before then. If the pain starts getting worse instead of better, get word to me. Or if you suspect fever. As for Mrs. Lilly, she'll be better in a week or she won't. My hope is she'll be yammering to get out of bed by the time I return. If she stays as ill as she is, she may remain an invalid. It's in God's hands.

"Let me emphasize that I meant what I said about finding Mrs. Wallace solitary living conditions. You'll need to be able to leave food at her door, and you must keep your distance. Consumption isn't highly contagious, but it's too dangerous to take chances with. Mr. Cook, let me know where to find her."

"Yes, sir," said Joseph.

"Now, one more thing. If Mrs. Wallace decides to press charges, I'll serve as witness. I've seen this sort of cowardly violence too many times, and I'm sick and tired of the moonshine excuse."

Despite her discretion, Vesta was unable to avoid Marcus's watchful eye. Her brother marveled at the mysterious pouch of coins she transferred from her apron pocket to Dr. Mason's hand. If Maylene didn't know the source of the money, Marcus intended to grill his sister.

CHAPTER TWENTY-FIVE

Maylene caught her breath when Marcus told her about Becky's illness. "What shall we do with her?" she asked.

"We'll have to build a cabin, a small one, easy to keep warm. It'll go up pretty quick with Lester and Caleb's help. It's a good thing Lester's job ain't started yet."

"You have a big heart, Marcus."

"Not at all, but I intend to protect my children."

"Is there somewhere she can stay in the meantime?"

"I spoke with Mr. Joseph, and he's gonna look in town. He rode down with the doctor and said he'll be back before nightfall."

"If he don't find a place, do you think maybe Mrs. Wallace could stay in the smokehouse for a while? Vesta and I can set out a basket of food every day—we won't have to go in. Mrs. Wallace can tend the fire, poor thing, but she'll have to leave the door open to let the smoke out."

"I'm afraid she'd damn near suffocate in there. She ain't breathing real good as it is. Let's hope Mr. Joseph comes up with something. By the way, do you know where Ma got money to pay the doctor?"

"Didn't I tell you? She's been saving every penny Mr. Joseph pays for us keeping the mare."

"No, you didn't. I figured he was freeloading all this time."

Maylene sighed as she returned to her sewing. At the rate the children grew, the need for new clothes never ceased.

Joseph did come up with something, but not what Marcus and Maylene anticipated. After making numerous inquiries, and getting the same, expected answer—that Hinton's exploding population outpaced its housing—Joseph walked back to the store and made another request of his boss.

Thinking, Don't it figure, Randall, I've found another way to make Marcus disgusted with me, Joseph said, "Silas, if I can buy it on credit, I'd like to purchase a stove and pipe. I've got a piece of land for sale up North, and I'll pay you back as soon as it's sold. It's a lot to ask, but I'd also like to borrow the wagon and team to take the stove up to the Lilly farm. My sister almost certainly has consumption and is going to have to live isolated from the family. All I can think of is to put her in the smokehouse for now. And if anyone should come by inquiring about her whereabouts, I'll be mighty grateful if you play dumb."

Silas agreed without hesitation, and Joseph arrived before dark with the wagon and a promise to keep looking for a long-term solution. When Vesta told him Marcus, Lester, and Caleb planned to build a one-room cabin, Joseph thought he'd misunderstood.

"What?"

"It's behind the house. They've laid the foundation and they're cutting chestnuts now. They've already hauled a few down to the barn."

Joseph stayed overnight, and he and Caleb cut a hole in the smokehouse roof and installed the stove the next morning. By noon, they had Becky settled on a fresh straw tick in her temporary home with *Moby Dick* and a cup of buttermilk. Although both her head and jaw ached miserably, she was so thankful to be away from Enoch, with her son unscathed, she muttered to her brother that she considered herself blessed.

Suzanne, who had revived enough to sit up in bed knitting, asked to see Joseph before he left. "I know you've got to get back to work, but come on Sunday, will you? Calvin and Nancy will be here, and we may as well tell everyone at once what went on the other night."

"I'm thinking of coming back tomorrow. I haven't asked for more than a couple of days off since I started this job. I'll take the wagon back and talk to Silas, so I suspect you'll see me in the morning. I want to help with the cabin. It'll go up faster, and I don't feel right sitting aside like an old grandpa."

"You *are* an old grandpa."

Joseph left with the conviction Suzanne was going to recover.

The construction progressed apace despite a snowstorm that swept in from the northwest. The men squared and notched logs in the barn, instructing Lester and Caleb in the precise shaping required for dovetail joints. Joseph and Marcus secretly admired each other's craftsmanship. Adept with axe and adz, both followed the ethic that a job isn't worth doing unless done right.

Marcus scolded himself for thinking how useful a heated workshop would be when Miss Becky moved out or…. No, he mustn't anticipate her death.

The father and son spoke little as the cabin took shape. Joseph assumed his presence caused Marcus's moody silence. In truth, the March storm imposed the heaviness evident to all, including Chase, whose worried eyes followed Marcus's every move.

Marcus couldn't help being reminded of a similar March storm, in 1864, when his brother Johnny caught pneumonia. Marcus had returned from furlough to find his brother ill and did everything in his power to nurse Johnny back to health. With growing desperation, he watched his efforts fail. Johnny's death had shaken him to the core, undermining his ability to cope with the War's harsh physical and emotional demands.

Maylene walked down to the barn to talk to Joseph but couldn't find a way to sideline him. She watched the flying chips and shavings of wood, complimented Caleb on his handiwork, and abandoned her plan to expose her husband's pain. The storm would end, and Marcus would relax.

Unaware of the balm they provided, Lester and Caleb chattered away like a pair of squirrels. A year younger, Caleb looked up to Lester, finding in him the brother he'd never known. He'd been a toddler when Amos enlisted and had no memory of him. And the teen had hundreds of questions, a storehouse of questions he'd never asked his father, not that Enoch knew much of anything about cabin-building or the proper running of a farm.

By the end of the week, Lester secured the roof's final cedar shingle and Marcus completed the chinking. Joseph put the new fireplace to work and transferred his sister to her diminutive but snug home.

Little did any of them, not even Vesta, know Suzanne had been disobeying the doctor for the past two days, sneaking out of bed to read and sew and knit before the fire. She wasn't about to let anyone confine her to a week of idleness for no good reason.

Through a haze of pain, Enoch heard voices and strained to make sense of them. But they faded away, leaving him alone on the cold floor. Opening his eyes, he saw that little remained of the evening blaze.

"Becky," he croaked, "feed the fire."

No reply.

"Becky!"

Raising his voice threatened to split his head open. "Damn woman. Where is she?"

Enoch crawled to a bucket of kindling and threw a few pieces into the waning fire, which brightened obediently. Even that minor effort left him dizzy and nauseated. He eased himself onto his side and swiped the top of his head with his fingers. He found it sticky with blood and bulging with a goose egg.

"What the hell?"

Enoch closed his eyes and hissed, "Someone on the porch. . . . Oh, Joseph! What brought him here, and why did I intend to shoot him? Something went wrong. I dropped the rifle! Why would I drop the rifle?"

Beyond that memory, Enoch dredged nothing from the murky, throbbing anguish of his brain. He spent the remainder of the night dozing, squandering the supply of kindling to avoid going to the woodbox by the door, and vowing to exact revenge on his brother-in-law, who must be responsible for his injury, as well as his wife and rifle gone missing.

March was always the worst month on the Wallace farm, and this March was worse than usual. Having gambled away the cow a month earlier, Enoch had little to subsist on but flour, meal, and eggs. It didn't much matter about the cow, anyway. The farm's steep pastures, badly overgrazed, bore erosion scars as if scratched by a giant cat. Both grain fields and pastures, polluted with thistles and locusts, looked more like chins in need of a shave than productive farmland. The hay supply wouldn't have come close to feeding mule and cow until spring. The mule and chickens would be lucky not to starve if Enoch didn't share the cornmeal.

As he recovered, Enoch grew tired of eating boiled eggs and tried his hand at biscuits and griddlecakes. But he made the fire too hot and wound up with dough burned on the outside and raw in the middle.

He cursed his wife for abandoning him and began thinking of how to retrieve her. Had Joseph taken her to Clara's or Ethel's? When Joseph heard that cough, he wouldn't want her staying with him. It angered Enoch to think one of Becky's friends might be receiving payment for room, board, and nursing care. It angered him that his so-called friends had banished him from the poker game he'd started more than twenty years ago. And it further angered him that Joseph had stopped sending Becky money.

And where was his useless son? He'd like to give him a beating he wouldn't soon forget.

After a few days, the headache subsided, and the remaining snow melted. Enoch saddled the mule and headed for town to inquire about Joseph's whereabouts. He didn't want trouble with Mr. Bennett or Mr. Crook, who had reason to be sore about the way he'd ejected their wives from his home the night he hit Becky. If he lost his temper with either one of them, they might call the sheriff, and he ruminated in a more temper-losing mood than usual.

His threat to accuse Becky of cheating had been nothing but bluff. She had two witnesses who would say otherwise. No, he had a score to settle. He would find Joseph and intimidate him into revealing Becky's temporary refuge.

For the first time in weeks, a smile stretched Enoch's mustache. The man looked forward to the encounter.

CHAPTER TWENTY-SIX

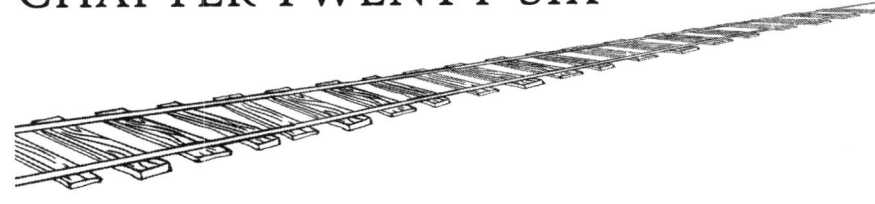

Maylene and Vesta skipped church to prepare Sunday dinner for thirteen—themselves, Suzanne, Marcus, Lester, Joseph, Caleb, Becky, Calvin, and the four children with teeth. Calvin's wife, Nancy, wasn't ready for the long, rough ride so soon after childbirth and chose to stay home with her newborn.

Vesta and her sister-in-law made stew of stillborn-lamb, ham, potatoes, onions, and the season's first greens. They opened the last jar of pickled green beans and baked cornbread, wheat bread, and cider-honey cake. The house smelled good enough to invite God Himself.

Yet most of the family, although appreciative of the meal, arrived with an interest that trumped food, namely, what happened on Broomstraw Ridge the Sunday before?

Suzanne, who scorned all attempts to keep her in bed, made her first appearance at the dinner table. Although lightheaded and easily fatigued, she refused to miss the occasion. She made her way cautiously down the steps and took her place, once Quentin's, at the table's head.

"Joseph, you've taken care of Becky?"

Joseph nodded. "Uh-huh, broth and buttermilk."

"Let's eat first. Calvin, will you say the blessing?"

All heads bowed, and Calvin, understanding the question to be a command, began with, "Heavenly Father...."

No one tarried with small talk but plowed through the food in a unified, goal–driven manner.

Suzanne, the last to set down her fork, pushed a plate of half-eaten cake away and said, "Joseph, why don't you start?"

"All right. As some of you know, I rode Cloud up Broomstraw last Sunday afternoon to rescue my sister, Becky, who suffered a broken jaw at the hands of her husband."

"Why'd he do that?" asked Johnny.

"Don't interrupt," said Suzanne. "Let Mr. Joseph tell his story."

"She'd sent her son, Caleb, with instructions to meet her at dusk in the henhouse, but I waited until well past dark without any sign of her. So I went to the cabin and knocked like this ..." He rapped on the table.... "hoping her husband, Enoch, was asleep and Becky would hear me. The second time I knocked, Enoch yelled for me to drop the pistol."

"You had a gun?" Sara Sue's blue eyes bulged.

"Your papa's. That rascal sneaked up on me from the side of the porch. The fog was so thick I could scarcely see him."

"Did you shoot him?" a riveted Johnny asked.

"No, sir. I had a rifle barrel pointing straight at me, so I let go the pistol and hoped I could talk some sense into that wild man. But before I had a chance, he said some nonsense and appeared ready to kill me. Suzanne, would you like to explain how you saved my neck?"

"I would. I walked up with Marcus's Enfield because I had a real bad feeling about the whole thing. I hid behind a tree and waited for dusk. I never did see Mr. Joseph until he showed up on the porch after dark. By then I thought maybe he'd sneaked off with Becky, and I was just about ready to sneak off myself. The fog was so bad I wasn't even sure it was him until Mr. Wallace come out of nowhere and started hollering at him. When I saw that rifle aimed at Mr. Joseph's breadbasket, I fired the Enfield, but with that fog and with my hands shaking so bad, my aim wasn't real good. I hit Mr. Wallace's rifle and knocked it out of his hands."

Johnny's mouth hung open. "Grandma! You shot at Mr. Wallace?"

"Yes, I did. And I don't recommend such behavior, you understand? I took the shot only because I thought Mr. Joseph was about to be murdered by a lunatic."

Joseph continued. "Then Enoch and I scrambled for that rifle, and I stomped a foot on the barrel just as Becky come out the door. Enoch didn't see her, as he was bent over trying to free the gun, and Becky brained him with a skillet. Knocked him right out!"

"Miss Becky?" Johnny had yet to shut his mouth.

"Holy Moses," said Calvin.

"That's right. I owe my life to your grandma and my sister, who are two of the bravest women I've ever known. But I didn't know it was your grandma fired that shot. It was your papa come running, and together we found her sitting with the rifle in her grip. We was both plumb staggered."

Knowing Maylene didn't want the children to know she'd abandoned them, Marcus inwardly thanked Mr. Joseph for leaving her out of the story.

"And it's not the first time Suzanne Lilly—Suzanne Harman, then—rescued me. I got into a fight with two older boys after school one day, and they were knocking the stuffing out of me. She nailed one of them with a rock—hit him right above the eye. He took off after her, which gave me a chance to get up and get away before too much harm was done. I believe I owe your ma and grandma my life twice over."

Joseph fixed his dark eyes on Suzanne. "It's a debt I don't know how I'll ever repay."

Marcus took in his mother, small and pale. He'd resented her unyielding authority as a child, but at this moment, when the entire family sat speechless, he marveled at her spine of iron and thought, Ma, if I were more like you, I'd have been a far better soldier.

Suzanne scowled at the admiring eyes aimed her way. She didn't figure God observed her in a heroic light, not with her history of temper, dishonesty, and adultery. She didn't want to tempt Him to put her in her rightful place.

"Before you all even *think* of putting me on a pedestal, I have another story to tell. It's one I ain't proud of, but you may as well know I've done Mr. Joseph wrong as well as right."

Joseph thought, Surely you're not going to humiliate me with *that* recollection.

"You know Mr. Joseph and I grew up together. We were the best of friends and spent many an hour as playmates on my family's farm. By the eighth grade, I'd set my cap for him and bet my life we'd marry in a few years. But we graduated that spring and went our separate ways. Mr. Joseph didn't visit the farm no more, and I never saw him except for rare times at the mill or store."

She glared at Joseph. "And then I couldn't get more than a word or two out of him."

"Why not?" asked Sara Sue.

"I went through a bashful spell," Joseph said.

"Bashful! You gave me such a cold shoulder I wanted to slap you. By the year I turned seventeen, I decided to take matters into my own hands, and the next time I saw Mr. Joseph at New Richmond, I invited him to come berry-picking with my friend Betty and me, up on Brooks Mountain above the farm, and he agreed.

"But I never did invite Betty, so you can see I lied.

"Bless his trusting heart, Mr. Joseph come to help fill the basket with blackberries, and I flirted shamelessly. I thought if I could get one kiss we'd be betrothed in short order."

"Did Mr. Joseph kiss you, Grandma?" Sara Sue climbed onto Marcus for a higher vantage point.

"No, he did not. Not only that, but he lectured me for lying to him and behaving in an unseemly manner. And I lost my temper and my reason so completely I hit him in the face and broke his nose."

"Grandma!" Sara Sue exclaimed.

Johnny beamed. He slammed a palm with a fist and said, "You whacked him good!"

"Young man, it was a wicked thing I done, and it spoiled our friendship. I'm fortunate Mr. Joseph has a forgiving nature."

Joseph absentmindedly scraped the table with the blunt end of his knife. "Not entirely. I was mad a good long time. But I blamed myself, too. I could have been flattered by your interest in me instead of self-righteous about the way you expressed it."

"What's 'self-righteous'?" asked Sara Sue.

"It's thinking you're better than someone else because you think you act better. It's no way to be with a friend," Joseph said.

"Did Grandma really break your nose?" Johnny asked.

"Look closely," Joseph said. "See how it's shifted a little to the left?"

They all stared, including Suzanne. She hadn't noticed.

"It didn't heal quite straight."

"I see it!" said Sara Sue. "It's a little bent. Grandma, were you sad you didn't marry Mr. Joseph?"

"Not for long. I met your Paw Paw the next year, and he swept me off my feet. What I was sorry for was the way Mr. Joseph and I parted company."

"Mr. Joseph, what did you do when Grandma hit you?" Jenny asked, braving her first direct question to Joseph.

"I wanted to hit her right back, but instead I cursed her, which wasn't much better. Then she ran off, and, adding insult to injury, she took the blackberries with her."

The children laughed. "Grandma, you were *naughty!*" Johnny couldn't conceal his awe.

"That I was, and disgracefully so. Now I'm about wore out with all this talk. Who's going to help Vesta and Maylene with the dishes while I go take a rest?"

Marcus had listened to the entire exchange as he chewed a cud of thought. Maylene scoured his pensive face and noticed the way Jenny examined her hands folded in her lap. Maylene's concern for her daughter's uneasiness was interrupted when she glanced across at Lester, nodding his head, a slight smile on his lips.

Joseph spent an hour reading to his mute sister while Suzanne napped. He returned to the house to find her sewing in the rocker, a basket of mending projects by her side.

"Shouldn't you be in bed?"

"No. I've had my week of uselessness, and I'm done with it. I admit I ain't back to normal, but I'm too well to live like an invalid another day."

"Where are the others?"

"Vesta's gone up to help with Georgie and play with the children. Marcus and Lester and Caleb are making a repair to the wagon, replacing the tongue. And Calvin's gone home, with strict instructions to say nothing about Becky and Caleb. I don't like those boys breaking the Sabbath, but there's work backed up, and they don't listen to me no more."

Joseph pulled a chair up next to the rocker and sat down. "You wanted to marry me?"

"I did, as a girl."

"You didn't mind the prospect of children who resembled me?"

"Joseph! Have you never become acquainted with a mirror? And look at Jenny. If her skin was a tad darker, she could be your twin. See what beautiful children you could father?"

"There's plenty of folks don't see me in a favorable light, but I hope that's not how they see Jenny.... Sounds like you didn't waste much time getting over me."

Suzanne reached over and patted his arm. "What I said was for the children's benefit. I was quite broken up, if you want to know the truth."

"There's a few missing pieces you don't know."

"Such as?" Suzanne continued mending a torn seam in a pair of Quencus's pants.

"For starters, I was bashful because I was so affected by you. My body lit up like a bonfire every time I saw you after about age thirteen. I'd get too embarrassed to speak."

"You did? I didn't realize. I thought you must favor someone else." Suzanne gave Joseph a sidelong look and a slight smile.

"And another thing. I come a'courtin' one day."

"No!" That stopped her in mid-stitch. "When?"

"The spring before our blackberry misadventure. I finally got up the courage to ride up one Sunday, but I was delayed because Pa made me escort Becky to a friend's house before I could leave. That was in the opposite direction, toward New Richmond, and set me back quite a bit. It was mid-afternoon by the time I got there, and I run into Homer Beckwith leaving your farm—an unpleasant surprise, to say the least. He said, 'Don't waste your time, Joey,' and laughed that put-down way of his. I pulled up the mare and must of sat there a quarter of an hour undecided what to do. I couldn't believe you'd entertain the likes of him, and I got madder the longer I thought about it. I ended up heading back home."

"Oh, for God's sake, Joseph! Why would you think for one minute I'd have the slightest interest in Homer Beckwith? He come that one time, and Mama made me let him stay for dinner. I gave him such a frosty reception he got the message loud and clear. You never saw a boy clear out so fast when Mama said, 'It was nice of you to come by.' You know, he'd gotten a haircut for the occasion, and I noticed he had a little scar above his eye from that rock I beaned him with. I figured that's why he always kept his hair down to his eyebrows, and my stomach hurt from trying not to laugh all through dinner.

"Goodness! You must have known I couldn't stand him!"

"Well, I didn't have a lot of confidence at that age. I didn't know what to think. His remark could be interpreted two different ways. Then the day we went blackberry picking, I knew you lied about your friend Betty getting sick, and you was sparking like a locomotive, which made me nervous as a cornered coon. You seemed so sure of yourself, I thought you must have some experience with romance, and I'd just that week found out about Becky being with child. I was a long way from being at my best, and I made some assumptions that were likely wrong and I've regretted ever since."

Suzanne avoided looking at him. "What you mistook for 'experience' was pure desperation. But maybe we'd have quarreled too much, anyway, and God spared us a lifetime of bickering."

"Maybe so. . . . Homer had a scar over his eye?"

"Plain as day."

And Joseph laughed. A deep, long one that shook him from waist to shoulders. Suzanne hadn't heard that belly-laugh since she was a girl. It warmed her more than the fire's heat and girded her for her question.

"Joseph, Lester will continue to live here, but he's taking work in town next week. Marcus can't manage without him. You've no place for Caleb in Hinton, and he can stay here. Why don't you stay, too? We need your help, and so does Becky. Of course, you can go when you buy your farm, but until then . . . will you?"

"I've been thinking the same thing. It's not right to abandon you with Becky and Caleb, and even if I found a place for them in town, Enoch may come looking for them there. They're safe here. I'll ride down tomorrow and talk to Silas. I hate to let him down, but he's the kind of man who knows family comes first. I'll ride back up with Doc Mason. I can rent a buggy later to fetch my things—the road's got to dry out first."

Suzanne released the tension knotting her shoulders. "Then it's settled. Good. And you won't need that buggy. You can take our wagon."

"Settled on one condition. I'll stay in the smokehouse. Caleb's bunking with Lester, and it's not proper for me to live with an unmarried woman and her daughter, even if we're 'kin.'"

"Suit yourself, but if you're still there when we butcher the hog, we'll have to throw you out."

"Merciless woman." Joseph stood. "If you don't mind, I'd like to be the one to tell Marcus."

The wagon repair completed and the soil much too sodden to till, Marcus turned to the repetitive task of spreading straw and manure on the garden. Joseph joined him, working in silence as he composed his short speech.

"Your Ma has asked me to live here awhile. I'm sure it's not what you want, but I have a responsibility for my sister, and I can't expect your family to look after her without my help. I couldn't find lodging for Becky, and I feel better about her being here. I'm concerned Enoch may come looking for her in town. I'll be staying in the smokehouse."

Marcus raked the soil's surface with a pitchfork, keeping his eye on the ground. "This farm belongs to Ma—she can do as she pleases."

He paused before continuing. "I ain't exactly welcomed you with open arms." He gestured toward the ridge with the fork handle. "The only pa I know is resting up there on the hillside. My father-in-law—I've known him all my life—is like a second pa, or maybe a favorite uncle."

Marcus braced himself with a deep breath and looked Joseph in the face. "I don't see how I'm ever going to think of you as my father, and I hope we can both make our peace with that. But I believe I've judged you harshly, and it shames me the way I've treated you."

Armed for combat, Joseph's brain balked, unable to reply to the unexpected change of direction. He must say something. "I'll be moving on, soon as I get my own place."

Then a question pressed against his skull, demanding to be spoken. "Why'd you come up Broomstraw that night, Marcus?"

Marcus grinned. "That's what Maylene wanted to know. I never seen her so mad at me. It didn't feel right, you going up there alone. I thought it could be a trap. But just about the time I figured Maylene was right, and I was being a damn fool, I heard the shot."

"You didn't even have a weapon."

"I had my hunting knife, not that I wanted to use it."

"I won't forget what you done. I don't expect you to think of me as a father, but I 'bout busted with pride that night, knowing I have a courageous son."

CHAPTER TWENTY-SEVEN

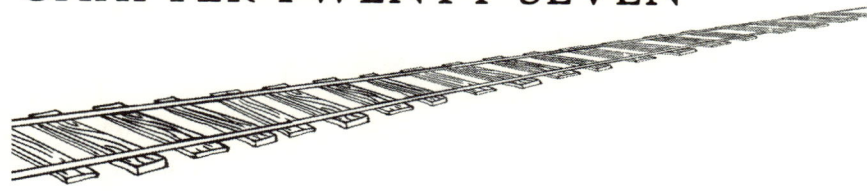

Sometime in the night, asleep in his new smoke- and bacon-scented quarters, Joseph dreamed he readied himself for bed at the store when startled by an unfamiliar man, who barged in as Joseph ducked behind the counter with the sickening realization he'd failed to lock the door. The intruder, his features cloaked by darkness, held a large hammer with which he began a rampage of destruction. He smashed the jar of pickled eggs, sending the contents splashing and rolling across the floor. Next, a large jar of pickles. He crushed the faces of dolls and tore cookware down from the ceiling. Unsheathing a knife on his belt, he sliced open bags of flour and salt and dried beans.

Joseph crouched and watched, horrified.

Another figure appeared and he, too, held hammer and knife. Briefly, he joined in the mayhem of demolition before the men approached one another, stalking in slow motion. Then both screamed and lunged, their blades thrusting.

Joseph turned away, sickened by the violence. When he looked back, the men lay face-down and motionless on the floor amid the wreckage of merchandise.

Standing over them, smiling, stood Randall.

"Randall!" Joseph bolted from his hiding place to embrace his friend. "My God, it's good to see you. I miss you bad."

He began to cry, and Randall began to expand. Joseph's nose reached his friend's bellybutton by the time Randall stopped swelling.

Randall shook with his familiar laughter and placed a hand on Joseph's head.

"Why are you laughing?" Joseph asked. "Are they dead?"

"Dead enough," Randall said. "They made their own justice."

Joseph then awoke and pondered the dream. Who were the men, and why did they kill each other? And how could death be justice for vandalism? Nothing made sense.

His arms around Randall's enlarged shape did make sense, however. He'd always considered Randall a friend but awakened to the realization he'd also been very much a parent, filling in for the father who'd forsaken his children in his grief nearly as successfully as his wife had forsaken them in her death. Joseph wondered if he'd served Randall as surrogate for the son he'd lost, and lay awake a full hour considering the men's bond in a new light.

Joseph's timing couldn't have been worse. Enoch chose that same Monday to ride his underfed mule down the muddy road, slipping and stumbling off the ridge to the gentler slope along Madam's Creek, to the Hinton ferry.

Along the way, he reviewed his plan, which he'd spent the previous day crafting. Talking more to himself than the mule he muttered, "Joseph ain't seen my face in decent light in at least thirty years. Now I've chopped off most of my beard. I'll find out where he works, must be the railroad. And follow him home and wait for dark to knock on his door. Ha! That fool won't know me 'til it's too late. I'll be inside before I introduce myself, all nice 'n polite. Listen up, Smitty, here's how it goes. I'll express my remorse over the whole regrettable incident, blame whiskey and sickness for my inexcusable behavior. I'll beg forgiveness for hurting Becky and vow to nurse her back to health. Promise to make it up to her, and Caleb, too. Say I'm beholden to Joseph for taking care of Becky, I'm desperate to see her. Could we please discuss the matter over a cup of coffee?

"The bastard hates me, but he's got some of Becky's stupidly trusting nature, yeah, enough to let a stranger in. As soon as I sweet-talk him into letting down his guard, I'll collar him, get my blade right under his chin, and make him tell me Becky's hiding place if she ain't there. Then I'll slit the meddlesome son-of-a-bitch's throat, take whatever money and food I can cram in these pockets, and leave in time to catch the last ferry. I got it all figured. Lucky thing I didn't spend the last of my cash on whiskey. If I don't find enough at Joseph's, I've plenty for the ferry fare. By the time Joseph's body is found, I'll be long gone."

Although he knew they were aspects of his scheme that might go awry, Enoch Wallace was confident he could kill a man by that grisly method. He'd done precisely that to a man in blue during the War.

Snowmelt and rain from Virginia had the New swollen and rising. The ferrymen used their longest poles and greatest effort to wrestle the vessel across turbid, roiling water. The craft strained and bucked on its tether as it made the crossing.

Joseph, ahead of Enoch, went straight to Dr. Mason's. Mrs. Mason said she expected her husband back from a house call in a couple of hours. Joseph detoured to the post office on his way to the store.

Enoch had no trouble locating his brother-in-law's place of employment—he asked one of the ferrymen. "You're in luck," the young man said. "He's been gone awhile and showed up just this morning. He works at the general store upriver 'bout a quarter mile."

By then, the sun had passed its zenith, and Joseph had completed a lengthy talk with Silas. He gathered the few belongings—including *The Count of Monte Cristo* in two volumes and a box of stationery for Becky—he could stuff into his saddlebags, along with his banjo, and sat on his bed holding a letter, a letter from a land agent in Harrisburg, Pennsylvania.

The offer, from a farmer with property adjacent to Randall's, was less than half the amount Joseph anticipated. The agent, a Mr. Delbert Klein, explained that the Susquehanna's major flood of 1865 had left logjams and piles of debris that must be removed. In addition, the cleared land had grown back to forest too immature for marketable timber. The property required significant labor before it would be productive. The letter concluded with, *Mr. Cook, I strongly advise you to accept this offer of purchase. I don't anticipate there will be another.*

Stung with disappointment, Joseph calculated what the money would buy. At the very least, he needed enough land to pasture Cloud and a cow. Enough for a hayfield and generous garden. He needed adequate woods for building material and fuel. He owed Silas for the stove now installed in the Lillys' smokehouse. He wanted Dr. Mason to continue attending to Becky and Suzanne. He'd have to buy a cow, a hog, chickens. . . . He possessed the skill to build a cabin himself, although Caleb would likely help.

He lay back on the bed, his hands behind his head. The money fell short. He'd be a pauper. Did he envision spending the rest of his life alone, in debt, reading his same collection of books over and over again? And what would he do when his health gave out, as the Charleston doctor had predicted?

Joseph pushed himself to his feet and stepped as an older man into the tepid daylight to fill the saddlebags and mount his mare for the return trip to Dr. Mason's.

Moments later, a thin man sporting shabby clothes and a cropped, gray beard arrived at Silas Hinton's General Store to check the daily hours posted on the door. Seeing that Joseph's workday ended at seven o'clock, he rode away, seeking a means to pass the hours until then. Having never seen a train, he headed for the railyard.

As he made his way back through town, across the tracks, past the stonemasons laying the courthouse foundation, and down to the railyard above the river, Enoch skirted the passenger platform and avoided eye contact with everyone he passed.

At the tracks, Enoch found the men on their dinner break. Having eaten nothing but four boiled eggs since dawn, he craved food and approached a worker pulling shut the door of a railcar.

"Young man, I come a long way to take care of some business in town, and I didn't bring enough food. I don't suppose you'd share a portion of your meal with me?"

Calvin Lilly answered, "I'd be happy to, sir, but I'm heading home for dinner. If you'll be around awhile, I'll bring you something. I'll be back in an hour."

"I'll wait. Much obliged."

Enoch wandered to the nearby freight depot, which emitted low voices, and tied his mount where the mule foraged on scraggly winter grass. Inside, he found three railroaders using a large crate as a table and three smaller ones as chairs.

A poker game!

Unable to resist, Enoch entered the warehouse and said, "Howdy. I'm waiting on a train. Mind if I join you?"

"You got some coins on you?" asked a fair-haired man.

"Sure do." Enoch rattled the change in his pocket for confirmation. "Bills, too."

"Well, pull up a box and we'll deal you in."

Enoch began winning at once and anticipated cleaning out the young greenhorns. He took care to cough into a rag he kept in his coat pocket, to conceal the blood. No sense getting himself spooked out of an easy windfall.

Soon, his luck turned, and he became the loser. Watching his earnings dwindle and baffled by his reversal of fortune, Enoch pressed on. Determined to win back what he'd lost, and more, he instead continued to lose.

Finally, down to his last few cents, Enoch stared in dismay at a pair of jacks. It was then he noticed a faint crease, exactly matched in location, at the top of each card. With rising fury, Enoch studied the hands held by the other men. On several cards, he discerned similar marks, nearly indistinguishable, placed at different locations. Without question, the high cards were being marked by a thumbnail.

He threw down his hand and jumped to his feet. "Goddamn it! You're scratchin' the cards. I can see it. Give me back my money! I won't play with cheaters!"

A dark-haired man, unruffled, said, "Looks like we've got us a sore loser. Quit if you want, but you ain't gettin' your money back."

"You're wrong about that!" roared Enoch.

Calvin came through the open door with a basket of food as Enoch yanked a pistol out from under his coat. The three rail workers dove for what little cover the crate provided as Enoch fired. The bullet missed the dark-haired man's head by the width of a candle wick and furrowed his back. Calvin vanished behind one of the wide, open doors as Enoch snatched a fistful of money, spun on his heels, and ran.

Kicking the mule with cruel blows, Enoch reached the ferry in no more than a minute. But as a man who'd spent nearly his entire life atop a mountain ridge, he lacked a vital piece of information—

the bigger the river, the longer it takes to crest. Although Madam's Creek showed clear signs of decreasing flow that day, New River continued to rise.

The ferry was closed.

Voicing obscenities, Enoch reined his mule downstream along the tracks, looking for a place to enter the thin strip of woods along the river. But he found the forested edge flooded and choked with logjams, which forced him into thicker growth upslope, and he made slow progress.

Meanwhile, Calvin sprinted to Sheriff Evan Hinton's office while the injured man's cohorts sought to give him aid. In less than an hour, Evan, his deputy sheriff, and the irate yardmaster, along with a pair of borrowed bloodhounds, gathered at the depot. As soon as the dogs had sniffed the playing cards and the spot where the mule was tied, they were off, with the mounted men close behind.

In short order, Enoch, squatting behind a sycamore, faced two triumphant dogs baying at full volume. He also faced two shotguns and a pistol, all loaded. He surrendered without a fight.

Joseph and Dr. Mason rode back to town from the defunct ferry when they heard a shrill voice cry out, "There he is!"

A ruddy-cheeked boy in cap and coat ran to them. "Someone was sent to your house, Dr. Mason. There's been a shooting at the railyard. Come quick!"

The doctor took off at a gallop, while Joseph trailed at a walk. Unable to help with the crisis, Joseph thought he'd stop at the depot to check for items addressed to the store. If found, he'd bring the wagon down.

Inside the building, a group of men stood awkwardly around the poker "table," which now held a shivering man curled on his side. One of the encircling men was Calvin, and Joseph pulled him aside.

"What happened?" Joseph asked.

"An argument about poker cheating," Calvin said. "I walked in just in time to see a man yell and draw a pistol and fire. Scared me half to death. I went for the sheriff fast as I could. Lit a fire under him—I suspect he'll find the scoundrel. Said he'd bring down a pair of hounds."

"Do you know the injured man?"

"No, he's a new brakeman. Ain't been here long."

Joseph overheard Dr. Mason say, "He's in shock. We need to get him somewhere warmer. Son, can you move your legs at all?"

Joseph said, "I'm grateful you were spared. There's men lose their heads over trifling things. But I didn't come to gawk. I come to see if there's merchandise for the store."

"I stacked it in the corner. There's bags of salt and starch and coffee. Vegetable seeds, too. A couple of boxes of garden tools. How are Miss Becky and Ma?"

"Better each day. We can't keep your ma in bed no more."

Calvin snorted. "That don't surprise me. You'll have your work cut out for you if Doc Mason wants her to keep resting. I'm mighty glad to know your sister's feeling better—I wouldn't wish that injury on no one."

"Nor would I. You know, I hate to abandon our music-making group. Maybe when things settle down I can ride down on Saturday nights and stay over if you have room. I'll be making my home at the farm a while and giving up my job."

"You can stay any time you like, and Lester, too. We've been so busy with Calvin Junior we ain't been playing much anyway. We'll get back to it. I'm right pleased to know you'll be living at the farm. Losing Lester, not to mention myself, is a true hardship. You'll be a godsend."

"I hope so." Joseph reached for a handshake. "Good to see you, Cal. I'll go for the wagon and be back shortly."

On his way out, Joseph passed the gunshot victim being hauled on a blanket by several coworkers to a waiting buggy. He saw the man's face and, stunned with disbelief and revulsion, stopped dead in his tracks.

He knew the man. He was Randall's assailant, Jimmy Browning.

CHAPTER TWENTY-EIGHT

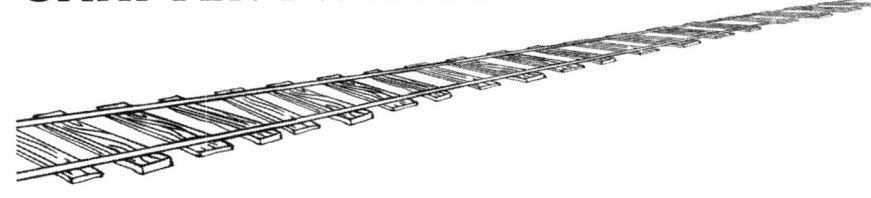

Enoch arrived at the jailhouse in time for supper, which consisted of a watery, tasteless beef soup and two thick slices of bread. He watched the guard toss a couple of sticks of firewood into the pot-bellied stove in the corner opposite Enoch's cell and shuffle away without a glance at the new inmate.

After eating his bland meal, Enoch wrapped himself in the one wool blanket provided, curled like a dog on his cot, and shivered as he waited for sleep. His illness worsened, and the day's stress left him spent. He might have felt relief that he no longer had to care for himself, but "care" was hardly to be expected in a jail cell. It was Becky's duty to look after him, and Joseph's to return her to him.

He'd told the sheriff he shot the man in self-defense, and the man's friends lied in their statements.

He must speak with his brother-in-law.

The ferry didn't reopen until Wednesday afternoon. That morning, Sheriff Hinton stopped at the general store.

Silas completed a sale and smiled at Evan. "What can I do for you, brother?"

"I'm here to speak with Joseph Cook."

Me? Joseph untied a bundle of newspapers fresh off the morning train. He stepped forward to shake the sheriff's hand, thinking, Did that horrid mother report some false accusation against me?

"How can I be of service, sir?"

"It's about our new resident at the jailhouse. Seems he'd like you to pay him a visit. I suspect it has something to do with posting his bail, which the judge has set rather high."

Joseph thought, No, it can't be. "Don't tell me his name is Enoch Wallace."

"That it is," said Evan with a grin. "Lordy, you look like you've just seen a ghost."

Joseph braced himself on the stack of papers. "He's my brother-in-law, and you may tell him there will be no visit. No bail. Only one more character witness at his trial."

"Happy to relay the message. Save a paper for me, Si." Evan bought a large pickle and left, munching and dripping.

Joseph spun in a whirlwind of thought. Randall, what the hell! Can you believe it?

Then the dream returned like a thunderbolt. *You knew!*

The two men vandalizing the store, then turning on each other. Randall calling them *dead enough*. Neither could continue his rampage of destruction. One would die in jail, while the other, assuming he avoided severe infection, contemplated a lifetime sentence in a wheelchair, paralyzed below his ribcage. *They made their own justice*, just as Randall had said.

But it don't bring you back, Randall.

Joseph felt the fine hairs on the back of his neck rise as he heard Randall's voice say, What makes you think I want to *be* back?

When a customer reported the reopening of the ferry that afternoon, Joseph made haste to Dr. Mason's, and the two men left at once, taking Enoch's scrawny mule along. Steady rain fell, darkening their wool attire as well as their mounts, but the day's mildness allowed them to reach the farm with little discomfort.

The first thing Joseph noticed upon their return was a lively chorus of spring peepers sounding from the pond. His stomach tightened with gladness. Whether from roadside ditch, ephemeral woodland pool, or farm pond, the quintessential voice of spring never failed to move him.

Dr. Mason chuckled at the diminutive new cabin, fragrant with fresh wood. Becky answered with a vigorous nod when asked if her pain had diminished. The doctor unwrapped the bandage, revealing a face less swollen but discolored with a new palette of yellow and ochre hues. Satisfied, he rewrapped Becky's face with fresh cloth, not quite as tightly as before.

What concerned him more than the jaw was the condition of Becky's lungs. "Are you coughing up blood?"

"No, sir." Becky answered like a ventriloquist through her locked mouth.

"But continuing to cough?"

"Yes, sir."

"Have you been walking?"

She nodded. "Down to the creek."

"Do you become short of breath?"

"Uphill, I do."

Dr. Mason felt the side of his patient's neck. "You're warm. Do you feel feverish?"

"Sometimes."

Dr. Mason sighed. "I'm afraid you contracted consumption from your husband, Mrs. Wallace. I saw him at the jailhouse yesterday, and there's no question about his diagnosis. I don't expect him to have many months left on this earth, but you are early in the disease . . ." He patted her knee. "I believe you may remain with us quite a while. I advise you to get out in the fresh air as often as you can. I'll be back next week to check on your jaw."

"Jailhouse?" Becky mumbled, her eyes darting to Joseph.

"I'll explain after we check on Suzanne," her brother said.

When Vesta told her ma Joseph and the doctor had arrived, Suzanne returned to bed. The last thing she wanted was a scolding.

"Dr. Mason," she said, sitting upright against a pillow, "I am much improved. I'd like your permission to get off this tiresome tick and resume my normal habits."

The doctor raised his eyebrows and lifted a wrist to check Suzanne's pulse. A minute later, he asked Suzanne to stand and checked her pulse again, noticing his patient's clothing suggested she had not spent the day in bed. He frowned at Marcus and Joseph, who simultaneously answered his rebuke with sheepish shrugs.

"Your heartbeat is stronger and slower," he said. "That's a good sign, but you must remember your heart has been damaged. You must avoid strain of any kind. Let the others lift heavy pails and jugs. When the garden work begins, I want you to take frequent breaks, and if you feel your pulse racing or become short of breath, stop altogether and rest. No more work that day, and less the next. You must listen to your heart, and never, never push yourself. Do you understand? Another heart attack could easily kill you."

"Yes, sir, and I thank you for coming. I shall heed your advice. Will you stay for supper?"

'It's good of you to offer, but the river will be rising again, and I'd best go."

On his way out, Dr. Mason asked Marcus, "Will she listen to you? She strikes me as a strong-willed woman."

Marcus laughed. "She don't much listen to anyone. But she does want to live. I think she'll be careful. We'll keep a close eye on her."

A brighter sky, without rain, greeted Dr. Mason as he left the house. As soon as he departed and Joseph disclosed the reason for Enoch's arrest, Marcus and Caleb saddled Blackjack and Reggie for a quick trip to the crest of Broomstraw Ridge, taking along the Wallace mule, "Mr. Smith," and a pouch of cracked corn.

At the Wallace farm, they collected Becky's clothes, which looked to Marcus more like rags than identifiable items of women's wear. They gathered cookware, a sewing basket, and Caleb's few belongings. After loading Mr. Smith, they fed and watered the desperate chickens, and were about to stuff them into meal sacks when Marcus said, "Do you mind waiting here a little while? There's a grave about a half-mile up the road I'd like to visit."

"Not at all," said Caleb. "I'll spend a little time with my brothers."

"Your brothers?"

"I never knew them. But there was three died young. Two was babies, but Enoch Junior lived three years. My sister Caroline told me Mama called him "EJ," and it just about broke her when he died."

"I had no idea. Your ma's had a hard life."

"Yes, sir."

"I'll be back shortly."

Marcus urged Blackjack into a canter, which delivered him to the slight rise on the right side of the road where a cluster of upright stones marked the Bennett family graveyard. Beyond, the sweep of high pasture dropping away to distant woods made a lovely sight. Marcus took note of red maples crowned with maroon blooms in the forest below and exhaled his satisfaction. Winter in its death throes.

He dismounted. A short search led him to a rounded fieldstone, or "dornick," marked with the initials and dates he sought—JB, 1811-1865. Jefferson Bennett, a fellow Thurmond Partisan Ranger, had served with Marcus during the War. Father of eight, in his fifties, he'd enlisted to fight alongside his eldest son. He'd returned home before the War's end and resumed his farming life before being shot dead by a Union veteran. A sad irony of his death was that it occurred the very day General Lee surrendered at Appomattox Court House.

Marcus removed his hat and knelt by the mounded grave. "I'm sorry I wasn't here to defend you, Mr. Bennett. You were good to me. May you rest in peace."

He wouldn't forget Jeff Bennett's way of taking young privates under his wing when they needed a pa. Although Marcus had resented the man's intervention when he staggered through months of depression following Johnny's death, he later appreciated the intention behind it.

Marcus pushed back his tawny hair, tossed by the wind. Whatever remnants of self-pity he held had been annihilated the night and day of Georgie's birth. What he'd suffered—hunger, cold, heat, exhaustion, anxiety, violence, guilt, grief, tedium, hatred, longing for Maylene, the pain of his wound—shrank to insignificance in comparison to Maylene's ordeal. He'd never endured such physical suffering. And through the three years, ended less than three weeks shy of his scheduled discharge by the War's close, he'd had the constant companionship of Corbin Radcliff, his calm, good-humored friend. Corbin, the husband of Maylene's oldest sister, Mary, had been conscripted with Marcus that spring of 1862.

But he rarely saw Corbin, who lived on his family's farm near New Richmond, along with Mary and their six children, a seventh on the way. It had become easier and more typical for the Farleys to visit the Radcliffs than vice versa, which offered the additional benefit of seeing another Farley daughter, Margaret, and her family, whose home neighbored the Radcliffs'.

No, Marcus did not feel sorry for himself, but there were moments like this when a piercing sadness pinned him to the earth, and he heard the sharp bark of gunfire, smelled stinging smoke, recalled cries of agony, and felt—without having witnessed the bulk of them—the thud of thousands upon thousands of men as they fell.

It'd be good to see Corbin, he thought.

Although his inner wound found no expression, it could be eased by being with his one friend who knew it.

Marcus straightened with streaks of mud on his knees and remounted his gelding. Finding Caleb waiting at the henhouse, he helped collect the chickens, and the duo rode back to the farm, arriving at dusk with their cargo of goods and squirming bags of disgruntled birds.

Although relieved his pa was locked up and prevented from doing more harm, Caleb became despondent with the hatred he harbored for the man, the disclosure of his mother's fatal disease, and the recognition that the only home he'd ever known was forever abandoned. As soon as Lester disappeared the following week to begin laying bricks, Caleb withdrew into a wordless world of despair.

Joseph encouraged him to read to his mother until Becky revealed her son was illiterate, thanks to Enoch's insistence he stay home to help on the farm. So, instead, Joseph interrupted his morose but hard-working nephew several times a day and told him, "It's time to cheer up your ma. Go down and talk to her a while."

Becky wrote letters to her son, letters for Joseph to read aloud, telling Caleb how proud he made her and how much he'd helped her cope with the harsh life imposed on them by a gambling- and whiskey-addicted man with little interest in farming or family life. She hoped in time they'd be able to forgive him.

She also wrote to her daughters, Caroline in Beckleyville and Lura in Oak Hill, as well as her friends, Ethel and Clara, telling them of her change of residence and advising them not to visit due to her illness. She made a point of telling each of her joy to be reunited with her brother and see Caleb free of his father, ending her letters with *I am taking walks and enjoying books and am happier than ever*. And the latter comment would have been true if not for her concern about her son.

To her brother, Becky made two written requests. She wanted Caleb to learn to read—the task would boost his confidence and serve as a distraction—and she longed for gravestones etched with her sons' names. At present, nothing but dornicks marked the burial sites. Becky explained that Enoch had refused to name any child until he or she reached the age of three months, thus labeling the two infants *Baby Wallace.* But she had named them after her brothers, William Adkins Wallace and Joseph Crawford Wallace. Enoch Jenkins Wallace, Junior, had lived long enough to earn his father's name.

No rush, Becky added to her note, *but someday. It will be a great comfort to me.*

Joseph promised to shape the stones the following winter and continued to read to his sister every evening after supper, seated on a chair in the open doorway. Often Quencus, the least talkative and most affectionate of the children, climbed onto his lap. If the boy began to shiver in the twilight chill, Joseph buttoned him inside his own coat and ran his hand across Quencus's curly blond hair, thinking the young head reminded him of that of a lamb. At those tender moments, Joseph felt like an honest-to-goodness grandpa.

CHAPTER TWENTY-NINE

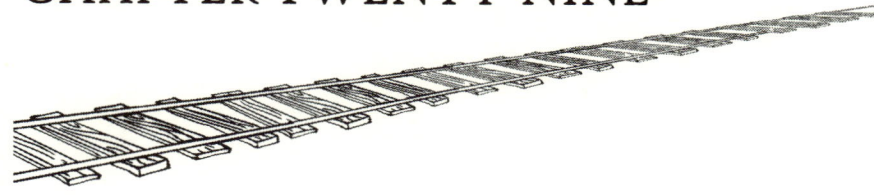

In addition to Lester beginning his new job, which caused Suzanne to grumble about Joseph coddling the boy by letting him ride Cloud each day, several other events marked the dawn of spring, 1875.

The family celebrated Jenny's eleventh birthday with butternut cake and a handmade present from her pa. Marcus carved a drop spindle, an object shaped rather like a child's toy top, used for spinning yarn. Jenny readily caught on to twisting the spindle and letting it fall as she fed in strands of wool or flax, the grown-up nature of the gift motivating her to master its use. The dress of homespun fabric Suzanne and Vesta had planned for her was diverted to Becky. They'd surprise Jenny later with a new dress.

That same week, two days of steady rain pushed the farm's run out of its banks. Beginning in a seep high in the woods, the little stream gurgled through the spring house before entering the pond in the lower corner of the pastures. On its way to Madam's Creek, it crossed the farm lane that led to the road and was easily forded by horse, mule, and wagon. A short wooden footbridge allowed the children to make trips to and from school with dry feet.

The run became enough of a torrent, however, to wash away the bridge.

The fourth "event" was Suzanne's announcement that the time had come for the family, herself excluded, to return to church. If the mud proved too much for the wagon, the family could ride down. With the added mule, only a few would be forced to walk.

Finally, it was Sara Sue who dropped a forkful of scrambled eggs on her plate that Thursday morning to exclaim, "Listen! Papa!"

She scurried around the table, grabbed Marcus by the hand, pulled him from his seat, and swung open the heavy door.

Marcus hoisted his daughter onto a hip. "How did you hear it, pumpkin?"

From above the cabin, near the top of the hayfield, came the clear, sweet notes of a meadowlark.

Marcus pressed his cheek against Sara Sue's smooth blonde hair. "It's spring for sure, now. Ain't that a glad sound."

Three days of wind dried the road nicely, and Marcus drove the wagon, filled with Lilly family members, to church. Caleb chose to stay behind with his mother, saying they would pray together.

Calvin and Nancy often attended the Baptist church, continuing up the creek to the Lilly farm every other Sunday, weather and Madam's Creek Road permitting. This was Nancy's first return to church after childbirth, although Calvin Junior stayed behind with his grandparents, and Nancy's nursing prohibited an after-church visit this week.

It required two benches to hold them all—Calvin and Nancy, Marcus and Maylene with their five children, Lester, Vesta, and Joseph. Red-headed Rachel, the second Lilly sister and wife of the Reverend Eli Goins, gave hurried hugs before her husband took his place behind the pine pulpit. Melva Farley, seated one bench ahead of the Lilly swarm, swiveled her neck to give Joseph a smile, which turned her face scarlet. Marcus and Maylene, aware of her flaming ears and neck, exchanged looks, shaking their heads.

Marcus felt proud of Georgie, who, awake and babbling, kept acceptably quiet through the early part of the service. Eli had gotten no more than five minutes into his sermon, however, when Georgie let out a hideous scream, spinning every head in his direction. Maylene tightened her grip as his tiny body went stiff, and she gave Marcus a look of panic. Georgie's back arched, his eyes rolled upward, and his limbs began to jerk violently.

"Let's go!" Maylene said, but they had to herd Jenny, Johnny, and Vesta before them to reach the aisle.

Quencus and Sara Sue began to cry. "Mama, what's wrong with Georgie?" Sara Sue asked, tears wetting her freckles.

Even Johnny snatched a handful of his mama's skirt as he watched his baby brother's terrifying epileptic episode.

Just as Maylene escaped the bench, a pair of hands snatched her baby from her. Eli lifted Georgie above his head and spoke with authority. "Brethren, pray with me! Lord Jesus, banish the Devil from this child! Satan, leave this child! In the name of Jesus, I command you to go!"

In a quiet voice, edged with iron, Maylene said, "Give him back to me."

Marcus's face paled like a morning moon.

Eli lowered Georgie to Maylene's outstretched arms as the fit subsided. The baby, too dazed to cry, lay limp as death.

Marcus said, "Children, go with your mama outside."

Eli paraded back to the pulpit, his arms aloft, as he announced, "Merciful Lord, we've witnessed a miracle! Jesus in our midst has driven a demon from a little baby!"

Parishioners murmured *amens* and *hallelujahs*.

But as the pastor resumed his sermon, Marcus interrupted. Standing with his hands clenched, he shouted, "How dare you! Using my son to grandstand? That there's the sweetest little baby in the world. There ain't no devil in him. He had a difficult birthing is all. I'm sick to my stomach by what you just done."

Marcus didn't wait for a reply from his dumbstruck brother-in-law but turned on a heel to go.

Joseph, on his feet, said, "Marcus is right. It's shameful to blame the Devil for something that's natural and can't be helped."

Marcus spun around. "I don't need your help defending my son!"

"Maybe not, but I have a right to defend my grandson!"

Marcus went a shade whiter, his mouth agape. A collective gasp arose from the congregation. From the corner of his eye, Marcus glimpsed Mrs. Nivens, shrunken and shriveled as the peas he and Sara Sue had recently planted, who smirked with pleasure at the juiciest gossip ever to reach her ears. Before him, a horrified Melva Farley clamped a hand over her mouth as her mother placed a comforting arm across her shoulders. Bob Farley sank with relief that his wife's concern for Melva prevented the spasm of laughter he expected to erupt.

Marcus couldn't get out of the little chapel fast enough, followed by the remainder of his family.

Calvin whispered to Nancy, "Do you mind if I go home with them? I'd like to get to the bottom of this. I'll tell Marcus I want to check on Ma."

"Please go," Nancy whispered back. "The suspense will kill me if you don't."

Catching up, Joseph said, "I'm so sorry, Marcus. Those words come out of my mouth before I could stop them—I didn't mean to say it."

Marcus stared straight ahead, walking fast. "Ma's going to skin you alive, and you'll get no pity from me. Maylene, how is Georgie?"

"He's coming around. He's better." Already on the wagon seat, Maylene had turned the team for home.

Marcus's thundering pulse began to slacken, and he blew out air as he took the check lines. The good in Mr. Joseph's revelation wasn't lost on him. At long last, Mrs. Nivens' rumors about Maylene had been exposed for what they were, vicious lies.

Even Sara Sue was uncommonly quiet on the way back, a journey of over an hour. Marcus noticed the resemblance to another return from church, nearly nine years earlier. That Sunday, Mrs. Nevins congratulated him for adopting Maylene's "squaw-baby" daughter, Jenny. Fortunately, only Marcus, Maylene, and Marcus's parents heard the remark, which Quentin shrugged off as ignorance. An enraged Marcus and a weeping Maylene, their denied wound gaping open, followed Madam's Creek with a similarly silenced family.

The exposure of their rift evoked Suzanne's confession.

As Joseph helped Marcus unhitch the team, he said, "This don't seem like dinner conversation. Will you talk to your brothers and sister in private? I'll discuss the matter with your ma after we eat."

"Whatever you want," said Marcus, resisting a smile. "By the way, Maylene's parents have known for years, so you've nothing to explain to them. With Ma, I wish you luck."

"I'll need more than that, God help me."

The grin broke across Marcus's face as he led Blackjack to the pasture gate.

"Ain't you early?" Suzanne asked. "I just now put the bread in to bake."

"Georgie had another fit," Marcus said. "We thought it best to go."

"I'm mighty sorry to hear that. It must have frightened the children."

"It did, not to mention Maylene and me."

"How is he?"

"Sleepy. Maylene nursed him on the way home, and he went right to sleep. She wants to stay with him, and I told her I'll bring her dinner up later."

"That's fine. Tell Jenny to go gather some fresh greens. Vesta's working on a mutton stew. I'll ring the bell in about an hour."

"May I borrow Vesta momentarily?" Vesta looked up from chopping turnips. "Jenny has a knitting question," Marcus lied. "It won't take but a minute. Then I'll send Jenny for the greens."

Joseph kept his sister and nephew company while Marcus, Jenny, Vesta, Lester, and Calvin assembled in the smokehouse, where Marcus fired the new stove. The family circled the heat, all eyes on Marcus.

"Is it true?" Lester asked.

"Is what true?" asked Jenny.

Marcus, his hands in his pockets, looked away before meeting his daughter's gaze.

"Jenny, honey, ... after you left the church, Mr. Joseph said something to back up something I said about Georgie having no devil in him. By accident, he said he had the right to defend his grandson."

"But Georgie ain't his grandson—maybe he just feels like he is. He must have said that to give his words more weight . . ." Her voice trailed off with growing doubt.

"No, Jenny-bear, it's true. Mr. Joseph is Georgie's grandpa and yours, too, because he's my father. It's like this. He come up Broomstraw back in forty-three, looking to say goodbye to his sister before he left for the railroad job. He stopped at the farm to say goodbye to Ma as well, and it happened she was alone with Junior that day. Mr. Joseph had no way of knowing she stayed behind when the family went to a funeral, on account of her being dead tired. Ma said Junior had kept her up all night fussing with a new tooth.

"Anyhow, they ended up doing something they oughtn't have, something they regretted, and I was the result of that mistake. We can all be shocked, and call it sin if we want, but I choose to make my peace with it as best I can. Pa never knew, and what's done can't be undone. We all know Ma loved him. She's lived with a weight of guilt enough to crush a woman less strong. I'll tell the others first chance I get, unless Ma wants to. After dinner, Mr. Joseph will talk to her about what happened at church. I hope her heart can withstand the strain. I'm afraid she'll blow her top. It wouldn't hurt to say a prayer for her, if you will."

Jenny crossed her arms and walked out of the smokehouse. Marcus called after her. "Jenny, don't say nothing to your sister and brothers just yet. Your ma and I will talk to them."

Calvin and Vesta stood too astonished to speak, while Lester nodded. Almost inaudibly, he said, "As I thought."

Marcus took long strides to the cabin, looking for Jenny. Maylene, who lay curled around Georgie, said, "She's upstairs."

Marcus found her on her bed, hugging her knees.

Without looking at him, she said, "I feel like you lied to me."

"I did lie to you, my peach, and it hurt to do it. But I made a promise to your grandma years ago I'd never divulge her secret. I couldn't tell you the truth without breaking that promise."

Jenny sat up as Marcus lowered himself to the edge of the bed. "I know you're too old," he said, "but will you sit on my knee a minute?"

Jenny complied but with arms crossed again in defiance.

Marcus continued. "You were Paw Paw's first grandchild, and he was crazy about you. And you are the one who'll remember him. I don't think Sara Sue recalls him at all anymore, and Johnny's memories are fading. It don't matter if he was your real grandpa or not, same as it don't matter if he was my real pa. He'll always be your Paw Paw and my pa.

"I don't believe I've heard you speak more than a dozen words to Mr. Joseph since we met him. And that's my fault. I didn't see it until now, but my coldness must have made you feel you had to choose sides, and that was wrong of me.

"Will you forgive me for that and for lying to you?"

Marcus had to lift his chin to place it on top of Jenny's head. He felt the glossy softness of her black hair, or imagined it, through his beard. A fist of sadness struck his heart as he considered this occasion likely the last he'd hold Jenny on his lap. But he pushed the thought away and said with an unseen smile, "It'll rest heavy on me if you don't."

"I will if you'll forgive Mr. Joseph," Jenny said.

Marcus suppressed a flash of anger. He'd grown up in a household in which children never told their parents what to do, never struck deals.

He lowered his head to meet his daughter's eyes. "You drive a hard bargain, young lady. But you may consider it done. I'm wore out carrying this grudge.

"Now, how about if you get a little friendlier with Mr. Joseph? Ma told me he thinks he makes you uncomfortable sometimes by looking too close at you. It's because you remind him so strongly of his mother, who died when he was a boy."

"I do? I look like my *great* grandma?"

"Evidently. And she must've been a right pretty lady."

That made Jenny smile. She stood. "Thank you, Papa."

Marcus rose reluctantly. "See you at dinner, honey. Your grandma wants you to collect greens. Take the little ones along to keep them out of her hair. I'm gonna chop some wood before Ma rings the bell."

The demand for wood was unending because fire was as much the lifeblood of farm existence as were rain and sun. Children learned to split and saw at an early age—Jenny and Johnny were already mastering the tasks.

As he swung an axe to splinter seasoned log sections into quarters for cookstove kindling, Marcus set aside his apprehension about his ma's reaction to Joseph's disclosure and mused about the many uses of fire. Fire for heat and light, fire for daily cooking and baking, fire for forging iron into various tools and implements, seasonal fires for making jams and jellies and apple butter, as well as preparing beans and beets for pickling. Fire to heat water for bathing, for washing clothes and dunking a freshly killed hog in hot water. Fire to heat irons for removing wrinkles from clothing, fire for curing meat in the smokehouse, fire to create steam to bend wood to desired shapes, fire for washing the fleece of sheep prior to carding and spinning, fire to make soap and candles, fire to distill corn into whiskey or condense maple sap into syrup, sorghum into molasses …

Little wonder stumps stood everywhere, marching farther and farther up the mountainsides from every farm. And the most ubiquitous sounds, next to those of water descending in countless runs and streams, issued from axe and saw.

Sabbath or not, Marcus never ceased to feel the pressure to prepare wood. As he lifted the axe to resume his labor after a short rest, he heard the clanging of the dinner bell.

Following dinner and its cleanup, Marcus said, "It's time for your grandma to rest. Let's go up to the cabin for a story. Quencus, it's your turn to pick a critter."

"A turtle!" Quencus said with a jump of excitement.

"A box turtle!" said Sara Sue. "When will we see one, Papa?"

"In a few weeks. You be on the lookout, and maybe you'll see the first one come crawling out of the dead leaves."

Johnny scuffed the floor with a foot. "Not a turtle. I want a story about a wolf, big and scary and mean."

Marcus put a hand on the back of Johnny's neck and squeezed. "It ain't your turn, young man, but you never know when a wolf might show up."

Lester said to Caleb, "Come on up. You'll be glad you did," as Vesta reached for her cloak.

Left alone with Suzanne, Joseph remained at the table.

"You looked troubled," said Suzanne, "and you hardly said a word at dinner. In fact, almost no one but Sara Sue did. Is it more than Georgie?" She seated herself across from him.

Into Joseph's mind flashed another time of awkwardness, although far worse, at this same table when he struggled to choke down a cup of coffee and tell Suzanne he was sorry about their fight and was leaving home, he presumed, for good. He was taken off guard that morning when Suzanne came around the table and touched his healed nose. He put his hand over hers, expecting the deafening drumbeat of his heart to wake Junior.

But that memory compounded his nervousness. Joseph swallowed it away. "I have a confession to make."

Suzanne's blue eyes, unblinking, narrowed as if she beheld a villain. "What have you done now?"

"At church this morning . . . Marcus grew angry when Eli took Georgie from Maylene and commanded the Devil to leave the child."

Suzanne frowned. "That sounds like Marcus. I'd have been infuriated myself."

"I made the mistake of agreeing with Marcus when he wanted to stand alone. He said he didn't need my help, which was true, but I was riled up enough to say something regrettable."

Joseph, aware of being short of breath and overly warm, paused.

"What in the world did you say?"

"I said I had a right to defend my grandson."

Suzanne's head moved backward an inch as she tucked her chin. "Lordy! You didn't!"

"I'm sorry, Suzanne. I didn't mean to."

Joseph steeled himself for an explosion. Instead, Suzanne stood up, a bit unsteadily, and said, "Will you excuse me a moment?"

She removed her cloak from its peg by the door and left. Joseph followed as far as the doorway to see her direction. Suzanne made haste to the privy.

Good Lord, he thought, I've made her sick. She's gone to vomit. What else can I do wrong? I'm the cause of her heart attack. I've brought a sullen teen and a sick, contagious woman into her life. Three more mouths to feed. I burdened Marcus with a lame horse and then a sickly mule and cursed him with emotional pain. And now I've revealed a secret sure to cause Suzanne shame the rest of her life.

What good have I done? Two pairs of shoes and a few borrowed books? Randall, I should never have inflicted myself on this generous family.

Joseph would have wept if it wouldn't have added to his humiliation.

But Suzanne didn't feel sick. She fled because of an urgent need to empty her bladder. The reason was not at all what Joseph suspected. Suzanne, overtaken by laughter, had to release urine along with mirth. She leaned forward until her head reached her knees and laughed with shaking shoulders and loud hoots. She hadn't laughed so hard, she didn't think, since the antics of Quentin's courting days. Before living with in-laws and bearing baby after baby drained much of the humor from her.

When she regained her composure, Suzanne returned to the house, where she found Joseph pacing. Her smile confused him. Even more, the giggle that followed it.

"Joseph, you look like a man approaching the gallows. Come sit in a rocker and we'll talk."

Once settled, Suzanne began. "You dear man . . ."

Dear man? The unfamiliar label confused Joseph further.

". . . you've relieved me of a tremendous burden. Ever since Jenny's birth, it's Maylene who's had to endure the rumors. Many thought Marcus couldn't possibly be Jenny's father, and I couldn't expose the truth. I couldn't hurt Quentin that way. When you started attending church with the Farleys, I'm sure tongues wagged again. Polly Nivens must've thought she'd ferreted out Maylene's secret lover at last. I'll never know how Maylene had the backbone to keep attending that church full of gossips. It's why Marcus went back. He stayed away after the War, except for the Sunday we persuaded him to attend Vesta and Louella's baptism. That's when he learned what was being said about Maylene. After that, he didn't want her going without him.

"I wish I'd been there to see Polly's squinty little eyes bulge to normal size." Suzanne giggled again.

"Now the truth is known. I'm free of the guilt I've carried about Maylene all these years. Polly and her gaggle of geese will have the time of their lives and let them. I never leave the farm no more. I don't give a damn what they say."

"Great God, you never fail to amaze me, Suzanne. I thought you'd be furious, and I was concerned about your heart."

"Hogwash. There ain't nothing wrong with my heart, but I do believe I'll take a little rest. Why don't you go up and see what's going on with that turtle?"

Joseph resisted. "I have a book."

"You also have grandchildren." Suzanne left the room without a backward glance.

CHAPTER THIRTY

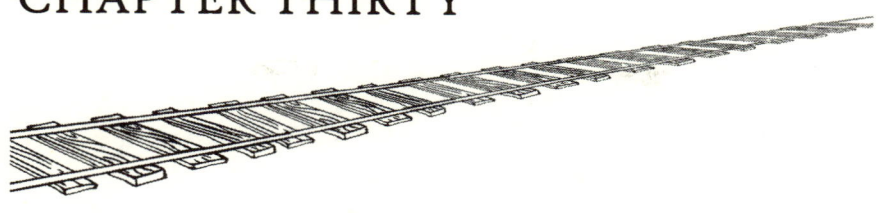

Spring burst forth at last. The apple trees bloomed in white and pale-pink blossoms, drawing droves of bees out of their hives. Barn swallows returned from their undisclosed winter home and began collecting mud for their nests in the rafters. Joseph and Caleb helped Marcus plant the rest of the early crops—wheat, oats, flax, cabbage, spinach, garlic, and lettuce, along with additional onions and peas. The pasture grasses thickened and greened.

For his children, Marcus made a temporary bridge from a split ash log, its flat surfaces facing up. And for Rachel's sake, he saddled Blackjack to visit Eli. Despite his fondness for all his sisters, Marcus couldn't deny his partiality for Rachel. She shared Quentin's good nature and boundless energy, and was the sister who had trailed Marcus, much like Sara Sue, as soon as she walked.

Both men expressed sorrow over their tiff and promised it would be forgotten. Although Marcus's rage hadn't dulled past powerful disgust, he recognized the value of putting the incident behind him.

Becky's jaw healed with a minor residue of swelling, and she began hoeing and pulling weeds, keeping her distance from the others. Caleb's depression lessened as conversations with his mother resumed. At Becky's urging, the teen began tutoring sessions with Joseph and Vesta, his complaints lacking vigor.

In addition, they were all relieved of the albatross of Enoch when he was convicted of attempted murder and sentenced to twenty years. Four witnesses, including the one he left paralyzed, made for a straightforward case. The sentence lacked relevance, as Enoch had little hope of serving a year before his demise.

Although Marcus and Joseph spent many hours together in the fields and garden, they remained uneasy and spoke only out of necessity. Both despaired that they would ever overcome their wariness. Joseph's desire to love his son prevented him from confronting the deep hurt of Marcus's rejection, while Marcus felt forever defiled by the circumstances of his beginning.

Marcus warned himself that Joseph had come to stay. Just as he had trained himself, with time and great effort, not to allow his brain to revisit aspects of the War, he must not return to the image of his conception in the same bed where his siblings were conceived, but so disgracefully with the wrong man. The tryst was none of his business, and he mustn't poison his children's relationship with their grandfather.

At length, Joseph told Suzanne he would not be able to buy a farm of his own. He had a new idea, to buy two acres of the Lilly farm on which to grow sorghum. He'd seen the demand for molasses at Silas's store, and he envisioned his plan as a way to contribute to the family's nearly nonexistent income.

Suzanne thought the suggestion absurd, but Marcus intervened, saying, "Ma, a man needs his own land to plant and harvest. Let him buy part of the buckwheat field. I believe he feels like a freeloader."

"That's ridiculous. He works himself weary every day. He's a great help to us."

"I know. But let him purchase the land. You know, he told me Cloud is the first horse he's ever owned. Think how he'll feel to plow his own land with his own horse."

Suzanne relented, and Joseph wasted no time getting the ground ready for planting. As a man who had always worked out-of-doors, he welcomed the sun and wind on his face, the sights and sounds of wild birds and domesticated animals, and the ceiling of sky. He relished his release from the confinement of the general store.

On the first of May, Joseph dragged the rockers onto the porch as the evening settled to darkness. He hadn't been alone with Suzanne in weeks. For several minutes, they listened to the cacophony of peepers, now joined by trilling toads, and enjoyed the dewy sweetness of a spring night.

Joseph considered telling Suzanne about Jimmy Browning but changed his mind. It still soured his stomach to picture the man's pocked face. It's between me and Randall, he thought.

He leaned back to study the sky. Without the moon, star upon star began crowding the heavens. "Yesterday, Jenny asked if I'll teach her the banjo. She was nervous as if I were a poisonous spider crawling up her arm. I told her it will be a pleasure, and we'll plan on Sundays after dinner for our lessons."

"She's not as obvious about it as Sara Sue, but she pays close attention to her pa. His avoidance of you affected her. She knew there must be a reason for it. But this is glad news. She will warm quickly to you, and she wants to, or she wouldn't have asked."

"Are you suggesting she's not interested in the banjo?"

"Not at all. She was about to make the same request of Calvin when he married and moved to town."

Suzanne changed the subject. "You know you can't stay in the smokehouse forever, and it don't set a good example for the children if you move into the house."

Joseph rolled his head along the rocker back to look at her. "Have you another alternative in mind?"

Suzanne's expression softened. Every object and sight on the farm reminded her of Quentin, yet there'd been a shift after the night on Broomstraw Ridge. She'd begun thinking more often of Joseph than of her late husband.

"You know I had to near die to get your arms around me—makes me shudder to think what it would take to get a kiss."

"Oh, for God's sake, woman. Is that what you want? I thought you'd smack me. Hold still a minute."

Suzanne stopped rocking.

Joseph twisted in his chair to plant a firm one on her mouth. "Feel better?"

"Not entirely."

Joseph sighed. "How did Quentin Lilly put up with you all those years?"

Suzanne gave him an impish grin. "I treated him better than I do you."

Joseph snorted. "No doubt! Then why in God's name do I love you?"

Suzanne took in a sharp breath. Joseph, impossibly handsome, virtually ageless with faint creases next to his mouth and laugh lines by his eyes, and she with her leathery face, with hair and skin the color of dishwater. Although Quentin had been an affectionate husband, he hadn't used those words since their honeymoon. Hearing them from Joseph wrenched her heart.

"What did you say?"

"You heard me. I'm not saying it again. I should've kept my job on the C & O."

"And missed meeting your family?"

Joseph stretched out his long legs. "I admit you're all getting stuck on me like cockleburs. My long-lost Suzy Harman, our old banter, cantankerous but irresistible. It's about time we let down our guard." Joseph paused a moment. "Despite the uncomfortable novelty of unbidden words popping out of my mouth, as they did at church."

"Joseph, you know I'd have slapped you silly that day you come up here and found me alone if you'd been ungentlemanly. I was the one started it. And I never would have behaved so ... inappropriately if I hadn't cared for you the way I did. I still find it hard to believe, what we done."

"Hard to believe, and hard to forget. I never shall."

"Nor I, although I've tried and prayed to forget. But, lest you anticipate romance, I must tell you I don't believe God cares for such behavior. Since you first come to dinner last year, we almost lost Sara Sue, then Maylene and Georgie. There was the frightful trouble up on Broomstraw, and Georgie's got his . . . condition. Louella had a baby born dead. I feel like God's warning me, like He's saying, 'Don't expect to be rewarded for what you done.' I've become quite wary of getting any closer to you."

Joseph gripped the rocker arms with both hands. "I feel like I'm riding a saddle with a loose girth. First you ask for a kiss, then you tell me God don't approve."

Suzanne shrugged off the inconsistency. "Well, I might of died before I got a kiss, so I took the chance. There's another thing. . . .

My body's changed. I ain't sound in a certain way, and you must put any notion of the bedroom out of your mind."

Did I bring up the bedroom?

"Your bladder?"

Pushing past shame to relief, Suzanne said, "It leaks like a barrel with a sprung stave. How'd you know?"

"Your frequent trips to the privy haven't gone unnoticed. It don't matter, Suzanne, though I'm sorry for your affliction. I'm not fishing for a repeat performance—there's something you should know about me. I developed a rash about two years ago, when we were nearing completion of the rail line, and I visited a doctor in Charleston. He said it was syphilis. I won't ever have intercourse again."

"From a prostitute?"

"Yes."

"I'm surprised at you, Joseph."

Joseph reacted to Suzanne's reversal from self-blame to self-righteousness. "Well, I regret the illness, but don't expect me to apologize for how I contracted it. I'm not going to apologize for being a man. There's women liked to spark with me, but they shied soon as I returned their interest. It's a rare woman wants to marry a man dark as me, and I never met one who wanted a husband who'd be forever on the move. I can't say I'm proud of the indulgence you find repulsive, but I didn't make a habit of it and spent most of my spare change on books."

Suzanne, after a moment of reflection, said, "Well, it ain't like I'm without sin. I've no right to judge you for it. What does it mean? Are you very ill? You don't seem ill."

"Not yet. The doctor said the disease sleeps, sometimes for a few years, sometimes for many. When it wakes up, I'll begin to decline in various ways. I may lose my sight and sanity. It won't be pleasant."

Suzanne placed a hand below her throat. "Oh, Joseph, I fear for you."

"And I worry about your heart, so we must put such thoughts away and be thankful we live."

"You've been spending too much time with Bob Farley. Sounds like something he would say."

"He's a wise man, but I'm expressing *my* opinion, and here's another. As for God's judgment, I believe you have it backwards."

"What do you mean?"

"I know I've brought trouble to you and your family and I regret it, especially your recent illness, which I intend to help you recover from if you'll allow me. But the trouble I take credit for is my doing, not God's. Have you spent the last thirty-two years so guilt-ridden you're forever looking for signs of God's disfavor? If so, I believe God has no reason to punish someone doing such a fine job of punishing herself. Sara Sue could easily have died, as could Maylene and Georgie. That unlikely shot you fired at Enoch saved my life. And you survived a heart attack, which many people don't. I believe God is trying to get it through that thick skull of yours that He's got your back. He's looking out for you and your family. And can you name a family sheltered from hardship and loss? Do you think the Good Lord has nothing better to do than conjure up ways to torment you in particular?

"I had a friend told me, 'You'll never be free of sorrow if you can't let the past be the past.' I don't always succeed in taking his advice, but it helps me.

"And I think it likely God brought me back to look after you, to remove your loneliness as well as mine. Miss Suzanne, if I'm able to live long enough, you can spend the remainder of your days with someone who cares for you."

Suzanne again brought her rocker to a halt, her vision blurred by uncustomary tears. As she waited for her speech apparatus to regain function, she pondered Joseph's words.

"You truly think so?" Her voice was not her own. Her foundation of self-understanding shuddered like Chase shaking water off her coat.

"I do. And I don't want to set a bad example for my grandchildren."

"Joseph, are you proposing to me? I can't tell."

"I suppose I'm botching it. I've never done it before. I'm offering my flawed self. You'll have to tell me if we're betrothed 'cause it's always the lady's choice. Well, almost always."

Suzanne placed a small, pallid hand atop Joseph's, broad and bronze. Joseph turned his hand over, allowing their fingers to interlace.

Suzanne, feeling a surge of desire she thought had died along with Quentin, withdrew her hand, pushed herself to her feet, and headed for the outhouse. Arousal, evidently, gave her bladder the wrong instruction.

Joseph waited until she was out of earshot to chuckle. "Is that a yes or a no?" Instinctively, he knew.

CHAPTER THIRTY-ONE

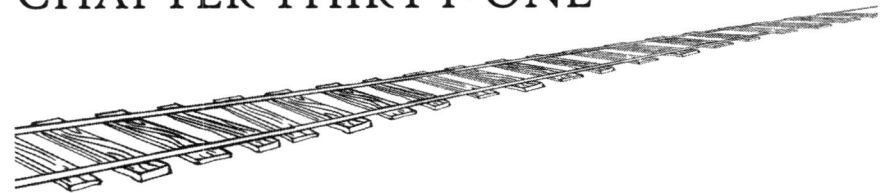

Marcus turned thirty-one and Johnny eight in April. They chose a fishing expedition as their celebration and awaited a fair Sunday. On Johnny's birthday, Marcus took his eldest son on a ramp-collecting excursion, leading the boy close enough to each patch that Johnny spied the vivid-green, blade-like leaves and thought he'd found the odiferous plants on his own. The capricious spring weather forced them to delay the fishing trip until the second Sunday of May, a glorious day saturated with birdsong and sunshine.

The family might also have celebrated the betrothal of Joseph and Suzanne, had they known of it. But Joseph remained in the smokehouse, and there was no outward sign of change. For now, the couple took pleasure in hoarding their secret. Besides, giving Marcus more time to become accustomed to Joseph's full-time presence made sense.

The fishing group, excluding Suzanne, Becky, and Chase, added Bob Farley after church and continued with a picnic lunch down Madam's Creek to New River, their wagon hitched to Reggie and a much-restored Mr. Smith. Melva, whose outrage concerning Joseph's amorality prevented participation, and her ma stayed behind. An annoyed Sara Mae told her husband she'd not miss another outing on Melva's behalf.

Maylene, with Georgie on her lap, shared the seat with Marcus and her father. Lost in conversation, none of them noticed when Johnny's sly hand stole Georgie's rattle. Johnny began offering the gourd back to his brother, only to snatch it away each time Georgie reached for it. By the third attempt, Georgie bawled.

"Johnny!" snapped Maylene. "Give your brother his toy."

"Do as your mama says," added Marcus, "or I'll have to warm your behind."

Johnny extended the rattle to Georgie in slow motion, grinning, his brown eyes fixed on his pa. Although he knew he'd get no more than one warning, he couldn't resist pushing the limit of his father's patience.

"I do believe," said Maylene, "Eli tried to exorcise the Devil from the wrong boy."

Her father chuckled, and Marcus smiled.

"It's a good thing he's willing to apply his efforts to farming," Marcus said. "I suspect we'll have more complaints about his school mischief from Mr. Waddell in the years to come."

He remembered precisely the words in the note Jenny had brought home a few weeks earlier.

> Dear Mr. and Mrs. Lilly, Johnny is a bright boy and very much liked by his classmates. As well, he is quick to assist the slower students. But he is more interested in dreaming up pranks than applying himself to his lessons. I request your assistance in correcting his behavior. Sincerely, Mr. G. Waddell

The river surged high owing to the wet spring, yet the water ran clear, its surface interrupted with bursts of whitewater. Spring's delicate greens reflected from and bordered the New, giving it a look of enchantment.

Maylene, her father, Vesta, and the children chose a location just downstream from the ferry, where the river spilled across a floodplain meadow. There its minor depth and slower flow allowed easy retrieval of any child who might topple in. The spot was not a promising one for fish, however.

Caleb's addiction to fishing was one of the few things Joseph knew about his nephew, and he hoped the day would coax the boy a little farther out of his cave. A bigger help, however, was Lester. Caleb talked to his new friend more than anyone else, and Joseph rejoiced to overhear the teens comparing notes on fishing techniques.

But a pang of missing Randall followed. Joseph hadn't gone fishing without him since his own teen years. Randall, who's gonna clean the fish? Maybe we won't catch any.

Lester and Caleb went upstream, and Marcus, following his ma's instructions, led Joseph in the opposite direction to his favorite fishing hole.

For a couple of hours, the men cast their lines near a beached batteau. A thirty-foot vessel with a long-handled rudder at its stern, the boat characterized a fleet once poled by men transporting goods up and down the river. Largely replaced by trains, batteaux had been ubiquitous when Marcus and Maylene were young, and most farmers lacked wagons.

Those were quiet hours, which suited both fishermen. While their silence often felt uncomfortable on the farm, it was natural and companionable on the river. They snagged two gigantic catfish and several chubs.

By the time the family reassembled and climbed back into the wagon, Joseph yawned with relaxation. Finding his place in the Lilly family might never feel like a done deed, but he'd made inroads during the past year.

Back at the farm, Marcus hunched on the edge of a bench outside the barn, cleaning fish. When Joseph approached after hanging up the harnesses, Marcus offered a second knife.

"Give me a hand, will you, Mr. Joseph? Caleb asked Lester to entertain your sister with his whistle, and Ma's impatient to get these fish on the fire."

Joseph sat next to his son, taking the slimy body of a catfish in his left hand, the knife in his right.

Don't make a fool of yourself.

He heard his mother's voice, "Joey, if you don't like it, you don't have to look."

Fast-moving clouds scudded overhead, splotching the surrounding slopes with a parade of shadows. One covered the sun incompletely, cancelling the pattern of lights and darks but allowing a shaft of brilliance to spotlight part of the mountainside, aglow with the lime-greens and peachy-pinks of emerging leaves.

Marcus followed Joseph's gaze. "I never get tired of looking up Broomstraw. Seems like it's different every time."

"It's a fine sight. I didn't like being away from the mountains. I don't believe a mountaineer ever feels at ease in the flatlands."

Sweat dampened Joseph's face and shirt as he slit open the fish. At once, his vision grew grainy, narrowing. He dropped the fish, then spread his knees and lowered his head between them.

"Are you all right?" Marcus asked.

"Just a little dizzy, it's nothing."

Marcus doubled over with laughter. "You're fainting over fish guts?"

"You oughtn't laugh at a man with a knife in his hand."

"I ain't laughing at you. Besides, you wouldn't kill your own boy."

"I'd consider it."

Marcus's attempt to stop guffawing failed completely. Tears ran down to his chin.

Joseph hauled himself to his feet, seething.

Marcus stifled his mirth, wiped his face with a shirt sleeve, and extended a hand. "I'm sorry, Mr. Joseph. Please accept my apology. For everything."

Take it, you simpleton! Joseph implored himself, yet his arm stayed soldered to his side.

The men's brown eyes, their sole matched physical feature, locked like the horns of battling rams.

Joseph burned with the rejection that had festered like a boil since the previous May. The strained skin now ruptured, spewing a foul fluid. He wanted to slug his son, not shake his hand.

Marcus, feeling struck, dropped his arm. "Never mind then."

"No, wait." Joseph reached for Marcus's hand, drew the younger man to his feet, and wrapped him a tight embrace. "I appreciate your apology, you son-of-a-bitch."

Marcus, momentarily stung by the words and irked by the fact that the top of his head reached the middle of his father's off-center nose, allowed the strength of the hug to quench his building flame. "I been called worse."

Joseph released him. "The truth of the matter is I'd sooner use that blade on myself than on you."

"That's kindly of you, Mr. J."

Mr. J? A nickname! Joseph might as well have been dubbed a knight. The angst of his conflicting emotions began settling like silt in the creek's ebbing surge.

A final chuckle escaped Marcus. "What made me laugh is I used to do the very same thing, skinning game or beheading a chicken. I dropped like a felled tree more than once and come close on many an occasion. Junior teased the hell outta me for it. Lucky for me, I outgrew it."

"It's an unfortunate trait."

"No argument there." Marcus returned to the bench. "I'll finish up here."

"I'll see if your ma has a chore for me—she generally does."

Joseph stopped. Was there time before they began planting corn and the other frost-sensitive crops when the blackberries bloomed? "Ever seen a stone-arch bridge?"

"Sure. I got around quite a bit during the War."

"I kept much of my toolkit when I left my job. I've been thinking of making a little bridge over the run, one that won't wash away. You think the youngsters would be keen on helping with that?"

"I know they would, especially Johnny. Though you might want to wait for fall when Sara Sue starts school. She'll ask so many questions you'll feel peppered with buckshot."

"I rather like her curiosity."

Marcus cringed at his obstinate refusal to express curiosity about Joseph Cook. "You built bridges?"

"All sorts of bridges."

"Huh. I wouldn't mind seeing those tools myself. If it's all right."

"It's not much bother."

Their meaning understood, the father and son permitted themselves a glimmer of a shared smile, and Joseph walked away.

ACKNOWLEDGEMENTS

I would like to thank the following people for their invaluable help: Jessie Reeder for her continuous encouragement, her donated photographs, and second round of photo editing. Bev Wright, a direct descendent of Jefferson Bennett, who proofread/edited the manuscript in draft form and provided sage commentary and unwavering support. Anne Barnes, for last-minute, first-rate proofreading I can't imagine how she squeezed in.

All the kind words and practical assistance concerning *Madam's Creek*, from too many to name, but especially my sister, Nell Foltz, and friend, Bev Wright. Your collective response helped me muster the inspiration to tackle *Broomstraw Ridge*. Friends and strangers who offered gifts of information about local history. Nancy Hopps, Austin Persinger, and the rest of the Summers County Public Library staff, not to mention many friends, who helped launch *Madam's Creek* and may indulge me again. Wendy Dingwall of Canterbury House Publishing, for her professionalism, guidance, and second "yes." The Lillys and their families who gave me a warm reception at the 2018 and 2019 Lilly Reunions (and thanks for your help, Nancy!). Sharyn Ogden, who helped me find relevant old grave sites (when we were supposed to be finding birds). Those dear hearts who have visited my social-media sites and offered support. As well as my cousin Steve, who personified persistence in the early years of his writing career, has never lost his creative magic, and made time to read my work.

Finally, those who have preserved and restored much of Hinton's and New River's history, with special thanks to Jon Averill, Ken Allman, Bill Dillon, Wayne Harvey, the City of Hinton, the Summers County Historical Society, the National Park Service, Summers County Public Library, and the Summers County Commissioners. And this warm-hearted New River community that honors, by remembering, those who came before.

Betsy Reeder

Betsy Reeder grew up in then-rural Maryland and later found her way to Central Appalachia, where she worked as a full-time biologist and part-time writer until her recent retirement. Her avocations include dog-walking, birding, volunteerism, spiritual exploration, natural history, local history, captivating novels, animals (both wild and tame), wandering the woods, and every second spent with family and friends. Although she aspired to be a poet, as she learned about the New River's landscape and history, seeds germinated that led to the writing of her first novel, Madam's Creek (Canterbury House Publishing, 2017). A sequel, Broomstraw Ridge, followed in 2019. Betsy Reeder is especially grateful for the present opportunity to spend more time writing and being a grandma.

Connect with Betsy online at:

BetsyReederWriter.com

Made in the USA
Middletown, DE
23 November 2023